THE COUNTESS'S ⌐
DISCOV⌐

The Discreet Investigations ⌐   ₊ay:
Book S.

ISSY BROOKE

AUTHOR'S NOTE

This book is written in British English. It has been edited professionally, but the grammar, spelling and vocabulary may be unfamiliar to some readers.

NORTHUMBRIA, APRIL 1894

Adelia, the Countess of Calaway, hid behind an ornately carved pillar in the hand-crafted wonderland that was Griseley Manor in the far north of England, and eavesdropped unashamedly on her daughter Margaret. She glanced across and noticed that one of Margaret's servants was behind another pillar, and when the startled maid turned her head to see herself mirrored, Adelia raised one finger to her lips and directed her own attention back to Margaret.

The maid smiled.

Margaret was standing in the large central hall of the manor house. This middle section of the building was ancient, having once been the seat of the old baronial family that Margaret had married into. It had been left to decline for many years but Margaret and her husband Ramon had taken on the renovation project with gusto and quickly updated it by basically taking it straight back to an idealised version of the Medieval period – which is to say, lots and lots of wooden carvings, dribbly candles and colourful tapestries, but absolutely no plague, lepers or out-and-out serfdom. It was often rather chilly, but there were always wolfhounds on hand if you needed to snuggle up to something warm.

A small figure of a girl was standing limply in front of Margaret and hanging her head.

Margaret said, tersely, "Iseult, last week I gave you that book and asked you to read it, did I not?"

"Yes, mama."

"Yet I discover today, from Nurse, that you have not been reading it. Explain yourself."

Iseult kept her eyes on the floor. In a small voice, bravely, she said, "Mama, you gave it to me on Friday and told me to read. And so on Friday night I read some of it. It was hard. And you did not say to read it again on Saturday or any other day. So I did not. I read something else instead."

Margaret sighed.

"It had dragons in it," Iseult added, knowing what would appeal to her mother.

Margaret kept her voice firm. "Surely it was obvious that you were to read a small section every night until it was finished? Of course it will be difficult if you do not even try to apply yourself. I should not have to spell it out and direct every moment of your day, Iseult."

Margaret then knelt down to bring her to her daughter's level and softened her tone of voice slightly. "Use your brain, child. Now go to your room and read some more and make a note of any words you do not understand. Tomorrow, ask Nurse to explain them to you."

Margaret nodded and quivered.

Margaret waited before standing up with a rush. "Iseult, did I not just tell you to go to your room?"

"Yes, mama."

"Then why are you still standing here?"

"Because it is scary to stand here and you said that brave

knights were scared but did the things that scared them anyway. So I am being a brave knight."

"You're ... what?" All of a sudden, Margaret started to laugh. She bent down again and gave the girl a quick, fierce hug, saying, "You surely have been sent to test me. Now go on to your room, and don't *ever* be scared of me, do you hear?"

As a command, it wasn't the easiest to follow. Iseult scampered away. Adelia sighed and stepped out from behind the pillar.

Margaret looked up but she didn't seem surprised to see her. She came forward, composing herself.

She was a tall, striking woman who had had an unfortunate childhood as far as looks were concerned but now that she was a woman of twenty-seven, she had grown into her angular cheekbones and strong jaw. The effect was one of Arthurian Queen, and it was compounded by her habit of wearing dresses that could almost be described as "gowns", in strong colours, with brocade and fur trims and a general air of the old Pre-Raphaelites about her. Down in London, she would have been accepted as a slight oddity. Up here in the rural north, who knew what the local folk made of her?

"Mother," she said, "are all children so stubbornly stupid or have I been unlucky?"

"Margaret, Iseult is barely seven. Seven! And you know that her remarks about bravery were very logical. She is a remarkably clever girl, indeed."

Margaret beamed with pride, her severe face suddenly sunny. "She is."

"Anyway," Adelia went on. "What book is it that you are insisting she must read? She is a precocious reader already. And you could barely get through a simple sentence until you were eight, you know."

"I do not believe that," Margaret said in shock.

"It is true. Ask your father. Be kinder to poor Iseult. You are expecting too much."

"I am not unkind. I love her very much. Did I not just tell her not to be scared of me? If I didn't love her, I wouldn't care if she could read or not. Oh, but it is so infuriating that I have to tell her something more than once! Why don't people listen?"

"Again, Margaret, she is *seven*."

But it simply wasn't sinking in, and Margaret's mind moved on to other matters.

She said, as she began walking away, "Anyway, dear Peter has come back from whatever he was doing earlier so you can meet him now. I know you'll like him, I'm sure, though he has his little ways. Don't we all? And did you meet Gwen earlier? Father is waiting in the dining room already, poised by the table like an absolute Roman glutton, and if we don't hurry, he will have ordered the servants to begin the meal and we shall have nothing left. This is nice, you know."

Margaret stopped suddenly and looked at Adelia squarely in the face. It was a shock. Adelia hadn't realised, until now, how little her daughter would usually do that during the course of a conversation. She was a woman more comfortable in talking when side to side with a person rather than head-on. "Mother, I am glad that you've come. It's such a long journey up here – we're practically in Scotland – so we don't get as many visitors as we'd like."

Abruptly she spun around and carried on, even more briskly than before.

"I thought that we were in Scotland," Adelia said as she tried to keep up.

"Sometimes we are. I mean, over the years, these lands have been Scottish or English or something quite separate to it all. Lawless lands!" Margaret said, a little excitement in her voice. She reached the dining room and flung the door open. "Here we are! Gwen! Peter!"

Everyone stood up, not just the three men but the small, auburn-haired woman called Gwen did so too. She dashed up to Margaret and Adelia experienced another shock. She watched as for the first time, she saw her stand-offish third daughter embrace a close friend with evident joy.

Margaret had had no real friends as a girl.

"Gwen! This is my mother, the Countess of Calaway. Mother, this is Gwen. Well, I suppose I must be proper. Miss Gwendolen Fitzroy-Harris. The Fitzroy-Harrises live up at the Old Tollhouse on the most picturesquely bleak road you can imagine."

Gwen smiled warmly. "Pleased to meet you, Lady Calaway."

"Pleased to meet you," Adelia replied, liking her immediately just because she seemed to make a light come on in Margaret's face.

"Oh, and Peter, of course," Margaret went on. Gwen went a little pink as Margaret said, "Peter and Gwen are to be married, you know. Come here, Peter, stop looking louche. Lord Peter Morland."

The introductions were done in a haphazard way, and they took their seats at the table before they were even fully concluded. The only person who did not speak was Ramon.

He was a strange man, and ideally suited to Margaret. Usually, Margaret was a taciturn and reticent sort of woman but tonight, in small and selective company, she was blossoming into a more confident young lady. She had never been so chatty before, and certainly could not be called vivacious or lively in normal circumstances, but there was a greater ease to her manner than Adelia had seen before and Adelia was pleased about that.

Margaret must be settled here and that is good, Adelia thought.

Ramon was not the sort of man to hold court, dominating a conversation. Instead he let his wife shine. Adelia watched him during the course of the meal, and noticed that he was far more comfortable talking quietly to one other person than being part of a group. But he laughed, he smiled, and he didn't seem unhappy.

Of all the matches she had made for her daughters, Ramon was the one who she had known least about. His family was rooted here in the north, scattered over a wide area, but Adelia had been impressed by them. Margaret herself had met him and suggested that she would not be unwilling to consider marriage if he was considered suitable; Adelia had taken on the challenge and arranged everything to everyone's obvious satisfaction.

Lord Morland and Gwen were also clearly in love, and their affections for one another were encouraged by Margaret who seemed delighted that they were planning a wedding for later in the year. Margaret had let Adelia handle most of the planning for her wedding, but it seemed that Gwen was far more independently-minded.

"I say we should hold the party here at the manor, and ignore what that old crone might say," Margaret said firmly. "And we can decorate the church how we like, quite frankly."

Adelia had been distracted and had lost the thread of the conversation. She said, "Which old crone is this?"

Margaret winced and looked across at Ramon. "Dorothy Talfourd. She's the mother of the local vicar." There was a note of something like distaste – or was it disdain? – in Margaret's voice.

Adelia wondered who she disliked more, the vicar or his mother.

Lord Morland was the most talkative of the group and he was not backward in sharing the general opinion of Dorothy Talfourd. "She thinks she's in charge," he said. "It isn't up to the Reverend Talfourd how we get married. But it's his mother who rather thinks that it's up to her, and you may rest assured she has very fixed ideas on how things have to be done."

"She is a curiously precise sort of woman," Margaret agreed. "You would think she was born to the nobility but Ramon knows her family, don't you?"

Ramon grunted. "Not really. I didn't grow up around here but they say her father was nothing but a labourer."

And now that labourer's grandson was a man of the cloth! Adelia was impressed. "The reverend has done well. He must be a determined sort. So he opposes your ideas for your wedding?"

Lord Morland was not impressed with the reverend's rise. He laughed with the hint of a sneer on his youthful face, his sandy moustaches curling upwards. "Oh, *he's* not an issue. He would say yes to me riding a white stallion up the aisle if I wanted to. But it's her. You know, when he stands in the pulpit of a Sunday and preaches, it's his mother you can hear speaking really, like some uncanny ventriloquist. His voice but her words, you know?" He shuddered dramatically.

"Well, we can't get married anywhere else," Gwen said, putting her hand over his. "My mother and father are far too old to travel out of the area. We shall do well to prise them out of the house down to the village, to be honest."

"Margaret said you lived in the Old Tollhouse?" Adelia said politely.

"Oh, yes. Just me and mother and father. The place might sound, from the name, like a wee little cottage but it's a rather rambling place that has been added to from decade to decade and it's positively dripping with the Gothic. I should invite you for tea, Lady Calaway, but my parents' health is often uncertain. They have good care and I am able to visit here often to see my dear friends."

Gwen was a birdlike little creature with eyes as large as a porcelain doll, and narrow lips in the most perfect bow. Even her speech seemed to flutter like wings.

Margaret smiled. "Friends? Would you visit as often if Peter was not staying here with us, for the moment?"

Ramon spoke and it was an uncharacteristic dig at Lord Morland. "It's a rather long moment, don't you think? At what point does a moment become a residence?"

"Hush, Ramon," said Margaret. "At least he won't drink our wine cellar dry."

Ramon shrugged in response. He was a clean-shaven man, though his hair was slightly too long and hung in straight curtains either side of his narrow face. He would habitually tuck the stray strands behind his ears, and they would almost immediately fall forward again as he bent his head to read a book or examine a newspaper. He wasn't bad looking but he wouldn't turn heads if he walked down the street – unlike Lord Morland, whose lithe body and muscular fitness seemed evident in every move that he made.

Ramon was more of a reader and a thinker than a mover.

Lord Morland seemed to be used to the teasing and though Adelia tensed, no one reacted badly. *Perhaps it was an ongoing joke*, she thought. *And what was that about the wine cellar?* It was then that she noticed that Lord Morland was not drinking alcohol.

"Well, I have to stay until May Day, don't I? I can't wait to see old Dorothy's face when your pet artisan unveils his project on the village green," Lord Morland said, and it set them all off laughing, all except Theodore and Adelia. They had only arrived that day, after a slow and leisurely journey of around a week, and were baffled.

"I have no idea what anyone is talking about," Theodore said, a little grumpily. He was tired.

Margaret frowned and Adelia recognised a flash of the old

character that she was more familiar with. Margaret huffed. "Papa, Peter just *said*. Do listen; it's polite. There is to be a surprise at the village May Day celebration. We want to return the fair to its more authentic roots. It's become awfully tawdry lately and it's such a disappointment."

"Authentic roots?" Adelia said. "You do know the origins of the May Day celebrations, don't you?"

"Of course we do. But Dorothy Talfourd has been clamping down on all that, claiming that it's pagan."

"She's right. It is."

"Mother!" Margaret exclaimed. "We're hardly going to be burning down the church and installing druids in a cave."

"I say, there's an idea. The druids in a cave, I mean, not burning down the church," Lord Morland said. "Unless *she's* in it. We could make an exception...?"

There was raucous, cackling laughter. Adelia did not join in. She frowned and she noticed that Theodore, too, was looking uncomfortable. Wine, brandy, sherry; indeed, all manner of drinks were flowing and although Lord Morland's glass was full of only some ginger and lemon, he too was relaxed and merry.

Adelia wondered, suddenly, if she perhaps preferred the old Margaret, the one who was quiet and reserved, the one who didn't speak out quite so openly. She had been closeted in her own world back then, so enigmatic and unreachable, but she hadn't been advocating local rebellion either. It was good to see she had made friends and established herself at last, but Adelia now thought that these friends were not bringing out the best in her daughter.

☙❧

ADELIA SLEPT RATHER WELL AND SHE WAS UP EARLY THE next day. She left Theodore lingering in bed and dressed in

comfortable walking clothes. Smith, her lady's maid, had trav-
elled with them and she advised Adelia to choose muted
colours and understated ornamentation. "We're in border
country now," she said. "The hedges are full of reivers and
raiders."

"Well, for one, that was all a long time ago. And secondly,
there aren't any hedges. But otherwise, I do take your point."

"I should come with you."

"Yes, that will make all the difference if I am set upon by
half a dozen armed men. No, Smith, you stay here."

"My lady, the people here have strange ways. They are
country folk."

"We live in the countryside too."

"No, my lady. This is ... *older*."

"You read far too many lurid novels, Smith."

"If only I had the time."

"Smith!" But Adelia smiled and left.

The April air was chilly. It was noticeably colder than it
had been in the south of the country and spring was a few
weeks behind. Griseley Manor lay to the south of the village
of Greyhaven. The road that led to the village was wide and
well-maintained, and as she approached the village she could
see why the access was so good. In front of her, running at a
right angle to the road, was a river and alongside the river,
before the road crossed it by the stone bridge, was a grey-
walled mill. It was low and not as large as the ones that were
spreading across northern and central England, but it was
busy enough, and she knew that it was a steadily growing
woollen mill.

She reached the bridge and looked down into the village.
Though it was early, it was already bustling. In fact the place
was almost a small town, with its coaching inn in the centre
opposite the green, and behind all of that were rows and rows
of workers' cottages.

Impulsively she turned left rather than go down into the village itself. The mill was to the right of the bridge and she left it behind as she followed a well-trodden path alongside the river. She could see a stand of trees up ahead and she was delighted to find a peaceful limpid pool being fed by the river. She couldn't see where the water left the pool, however. It was as if the river simply filled the pool up but it never overflowed, like a magical cup in the Arthurian legends.

Two swans turned lazily on the still water. A willow hung low, its long thin leaves half-submerged. She gazed on the scene for a little while, letting its calmness refresh her, and then idly began to walk further along the path, aiming to complete a circuit of the pool if possible. But the path wound into some trees and she stopped abruptly when she saw a stand of three hawthorns, twisted and old, their branches distorted in unnatural shapes. The tallest one of the three was particularly unsettling and something about it made her shiver.

Tied to the branches and twigs, in amongst the emerging spring leaves, were scraps of coloured fabric. An invisible breeze seemed to lift the edges of the rags and she didn't like it at all. She turned around and walked very quickly back to the more open side of the pool, and nearly screamed when she saw a figure up ahead who was dressed entirely in black.

Almost immediately, and to her relief, her rational sense caught up with her irrational and emotional reaction. It was a man of the cloth, in his early middle years, and he was standing with his hands on his hips and staring at the pool as if it had personally offended him.

She approached noisily so as to not startle him, but startled him anyway when she extended her hand and said, "Reverend Talfourd, I presume?"

"Yes! How did you know?" he said, wide-eyed like he had been caught.

"Well, I didn't think the village had two reverends. Adelia, Countess of Calaway."

"Oh! Ah! Mrs Alfoxden is your daughter. Delighted." He had an educated accent, and polite manners. He pressed her hand lightly. "You're staying at the manor?"

"Yes. I must ask, what is the meaning of the tree down in the hollow that's all covered with rags?"

He knit his brows together. "The villagers here are somewhat backward in their beliefs," he said. "It is as if a thousand years of the word of our Lord has not happened. Do not let it alarm you – it is a silly and meaningless superstition and I am called here to root out such practices. None of it has any power to harm you," he added.

"I never believed that it might," she said in surprise, though she wondered if that were strictly true. But now, standing in the early spring sunshine, in the company of a churchman, yes – to remember the trickle of fear she'd had a few moments' previously now seemed ridiculous.

"Called here?" she then said, to change the subject. "How very interesting. From where do you originate? Is it a very different sort of place to … to all of this?" She glanced around. The chimney of the mill was short, and dwarfed entirely by the ring of hills that rose in circles of steepness to enclose them in this valley of grey-green scrubby grass and brown-black river water.

"Not entirely," he said. His mouth twisted downwards, an open expression of disgust. "In fact I was raised in this very place but left to study at Cambridge. Once I had been ordained, after a short period elsewhere, I found my path to return here and I took my place among the people once more."

"The people? Your people."

"I … suppose so." He didn't look very happy about it.

"And I hear that your mother is well-known in the village,

too. She must be very pleased to have her son back in the fold." Adelia wanted to say something about his rise from humble origins but didn't want to cause offence.

"My mother. Yes. She is." His gaze slid past her, then, as he sought an escape from the conversation.

She realised that she must have been disturbing a private moment of reverie. Perhaps he sought peace by this particular pool and she had upset his morning meditations. She made a move past him but as she went, she spoke again.

"I am very glad to have made your acquaintance and you shall certainly see me in the pews for as long as I am here at the manor. Might I also pay a call upon your mother?"

"No, she – yes, of course, no, she's quite old now of course, but would appreciate the company, however, yes, certainly." He looked like a startled rabbit.

"Thank you," she replied, choosing to take his confused stream of words as a "yes" though it was debatable. "Good day."

He murmured a strangled response and she sailed past him, heading back along the path, wondering why on earth he felt he had been called to come back to a place he so clearly hated with every fibre of his soul.

A group of very serious looking men were gathered outside the mill as she went past. They were holding files, folders, rolled-up sheets of paper, rulers and all manner of other paraphernalia. One was pointing at the river and gesticulating while the others nodded sagely.

Adelia had a vague recollection of hearing Ramon speak to Theodore about changes planned for the mill's operation but she had not got into the details, and the overall impression she'd been left with was that the changes were not good ones. Ramon and Margaret had suggested that these improvements were not to be welcomed but she saw no lack of enthusiasm from the men outside the mill.

She crossed the stone bridge over the river and headed towards the village. Directly in front of her was a large green space though she was less delighted to see a set of wooden stocks in one corner by the road. She hoped they were only there for decorative and historical purposes now, rather than the public shaming and punishment of wrongdoers.

At the far side of the green was a looming grey house surrounded by trees and alongside that was the church. She did not head that way. Instead she veered to the right where the Mason's Arms lay in the centre of a row of shops.

She was curious to discover what retail offerings the village harboured. She was pleased to see a very well-stocked general store, plus a pharmacy and an ironmongery. She was peering in through the small-paned window of the grocer's when a woman of terrifying antiquity accosted her with directness.

"Good morning. So who are you, then?" the ancient relic asked.

At first Adelia wondered if this could be the famed Dorothy Talfourd but on second thoughts, it was deeply unlikely. This old lady was dressed in layers of roughly spun tweed cloth and her accent was rolling and thick. She had a whiskery chin, pale rheumy eyes, and a voice without a hint of age in it.

"Good morning." Adelia introduced herself and extended her hand.

The woman seized it but did not shake it. She twisted Adelia's wrist so that her palm was now uppermost and peered closely before laughing. "I was about to tell you you're dead but you're wearing gloves! Ha! Ha! Oh, my eyes. Take them gloves off and let me see your lines. I'll read you your fortune, pet."

A man emerged from the shop and interrupted them. "Leave off, Nanna, let the visitor bide. You're up at the manor, are you not?"

The woman addressed as Nanna said, "Jack, she's Mrs Alfoxden's mother!" She widened her eyes as if she'd said something significant.

"And you didn't read that in her palm. She told you so, and you're not fooling me." Then, to Adelia, he said, "I am sorry for the state of this auld harridan. Nanna Black's the scourge of the village, isn't that right?"

"And Nanna Black is your grandma, Jack, and not too auld to put you over my knee, see if I don't!" she retorted, but both were laughing.

Jack grinned at Adelia. "Don't mind her. She's everyone's grandma. Were you looking for anything in particular?"

"No, just browsing, thank you."

"You'll want for nothing, up at the manor, I reckon," said Jack.

"Aye," said Nanna Black, "anything that money can buy, perhaps. But not the other things."

"What other things?" Adelia asked. She was fairly sure that the old lady was simply playing into the common perception of the ancient village soothsayer and her grandson, if he was that relation to her, was acting the part of a yokel. But there was something unsettling about the pair, nevertheless. Perhaps the memory of the rags on the hawthorns was having more of a lingering effect than she cared to admit.

With an apparently abrupt change of subject, Nanna Black said, "How is the wee girl? How is our Iseult?"

"She seems well, thank you."

"Aye, aye," Nanna Black said, nodding at Jack. "Good to hear. Mind that you tell us if she ails and we'll see her right."

"Oh," said Adelia, speaking to Jack. "Are you the pharmacist?"

He burst out laughing. "Nay, pet, I'm down at the mill."

"We have ways," Nanna Black intoned. "We've kept her safe so far, in our own way. Tis not a task they'd thank us for, but it has to be done, right enough."

Adelia wanted to ask, *what ways? What tasks? What has to be done?* And she thought of the scraps of fabric, and decided that she didn't want to know. Instead, she said, "Ahh, yes, the mill. I saw a lot of men outside it just now."

"The engineers. Aye. We're hoping for an engine, you see, so we can keep up with the other mills. They've all had them for years and years now, and it's time we brought the steam power here too, make us more productive, like."

Adelia was astonished. She'd assumed the place already worked under steam power. "Oh," she said. "But why are people saying it's a bad thing?"

Jack glowered at her. His mood had turned. "*Nobody* says it's a bad thing. It can't come soon enough for the likes of us. I must get on." He lightly touched the tips of his fingers to the edge of his hat, and stormed off.

She noted that at no point had he removed his hat to her nor addressed her as "my lady."

"I am sorry," she said to Nanna Black. "I have offended him."

"Not you. It's them. Oh, we'll look out for wee Iseult, right enough, for the bairns are always innocent but your daughter now, and her husband, they ought to be taking more care. Up in the manor, they have a responsibility to us as much as we have to them, you know. His family's always been here, in one way or another. There's a pact. An understanding."

"Of course." Adelia knew that very well and was disappointed to learn that Margaret had not apparently learned the lesson. It was something that was hammered into the upper classes – the lower orders owed them fealty and loyalty, but there was a price to be paid. The upper classes owed their dependents protection and understanding.

"I shall speak to them," Adelia said.

"You do that," Nanna Black said roughly. "And while you're at it, you ask them this: why can we not have jobs like the rest of the country? We *need* that new engine. We need the mill to expand. You tell your daughter that, pet. We're not here to starve and look pretty to feed her fantasy."

"What fantasy?"

"The stuff in her head. I'm half-blind and can still see it. Now you go and have another look at her."

And without another word, Nanna Black spun around and left.

Adelia no longer felt disposed to browse in the shops. She gathered herself and set off back to the manor.

IT WAS SHAPING UP TO BECOME ONE OF THOSE WARM, bright, cheerful sorts of spring days. In spite of Adelia's lingering concerns about the potential for a rift between the village and the manor, she found a bounce in her step as she made her way back. Her stomach rumbled. Smith would have kept some breakfast aside for her, no doubt, and she increased her pace.

Griseley Manor lay behind imposing high walls but the huge black metalwork gates stood permanently open. A long driveway led from the gates between rows of neatly clipped trees, sweeping up to where the manor itself sat on a low rise. Perhaps it would have dominated the village better had it been on the top of a hill, but up here in the wild north, it would have become an inhospitable place for most of the year.

Ramon Alfoxden, the master of the house, was one of a horde of sons of a huge, wealthy and variously-titled family that spread its tendrils and scions across much of Northumbria and the border country. Though Ramon himself had inherited no particular titles to speak of save the usual courtesy designations – the Honourable this or that – he was in all other respects the de facto baron of the lands around Greyhaven at least.

His estate was relatively small, and turned over mostly to grazing animals, but he had extensive grouse moors too. He lived off the money from his inheritance, his rents, his farms and the shooting rights that he leased. As far as day to day business went, he worked few hours and seemed to have very little stress.

Adelia thought then about Lord Peter Morland. He was a happy-go-lucky sort of chap and she had a vague idea that he, too, was part of the same family, perhaps a distant cousin of Ramon's. She couldn't recall anything definite about his background and he had never crossed her path in London. He was quite a bit older than Gwen who was only in her early twenties, as far as Adelia could tell, and he had referred to time spent aboard – Moscow, Paris, even New York. So he was well-travelled, educated, and lively. Gwen could do worse, for sure. Adelia wasn't certain where his money came from, but he clearly had enough of it.

Her musings were interrupted by noises coming from a low building to the right of the manor. She veered off course, intrigued, and found herself in the open doorway of a woodworking workshop. She inhaled deeply. There was something so very comforting about the smell of recently-cut timber.

She opened her eyes and realised the noise of chiselling and hammering had stopped.

A lithe young man was staring intently at her. He had closely-shorn dark hair which made his face look almost fey in the shafts of golden light that were slanting in through the large windows. The shutters had been folded back to let in as much light as possible to work by. He was dressed in the timeless uniform of the craftsman; a loose linen shirt, brown trousers, and a leather apron.

He also wore the casual confidence of one who was utterly the master of their craft and their space.

She apologised for the intrusion immediately. Somehow, a craftsman's working area was understood to be sacred. Wealth and title might open many doors but the tradition of an artisan was a special one and their workspaces were not to be meddled with. Perhaps it was a romantic notion, but it felt inviolable nonetheless. She introduced herself as she backed away.

"No, wait," he said, his voice warm and rich with a northern accent. "Stay, if you want." He sounded similar, but not quite the same as the people she had met in the village.

"I don't want to disturb you. Sorry. I was attracted by the – by the smell."

He laughed with a snort, but it wasn't mocking. He nodded and looked down at the huge wooden pillar lying across half a dozen trestle tables. She wondered how she had missed it when she had first entered. He rested his narrow hand lightly on the wood and smiled at the work he had been doing with a gentleness that he certainly had not bestowed on her.

"Goodness," she said. "Is it a ship's mast?"

"It was, once," he replied. "Come and see. Mrs Alfoxden wants a maypole for the May Day fair, and it has to be special."

Adelia could see, now, the carvings which writhed up and down the huge piece of wood. There were echoes of the Green Man, a common enough sight in churches of course. And there were more countryside images – foxes, squirrels, deer, crows and mice. Tree leaves – oak, ash, sycamore and rowan – half-hid female figures in long narrow gowns. It was a beautiful cornucopia of agricultural fertility.

Something about it nagged at her, however. Something about it was off, yet she could detect nothing wrong in the beautiful carvings.

"And this is to be the surprise, is it?" she said, now understanding what the previous night's conversation had been about. Reverend Talfourd had to be against this. Indeed, it was his job to be against this. As for what she'd heard of his mother...

But the village, surely, had to love this. From what she had seen of Nanna Black, surely this kind of thing was exactly what they would appreciate?

Then Adelia thought that she understood. Perhaps this was Margaret and Ramon's way of building bridges with the rural people. Nanna Black had hinted that the Alfoxdens didn't take their role seriously, but perhaps Margaret knew that, and was making amends. Maybe Nanna Black and the others didn't know about the maypole yet.

She felt more kindly towards her daughter again. She had underestimated Margaret.

But she looked again at the carvings. Fields of corn, fields of wheat.

Oh, she realised. *None of that was grown up here.*

Before she could ask about the themes that the craftsman had carved, they were interrupted.

"Mama! So you've found my tame artist, have you?" Margaret said as she slipped almost silently into the workshop, summoned by Adelia's thoughts.

The craftsman turned his face away. And who could blame him? An artist was no one's tame pet.

Adelia said, "I don't know about that. I was admiring this piece of work, however."

Margaret went over to the craftsman and slipped her arm into his, in a familiar gesture that surprised Adelia. But then she realised it was one more way that Margaret was showing ownership of the craftsman, not friendliness. Well, one person's good intention might be interpreted quite differently by the other person on the receiving end of such an action. The man smiled briefly before dipping his head and carefully sliding his arm free.

"Oh, Charlie, you're such an old-fashioned sort. Mama, tell Charlie he mustn't be like that," Margaret scolded.

"I shall do no such thing. Let the man get on with his work," Adelia said.

He nodded and turned back to his tools, picking up a hammer and a chisel.

Adelia went on, saying to Margaret, "It is beautiful. But you must know that the Reverend will be appalled at this because of its pagan connotations – do you think it might cause a rift within the village, perhaps?"

"How so?"

"I have met a few folks this morning who will likely enjoy this, but if he were to preach against it, you will alienate a good proportion of other people, the church-going sort. You said last night that this were to be a surprise and you treated it as a good joke, but I wonder if you ought to perhaps work *with* Reverend Talfourd, not against him. For the sake of local harmony if nothing else. I am sure many of the villagers will support you if you go about this in the right way." *Nanna Black, for example*, she thought.

"If it were just a case of working with the Reverend, we would have done so already," Margaret said. "Did I not make that plain last night? It is his mother who is the problem."

Charlie's chisel slipped. He straightened up and paused.

"What is it? Are you hurt?" Margaret asked, although Adelia suspected she was more worried about damage to the maypole.

He didn't reply to her. Instead, the mention of Dorothy Talfourd seemed to have sparked something in the craftsman. He stared hard at Adelia. "My lady, forgive me, but may I ask a question?"

Margaret rolled her eyes. "Charlie, are you still obsessed with the Arbury family?"

He ignored her and carried on. "Do you know anything about the Arburys who used to live in this area?"

"Goodness. I am not the right person to ask," Adelia said in surprise. "Surely Ramon knows? He is local."

He ignored her question. "The Arburys are an old family, or they were. They don't even exist anymore," Charlie said. "Arbury House is derelict. But if you hear of anyone with the surname, will you let me know?"

"Of course," Adelia said, thinking that would be very unlikely. But what else was she going to say? She searched her memory. Maybe it did ring a bell. The more she thought of it, the more she wondered if she *had* heard of an Arbury. But she didn't say anything to Charlie. She'd make a few enquiries and be sure of her knowledge before she let the young man know.

He was still staring. "Please," he said. "It is important to me."

Margaret said, "Charlie, mama has agreed – you don't need to press her on the matter." For Margaret, a person only had to be told a thing once, and they were expected to know it forever.

To soften her daughter's impatience, Adelia smiled at the craftsman.

"Yes, Charlie ... I'm sorry, what's your surname? So that I might find you again?"

"Charles Webb."

"Of course you'll find him again. He's going nowhere, are you, Charlie?" Margaret said.

He turned away and picked up his chisels.

❦ 3 ❧

T heodore enjoyed a hearty breakfast, indulging in all the very best that the area could offer. The sausage was a slab of meat cut in a square, called a Lorn sausage, and it was served with a relish made from red onions and tomatoes that had been grilled to a lightly blackened sweetness.

Where had the tomatoes come from at this time of year, he wondered idly. There were hot rolls, yeasty and fresh from the oven, with a choice of butter, cream, jam and marmalade. He had to refuse the offer of fried potato cakes and eggs, and was tempted by the suggestion of asking for lamb's kidneys but decided to try them another day. His clothes were straining.

"Do you have this spread every day, or are you trying to impress us?" Theodore said to Ramon.

Ramon looked up from the book that he was reading. As far as Theodore could see, Ramon was always reading something. Every room in the manor had a pile of books, and if Ramon found himself near to them, his hand would automatically snake out to pick one up, even in the middle of a conversation.

"Our cook is a marvel," Ramon said, only half paying attention. He could read and talk at the same time, it seemed. "But we are lucky to live where we do, right in the middle of a very special kind of abundance."

"Well, it's delicious."

"Thank you. People tend to think of this area as wild and empty, sparse and devoid of life, but it's positively teeming with good things – and potential. Sadly, that means the march of progress is upon us, whether we like it or not." He put his book down, and tapped his finger on one of the newspapers which had been brought in that morning. This one he had spread flat on the table alongside his plates. "Steam engines!"

Theodore buttered another roll. "But we've had engines in one way or another for over a hundred years," he said. "They are jolly useful and you can't deny that our engineers are the finest in the world. Our manufactories are bringing wealth and employment to everyone."

"With respect, sir, they bring misery and death to many. They bring wealth to the mill-owners and force employment of a most inhumane sort onto the common man. It is not how one should live. I have been in these places, sir – have you? Children, barely older than our Iseult, running in among machines that at any moment threaten to tear their limbs off. Fourteen hours without seeing the sun or a breath of wind upon the cheek."

"But the Factory Act prevents –" Theodore started to say.

"Oh yes, yes, the children have to be ten years old at least but who checks? And all that they produce is sold at vast expense – they are denied even the pleasure of owning what they make. In short, sir, it is a hell that man has made, and enslaved the freeborn Briton."

Ramon spoke in a low voice, quickly, as if such a stream of words had to be got out of him in a hurry. He tutted at the end, and pushed the paper away from him. He picked up his book, not inviting a reply. He had spoken his mind, and that was that.

How very like Margaret, Theodore reflected. In fact, most children were now staying at school until the age of twelve and hardly worked more than ten hours in a day. It was a far cry from the conditions that children had suffered when he'd been a boy. But Ramon was fixed upon the ideas of the thing, not the reality.

He remembered much of the conversation they'd had the previous night. Both Ramon and that Morland fellow had been vehemently against the introduction of a Corliss engine at the mill. Currently it was barely a mill at all, but Ramon seemed to glorify the work that went on there and in the rooms behind people's cottages and houses. Half of the village were woollen spinners and weavers in one way or another, but Theodore knew they could no longer compete against the mass-produced cloth of other towns. He shook his head and thought, privately, that it was a wonder the village had survived as long as it had.

He excused himself, and took a walk down to the village to see it for himself.

❧

THERE WAS ANOTHER REASON FOR THEODORE TO VISIT THE village of Greyhaven. He didn't bother to look too closely at the mill; nothing could be seen of the workings from outside, and anyway, he knew most of the cloth was currently being produced in private homes, in an old-fashioned and very inefficient way. He took note of the inn and thought it looked respectable enough to patronise later, perhaps. There were a handful of shops of no interest whatsoever, and a village green that looked reasonably well-kept. The people that he saw were poor, however, and many had need of medical or dental attention.

He wondered if Adelia would let him loose with his doctor's bag.

He asked a toothless rustic for directions and once he had deciphered the atrocious accent – he was sure they were putting it on just to rile him – he was able to find the house he was looking for.

It was relatively new, huge, ostentatious, and very much exactly how he expected Beaumont Sloane's place to look.

The door was answered promptly by a neat young girl who took him politely into a reception room. He heard a loud voice shouting, "Who? Who is it? What did you say?" Then brisk footsteps, a cough, and the door was flung open.

Beaumont Sloane was around thirty years old, with a rugged and tanned face from an outdoor life. He stared at Theodore blankly.

"Morning, sir. What can I do for you? I don't contribute to any silly subscriptions, you know, and you're wasting your time if you're here to convert me."

"What on earth do I look like I'd convert you *to?*"

"I don't know. What's your name? My maid is useless."

"Theodore Caxton, the Earl of Calaway."

Sloane narrowed his eyes and then burst out laughing. "Good heavens, forgive me, my lord! Ha! Lord Calaway, you are most welcome. Sir John Arbuthnot put you onto me, didn't he?"

"He did, but we have also met, if you recall. Naseby's, last summer?"

Sloane shook his head, but he was smiling. "I don't

remember a thing that happened at Naseby's and it's probably for the best. I was drunk before I even got there, and things only got worse from that point. I settled one lawsuit quietly. Did I try to fight you?"

"No, but you asked me to ask my wife to find you a new wife of your own."

"Did I? Ha! And has she?"

"I mentioned it to her, and she was surprised, as she understood that you were already married."

Sloane's easy manner slipped and a darkness lowered his brows. "I am, but she's unwell."

"I am a doctor. Might I assist?"

"It's nothing physical. You can help me get her committed, though. We have no children and in her current state of hysteria, we're unlikely to get any. I have to think of the future, you know? Do you know of any approachable asylums?"

"Er, no, not in this area," said Theodore, quite taken aback by this turn of events.

"Let me know if you hear of one. And it doesn't have to be local. In fact, it would be easier all round if it weren't. I'll send her to Timbuktu if I have to!"

"Of course," said Theodore, who had now decided he had absolutely no intention of helping this man throw off his wife.

"Good, good. Got to think of tomorrow, you know. The future. I am a *vastly* wealthy man and what's the point if I can't leave it all to a strapping son? Oh, you look a little uncomfortable – my talk of money, is that it?"

It wasn't and Theodore just nodded and smiled. "What line of business are you in?"

"Oh, I inherited half of it and I've made the rest through investments. I own half the cottages around here – yes, me, not the Alfoxdens. I bought them up bit by bit as the Arbury family sank."

"The who?"

"Oh, years ago, the whole area was under the thumb of a terrible old family called the Arburys. Good riddance to the lot of them. The Alfoxdens, however..." Sloane cocked his head. "You know them, I think..."

"I'm staying there. Margaret, Mrs Alfoxden, is my daughter. So we are, in fact, related to them."

"Yes! Yes! I see it now! Well. That *is* interesting."

"How so?"

"I don't have a great deal to do with them, to be honest. I socialise in Newcastle or Edinburgh; I spend most of my time away from here. You were lucky to catch me. Nothing happens here and I don't understand why they bother to stay."

"The landscape is rather bleak but I understand the shooting to be good, in season."

"That's the only thing going for this northern hellhole. I'll be straight with you, I've nothing against the Alfoxdens as such, but I don't really agree with all their talk of craft like it's some sacred thing to work with your hands. It bloody well isn't. They glorify labour because they haven't done a day's work in their life and if you see one of them with a spade in their hands, then they're playing the part of a worker for a few hours but it would be a different and sorrier tale if they had to dig a field for even a full day."

Theodore burst out laughing. Nothing that Sloane had said either offended or surprised him. "I agree with you completely," he said.

"We understand one another! Capital!"

"So you're supporting the installation of the Corliss engine at the mill, I presume?" Theodore went on.

Sloane was just crossing to ring the bell to summon a maid, perhaps to call for refreshments to be served. He stopped and turned. "You presume?"

Theodore felt the atmosphere in the room turn chilly.
And it truly must have plummeted in temperature for
Theodore to have noticed it.

"You suggested that we were on the side of progress?" he
said hesitantly, wondering how he'd gone wrong in the
conversation.

"Ha! I'll tell you this for free – that bloody mill is the one
thing, the *one* thing where I have common ground with your
Alfoxdens."

"But they are against it."

"Yes! And so am I!"

"But why?" Theodore asked in amazement. "It will bring
increased efficiency and more control over the workforce.
Without it, this village will die."

"That is progress, too," Sloane barked. "All things come to
an end, don't they? Can't fight that. Maybe this village needs
to die."

"While I agree in principle, there is no reason to allow
this village to die in this way right now, if it is preventable,"
Theodore said.

"That engine is a waste of money and the people here will
never take to it. And it's too far to the bigger towns. And
there is too much competition out there already. No, sir, the
mill is a lost cause and the engineers need running out of the
place, I tell you, before they destroy everything!"

Theodore took a step back. Sloane's face was puce now,
and spittle was forming in the corners of his mouth. For all
his talk of a hysterical wife, it seemed that Sloane was not
emotionally stable himself.

Sloane mastered himself at last. "Forgive me. It has been a
trying time lately. My wife ... the mill ... business matters. You
understand, I'm sure." He showed no sign, now, of ringing for
refreshments.

Theodore accepted his apologies and took his leave.

Beaumont Sloane sober was as loud as Beaumont Sloane when he was drunk, Theodore realised. Theodore resolved not to seek out the man's company again, at least, not unless they were in a larger group. Alone, the uncouth man was something of a barbarian.

❧ 4 ❧

When Theodore got back to Griseley Manor, he found Adelia writing letters in the little suite of rooms that had been assigned to them at the back of the house. They had most of the upper part of one wing, which seemed excessive, but Theodore knew that Ramon and Margaret just wanted to make them comfortable. And, like the expansive breakfast, perhaps they were trying to impress others, just a little. But it was natural for the children to want to show to their parents that they had "made it" in life.

Adelia looked up briefly but carried on writing and he settled himself in a chair by the window, overlooking a court-yard, while she finished.

"Smith said you had gone into the village. I am surprised that we did not meet; it's not overly large," she said at last as she signed the letter with a flourish.

"It is large enough. Anyway, I went to see Beaumont Sloane. Sir John reminded me that he lived up here. I paid him a call, unannounced and uninvited, but I shan't be hurrying back. He's trying to get his wife committed."

"Poor woman! Committed? Is she so dreadfully unwell that I could not call upon her, do you think? I could offer a crumb of solace, perhaps."

"I do not know the extent of her malady but I suspect that he would not welcome it. He doesn't welcome much, if I am honest. He's opposed to the new steam engine, which was very strange indeed, because in all other respects he was talking keenly about progress and the future."

"What was his objection?"

"Honestly? It was vague and unconvincing. That looks like quite a stack of letters – to whom are you writing? Harriet, I suppose?"

"Harriet, yes, and Charlotte and Dido, too." Adelia sat back in her chair and tapped the pen nib thoughtfully on a piece of blotting paper. "I don't suppose you have ever heard of a family with the surname Arbury?"

"Arbury? Oh yes, I know all about them," he said smugly, just to watch her jaw drop.

"Theodore! Don't look so pleased with yourself. You are up to something."

"I'm not," he said with a laugh. "No, it's just that it's the second time today that I've heard the name, that's all. According to Beaumont Sloane, the Arbury family used to dominate around here but he gave me the impression they were rather unpleasant and they fell into decline. He was able to buy many of their properties, which now give him a jolly good rental income. Indeed, he owns half the village."

"So there are no Arburys left here now?"

"Not as far as I know – but surely Margaret and Ramon would be the people to ask."

"I was with Margaret when it came up." She quickly told him of her encounter with Charlie Webb, the wood-worker, and his plea for information about the Arbury family.

"So you're writing to ask if anyone we know has heard of them?" he said. "Sloane said that there were none left now."

"I promised that young man I'd ask. It's the least I can do. And I am sure I have heard the name while we were in London. But that's the problem with memory; the more I think about it, the more I can convince myself that I *do* know it but maybe I've just thought about it so much that I am remembering thinking it. Does that make sense?"

"No, not a word of it."

She smiled. "I do know one more thing that you don't, or you would have mentioned it by now."

"Maybe I do know it, and am waiting to spring the surprise upon you," he countered.

"Go on, then."

"No, you speak."

There was a stalemate of around two minutes before he broke first, as they both knew that he would. "I don't know anything else," he admitted. "You win."

"Excellent! Are you ready for another walk?"

"Where to?"

She stood up, and he realised she was still dressed in her walking gown. "We're going to see Arbury House, of course."

ADELIA TOOK THE LEAD. THEY WALKED BACK THROUGH THE village and this time took a road that became a track, leading past the church and up towards a dense stand of stunted trees. As they got closer, they could see there was a crumbling wall held together by ivy, some twisted rusty gates, and beyond that, a wilderness of bushes and rambling shrubs that hid the rotten shell of a derelict house.

"Margaret told me about it after we had met Mr Webb, the craftsman," Adelia told Theodore as they picked their way towards the gates. Later in the year, they would struggle to even get this far; she could imagine the thistles and nettles would be shoulder-height and quite unforgiving.

"Oh, this maypole? Ramon mentioned it."

"That's right. Anyway, she said that she's already told Charlie Webb everything anyone knows about the Arburys but the lad won't give up. They used to live here but it's been abandoned for years. There might have been a son, who would be in his late twenties now if he is still alive, but no one around here knows anything more than that, and they won't speak of it."

"How intriguing."

"Perhaps. Or it's the same old story of ruin and neglect. That said, it *is* intriguing. Why does this Charlie Webb want to find out about them? What could the Arburys possibly mean to him?"

"He's probably inherited an unpaid bill and wants the money," Theodore said. "Shall we try to get in?"

She looked at the shambolic heaps of rubble held together by ivy.

"No. There's no roof on the place and it looks quite unsafe," she replied. "I think we ought to leave it now. I only wanted to see it, at least from the outside, and ascertain the extent of its decline. I need to go to the Post Office to send these letters anyway."

They lingered for a little while longer, absorbing the gloomy atmosphere of decay, until she was thoroughly depressed and unsettled. Then she slipped her hand into Theodore's and he squeezed it and led her away from the shadows, back into the light. She let go before they reached the village itself, of course.

"I was meaning to say to you that I think some of these locals need a little medical attention," he said to her in a whisper.

Not a whisper that was quiet enough, apparently, because she hushed him quickly and at least one head turned their way with a frown on their face. It was a young man, skinny as a rake and with a pock-marked face. He took in their well-cut, clean clothing, and threw them a mocking salute before then flicking them a far ruder gesture and breaking into a run, leaping a fence with a laugh and disappearing.

When they went into the Post Office, there was already a queue of people but as soon as the door jangled, everyone turned to look at them, and then, as one, they silently parted like a sea, pressing themselves against the walls so that Adelia and Theodore almost had an honour-guard to lead them to the counter.

Adelia protested, saying they would wait like anyone else, but the villagers looked mulishly at the floor and the Postmaster shrugged helplessly, gesturing for them to come forward.

It was all very, very unpleasant. There was obsequiousness there, yes, but it was layered over something else – resentment, perhaps? Adelia told herself it was only her imagination. She conducted her business as quickly as possible and they hurried out.

No one had said a single thing for the whole time they were in there. She wished, suddenly, that Nanna Black had been present. The old lady might have been strange and direct but at least she hadn't treated Adelia like these villagers were doing. It wasn't really deference, but nor was it an out-and-out rudeness. It was something quite different, and quite rural.

It was what Smith had warned her about. And maybe it wasn't just her imagination. She hadn't imagined the rags fluttering on the hawthorn, nor Nanna Black's intimation that Iseult was somehow cared for by the village in unspecified but unsettling ways.

Smith had been right – as usual.

Adelia and Theodore walked briskly out of the village and she had to force herself to slow down. "We don't want to look as if they have chased us away," she said, pausing on the bridge to gather her thoughts if not her dignity.

"It is the most decidedly odd, contrary, contradictory and unwelcoming place I have ever been," Theodore declared. "And that's saying something, for I've spent time in Parliament. They cannot always be like this."

"I do agree. Maybe your Beaumont Sloane had a point about not bothering with improving things here. Perhaps the people would do better if they moved to a larger town."

"Perhaps we caught them at an awkward time," Theodore said, inclining to be charitable.

"I admire your keenness to see the good in everyone."

As she spoke, she looked away from the mill that loomed to one side, and let her eye travel down the path that ran along the river towards the silent hidden pool. She thought about the hawthorns with their dark twisted trunks and grasping branches, and the scraps of fabric that fluttered there, signifying something – but what? What exactly were these the secret rites that Nanna Black had alluded to, performed to keep Iseult safe? What would happen when Margaret and Ramon unveiled the maypole at the May Day fair? Reverend Talfourd and his mother would be furious.

But what of Nanna Black and her ilk?

They could welcome it – or resent the intrusion.

Then Adelia shook her head and laughed at herself. Nanna Black was playing a part, nothing more. She was indulging in a game to try to bamboozle and scare the posh folk from down south. She had to take a leaf from Theodore's book and see the positive in people.

Secret rites? Nonsense. And there was no way that a

thirty-foot-high carved pole could be erected in secret on the village green, anyway – could it?

DINNER THAT EVENING WAS ANOTHER FEAST, INCLUDING langoustines cooked with saffron and wine and garnished with more extravagantly unseasonable tomatoes. The side dishes included such local delights as sea kale, dressed with mustard, and the meal was finished with something called "Border Tart" which was made with currants and walnuts, and served hot with a dish of thick cream.

Iseult was brought down to say goodnight to everyone before being packed off to bed. Gwen had not joined them from her home at the Old Tollhouse this evening, but Lord Morland was still staying in one of the guest rooms.

At the end of the meal, the table was cleared but they remained where they were as the fire was warm and the atmosphere convivial. No one saw the need to move. Conversation remained light, with Lord Morland speaking the most. Margaret chattered a little about her views on the pure honesty of a return to old-fashioned craft values while Ramon was happy to speak in a quiet way to Theodore on various light topics, a book clasped on his lap like a child would cling to a comforting doll. Adelia was on her best behaviour and she found that she did enjoy herself. Everyone seemed very happy.

And when Adelia asked Margaret about the family's relations with the rest of the village, she didn't seem particularly bothered at all. In fact she didn't recognise that there was a problem and so Adelia chose to let the matter drop. She'd done enough meddling in the lives of others, and of all her daughters, Margaret was the one who would most resent any interference.

The next day, a travelling dressmaker arrived to help Margaret with her new wardrobe for the coming year, and they closeted themselves off in an upper room. Iseult was, presumably, being bored stiff under the far too early tutelage of the nameless woman known only as "Nurse" whose role, it seemed, extended into governess and general tutor. At least Iseult's clever precociousness was being fed, to Margaret's credit as a mother.

Whatever Lord Peter Morland got up to during the day was a mystery, as Adelia only saw him turn up at mealtimes. He alluded, vaguely, to "business" though he was often sweaty and smelled of horses. Adelia guessed that he might be mostly riding to and from the old house in the hills where Gwen lived. Ramon had gone into a local town for the day, presumably to buy books, and Theodore had gone with him.

Adelia found herself at a loose end. She wandered out into the courtyard and could not hear anything coming from the workshop, although the doors and shutters were open. She peeped inside, and her movement startled Charlie Webb who was sitting hunched on a stool, his head bowed and his hands knitted together almost as if he were praying.

"Lady Calaway!" he said, and smiled in welcome though his facial expression remained flat and almost gloomy. His smile itself was brief. "Mrs Alfoxden is unexpectedly engaged all day, isn't she?" He sighed.

"I believe so. Is there a problem with the project?"

He didn't even glance towards the carved maypole. "No, there's a problem with what she'd promised she'd help me with."

"And what was that?"

"I need to go and see the parish records."

"What prevents you?"

"Who prevents me, more like."

"The Reverend Talfourd cannot bar you or anyone else from the records," she said.

"You would say that. You're rich and no one would say no to you."

"In that case," Adelia said, "let us go together, you and I. Would that please you?"

He straightened up, his eyes shining with intensity. "My lady, I'd be forever in your debt. Please. May we go immediately?"

"Almost immediately. I shall change, and let my maid know where I am going."

৩৫৩

ADELIA TRIED AGAIN AND AGAIN TO DISCOVER WHY Charlie Webb was so keen to look at the parish records. She asked if it were to do with the Arbury family but he wouldn't even admit that. He replied to her queries with short non-committal answers and if she'd pushed any harder, she would have had to have been quite rude.

They ended up walking in total silence through the village. People glanced their way and looked away again hurriedly. Someone made a strange motion with their hands, and she had the impression of warding off evil. Or maybe that was just her imagination, and it was a typically obscene and everyday gesture from one rough sort to another.

They skirted around the edge of the village green and avoided the rectory, heading first for the church itself, and they were in luck. The Reverend Talfourd was at the far end by the great brass lectern, sorting out a pile of ragged-edged hymnals. He jumped as they entered the cool gloom of the church. Adelia looked around but if there had ever been stained glass in the windows, it had all been removed, and the panes were plain and transparent. Indeed the whole building was sparsely furnished and not decorated at all, verging on the non-conformist, with not a hint of the more lavish ornamentation she was used to from the Anglican churches around her home in the south of England. It was a little bare, and not at all welcoming.

And equally unwelcoming was the vicar.

"Oh," he said, as if people never came into the church. He remained standing stock still, a book clutched in his hand like a talisman. He did try to smile but it seemed flat and as carved as a church grotesque.

"Good morning," Adelia said, taking a few steps up the aisle. Charlie Webb crowded in behind her, almost treading on her skirts. "I was hoping to access the parish records."

"They're locked away."

"Excellent. I am glad to see you take the security of such valuable items seriously," she said, and folded her hands together in front of her to make it very plain she was waiting for those records to be promptly unlocked.

"I mean – well, of course, it can be arranged. What are you looking for in particular? If I know what you need, then I can have the correct books brought out. There are many volumes, you see..."

Adelia turned her head to see what Charlie was going to say in response. He was still behind her.

And behind him, in the doorway of the church, was a woman dressed entirely in black like the deepest of mourning, resting her weight on a walking stick. Her voice was croaky and had a high-pitched whistle at the end of each laboriously-spoken sentence.

"Who is this?"

"Good morning," Adelia said, and paused. When it became evident that the Reverend Talfourd had completely lost his manners and was going to say nothing, she introduced herself and Charlie Webb.

. . .

SO THIS, AT LAST, WAS THE FAMED DOROTHY TALFOURD, A woman of working stock who had somehow raised a son to the Church. She must have worked hard to afford the education he needed. Perhaps the reverend was uncommonly gifted and had been awarded scholarships, though any gifts were not exactly evident so far.

The woman began to advance upon them, her stick striking the stone of the floor with the regularity of a grandfather clock. "That Charles Webb has been asking questions before. He got no answers. He needs to learn that there *are* no answers and that his questions are nonsense. Pure nonsense. I'd say he was ill in the head but that suggests there is a cure. There is no cure. No cure. No answers."

Her breathing became ragged with the effort of walking and talking at the same time. Her sentences were now nothing more than staccato words fired out at them like lead shot.

"Mother..." whispered Reverend Talfourd. His low voice was swallowed by the lofty empty building. If she heard him, she gave no sign of it.

She had reached Adelia and Charlie, who now scurried around so he was at Adelia's side and slightly half a step behind her. The old lady leaned heavily on her stick and glared at them.

"Mrs Talfourd," Adelia said in her most reasonable voice. "We are sorry to have caused you any alarm or distress, but I can assure you that–"

"You can assure me of nothing. Get out of this church."

That shocked Adelia. "I say." She floundered for words. "I say! One cannot be ordered out of a sacred building. This place is open to all."

But Mrs Talfourd paid her no heed. She grunted and

picked up her stick, and began to jab it quite violently towards Adelia's stomach. Her movements were wayward and her balance unsteady, and Adelia had to retreat to stay out of the way. *Any minute now*, she thought, *the Reverend Talfourd is going to step in and stop all of this.*

Any minute now.

Surely?

The end of the stick caught her a blow on her arm. The shock hurt her the most. "Ow! What do you think you're doing?"

"Get out of this church!" the old lady repeated, swaying as she lurched forward once more. "He is not welcome here!"

Adelia stepped to one side, colliding with Charles Webb.

They had no choice.

They left, with no grace or dignity left. They rushed past the gesticulating old lady, and almost ran out into the open air. Two young boys were sitting on the wall by the entrance to the churchyard, and they laughed and hollered in an incomprehensible dialect as Adelia and Charlie went past them. It seemed that half the village was out of doors for no real reason, and Adelia felt every set of eyes was on them as they took a short cut straight across the village green. As they reached the wooden stocks, the jeering and chatter suddenly fell away. Adelia stopped and glanced back.

Mrs Talfourd had appeared by the lych-gate of the church and the two boys were nowhere to be seen. She raised her stick unsteadily in the air.

Somewhere, a crow called, its hoarseness scratching the ears of the listeners.

Charlie muttered something which might have been anything from a spell, a prayer, to a curse.

Adelia didn't want to see any more. She picked up her skirts and continued briskly out of the village. She wasn't *fleeing*, exactly. But she certainly wasn't lingering.

"Mr Webb, what was all that about?" she gasped as she went. "I say, Mr Webb! Mr Webb!"

But he wouldn't speak to her. As they passed the inn, he veered inside, and left her alone to walk back to the manor as fast as she could.

5

The following few days passed uneventfully enough. Adelia did not see Charlie again, and she was glad of it in a way, even though she wanted some kind of explanation from him. The whole incident with Dorothy and the Reverend Talfourd was both embarrassing and infuriating, though when she'd relayed it to Margaret and Ramon, they had laughed, as if it were perfectly normal to be cast out of a holy place.

Only Theodore had been pleasingly angry on her behalf but she didn't press for him to seek any reparations. Yes, she had been rudely treated and she felt bad for Charlie too, but she had already decided that she would not be going to the church on a Sunday, in spite of her earlier promise to the Reverend. She would not set foot in that place again.

"If there are any witches in the area, I'd lay money on Dorothy Talfourd by the sounds of it," Theodore said. Adelia had calmed him down from his initial burst of indignation at the slight that had been made against his wife. He was still annoyed, but he was choosing to see the funny side.

"Witches?" Adelia replied, alarmed. "Who mentioned them?"

"You did."

"When?"

"The hawthorns that you saw. The way the villagers are. Their talk of *protection.*" He grinned suddenly. "All utter poppycock and designed only to alarm the incomer, of course."

"You don't think that there could be anything in it?"

He stared at her so long and so blankly that she felt quite silly, and dropped the matter.

She put all of the unpleasant experiences out of her mind. Once she set herself to it, she found that she was able to actually relax and enjoy her time in Northumbria as a real holiday. She kept up with correspondence, went for long walks, sat in the sheltered areas of the garden when the weather permitted, read books, and to her absolute astonishment, found great pleasure in having conversations with Margaret.

She had long considered Margaret to be her most difficult daughter. Mary, the first-born, had been so ill and frail, but then sensible and solid Dido had come along and taken on the mantle of the "eldest" in all but number of years while Mary was happy to be the coddled pet of the group. Next to be born was flighty Felicia with her anxieties and her girl-ishness.

By that time, Margaret was four years old and already serious, asking strange and difficult questions about how the world worked and *why* it should be so, and what would happen if it wasn't, and how that might be made to come about. Felicia's emerging silliness was a blessed relief, if Adelia were brutally honest with herself. Attentions of the family focussed on Mary's fragility and Felicia's attention-seeking drama, while Dido quietly read books and formed close friendships and Margaret just ... what? Amused herself, withdrawing into her own world as she didn't get any satisfying answers out in the real one.

Then came Anne, Charlotte and Edith, all so much younger than Margaret and all very different too, but in spite of their opposing personalities they made a little cluster together, again excluding Margaret from their coterie, though Margaret had seemed to be content enough.

Perhaps, Adelia thought, *I didn't enquire deeply enough. Perhaps, shamefully, I didn't want to have to deal with the results of my enquiries.*

Then she shook her head. Margaret had turned out well; she was married, she had an intelligent daughter, and friends too. Not the finest friends, perhaps, but friends nonetheless.

❦

"DO YOU EVER WRITE TO ANY OF YOUR SISTERS?" ADELIA asked Margaret as they worked together in the kitchen, getting in the way of the servants who were more than capable of packing up a picnic for them all. They had decided, at the last minute, that the weather looked to be uncharacteristically beautiful that day, and so they were to have a long lazy afternoon in the grounds of the manor. Ramon had already warned them all to make the most of it, as Northumbria had a habit of lulling one into thinking that spring was definitely bedded in before turning on everyone and letting winter descend once more.

"Of course I write to them," said Margaret as she wrapped a large game pie in some chequered cloth.

"You do?"

"Why do you sound so surprised?" Margaret asked. "They even reply to me! Honestly, mother, I am not blind nor stupid. When you arrived here, you spent the first few days tiptoeing around, starting conversations and then stopping abruptly as if you were afraid to speak. I can only imagine that you think I am some kind of prickly and sensitive monster whom you are desperate not to offend."

Adelia hoped that the hot blush of shame that she felt did not show on her face. She would not have expressed her feelings in such a blunt way, but yes: Margaret was correct. And it did Adelia no credit at all.

"I'm sorry," she said, fighting her urge to explain herself or try to justify it. She lost the fight, however, and went on to say, "But you must admit that we have not been very close and so I wanted to take care not to ... I mean, obviously, you are all grown up and I want to respect your house and ... sometimes you have been ..."

"Lottie wrote and said that you had argued with her while you had stayed in London."

"I did."

"And you were absolutely furious with Edith when she had that public outburst at all her husband's relatives. You actually locked her in a bedroom."

"Well, it wasn't quite that dramatic ... no, I admit it, I did. But she did behave unforgivably."

"So I hear and you did the right thing. I'd have locked her up too. But you really must stop treating me like I might explode, mama. I have definite opinions and Gwen tells me that some people find that intimidating until they get to know me, but you are my own mother. So stop acting as if you could say the wrong thing and I will have a fit. I have never had a furious outburst in my life."

Somewhere, a maid quietly giggled and another coughed. Adelia tensed – and then realised she was doing exactly what Margaret had told her not to do. She glanced up at her daughter to see if she was aware of the servants' quiet mockery.

She was. And she was smiling.

Adelia relaxed in a rush, and spoke honestly. "When you were a girl, a young woman I suppose, after Dido had left home, and Mary was spending time in that sanatorium, you became so abrasive and difficult. If I said something twice, you positively sneered at me for my idiocy; you could not bear to be questioned or contradicted; you assumed that everyone ought to be as quick and intelligent as you, and if they were not, then you felt they were deliberately behaving in a way to annoy you."

"Mother," Margaret said, speaking in a restrained way, but frowning. "That was above ten years ago. I had been left as the eldest daughter. The others were so much younger, and silly, and the centre of everyone's attention besides. I had no one to talk with. I longed to be at papa's side and learn from him but he was always so busy."

"He was engaged in business..."

Margaret held her hand up. "I know. I do not blame him. He was more present than many fathers. All the talk around me was of marriage and my future as a wife, but I did not care for any of that, until I met Ramon. I was lost, utterly lost. And yes, people talked to me as if I were stupid – you might suggest that they weren't being deliberately patronising but they were, they really were – and I simply could not bear it."

Adelia didn't know what to say.

Margaret piled up some of the last of the stored winter apples in a basket, arranged prettily in a nest of straw. "But I do concede that I don't suffer fools gladly," she added. "It has been mentioned to me. I shall do better. But you must allow me to have changed, and to continue to change."

"I will. I do." Adelia seized her hand impulsively and squeezed it.

"Oh, mama, enough," Margaret said, a little crossly, shaking herself free almost immediately. She softened it with a smile. And she'd said *mama* not *mother*, which was something. "I shan't change into *that* sort of woman though. The sort that likes having her hand patted. I pat hands – hands don't pat me. Come on. Let's get this outside."

She stood back and the servants came forward to subtly rearrange the things Adelia and Margaret had done wrong. Adelia and Margaret inched backwards, and found themselves eased out of the kitchen by gradual degrees.

❦

THE AFTERNOON WAS TRULY DELIGHTFUL. LORD PETER Morland brought Gwen, riding across the lawns on a huge white horse with Gwen sideways-on in front of him, clinging on and giggling. They might have been engaged to be married, but they were not yet man and wife, and it was a shockingly indecorous sight.

Adelia bit her tongue. Who was there to see this impropriety? It probably didn't really matter. And then she thought, *goodness, I must have absorbed some new attitudes from the time I spent with those Bohemian artists.*

Theodore, bless him, hadn't noticed a thing.

Ramon was content to sprawl on a rug, only three books close to hand, and he was playing a lazy game of quoits with little Iseult. She was more than happy to do all the running around. Her nurse and various other servants were clustered a little distance away, sitting on chairs and pretending to be busy with darning and so on. Really, they were all just enjoying the sunshine.

Chairs had also been brought out for the women but only Adelia sat on one. Margaret was content to sit on the ground like a common model in a Renoir, and Gwen followed suit, making Adelia feel slightly odd as she was higher up than everyone else.

Even Theodore decided to tumble to a tartan blanket,

though she heard his knees crack as he got down there, and he never seemed to get entirely comfortable. But once he was down, he was down; and the longer he stayed there, the more likely it was that he'd need assistance to get back to his feet. He was certainly not going to admit that he was now stuck.

Adelia made an effort to be natural and relaxed. She listened, more closely than she had done before, to Margaret as she talked about her hopes for the future of the village.

"But these dreams that you have," Adelia said, "all this talk of honest toil and true craftsmanship – well, it's all very good and I heard a lot of it in London, too. But what do the villagers here think?"

"Firstly, mama, I am not a dreamer," Margaret said firmly. "I never have been. You *know* that I am not frivolous like Mary; I don't have my head in the clouds like Felicia. I don't know why you insist on thinking that I am silly like them."

"I didn't say…"

"Anyway," Margaret went on. "I am sure that many of the villagers support us. Indeed, I am more than sure. I know it. They too dislike the impositions laid upon them by the pernicious influence of Mrs Talfourd. They resent her. Remember how she treated you, throwing you out of the church? For a labourer's daughter, she has ideas above her station."

"What did her husband do?"

"Die as quickly as possible, I believe." Everyone laughed.

"No," said Adelia, not laughing along. "Was he wealthy?"

Margaret looked blankly at Ramon. He said, "I cannot remember Mr Talfourd. He wasn't a man of any means or significance. She married well enough, I suppose."

"Any other relatives?"

"Oh, mother, who cares about that old witch?" Margaret said impatiently.

Ramon was frowning. "Her sister was the local midwife."

"There," said Margaret. "Witches, all. As for the villagers, they pay her no heed at all. They are concerned about the lack of work and how the young people of the village have to leave to get work in other places."

"So why not allow the mill to be improved? A new engine means more machines which means more work," Theodore said, perhaps bored by the talk of people and wanting, instead, to speak of engines.

"It's the wrong type of work. Soulless, deadening, repetitive, dulling. There is no heart to work like that."

"But there is money," Theodore said. "Of all of us here, I suggest I am the one with the most contact with the lower orders of society. I have *seen* what poverty does to a person, to a family. I have *seen* what happens when there is no work. And I've only seen a fraction of it, because the truly poor never called me as a doctor; they could not afford me. All they could do was let their children die. Dull though a factory job is, it is *work*. And that can mean life or death."

Adelia smiled at him. He *did* feel for people, in his own way.

"But our plan involves work for all, too!" Margaret said with passion. "I really believe we can create a centre here for craftsmen of all types to create beautiful and honest goods for sale. It has happened in other places. People will pay for genuinely produced work that is the labour of love."

Adelia furrowed her brow and decided not to argue back. Instead she said, "Well, I don't know enough about the whole thing so I shall leave it to you."

Theodore snorted. "We are not living in feudal times!"

"And thank goodness for that," said Gwen, even though she was dressed as a Medieval maiden and had just ridden in the arms of her Arthurian knight.

Talk turned to more idle matters as Gwen began to discuss the best flowers for a bride's hair, and Ramon spoke of the hothouses he was having built, and Lord Morland was content to lie flat on his back and let Iseult throw grass and daisies on his face.

And suddenly a visitor arrived.

He came striding across the lawns, pursued by the butler who was in a flap. The manservant was crying, "Sir, sir! I say, let me announce you!"

The stranger laughed and almost danced his way up to them. He was dressed a suit that was the most alarming shade of mustard yellow seen outside of the fields of Norfolk. He had longish hair that curled and bounced, a walking cane of purest black, and a smooth face. He carried a round black hat in the same hand as his cane, clenched between two fingers, and with his spare hand, he waved a broad hello as if they were all long-lost friends.

He reached them and bowed very low. "I am so sorry to interrupt your meal *al fresco* but my, my, what a perfect picture of a pastoral idyll! I had no idea that *the north* could be so appealing. I grew up here and I can tell you that the first eighteen years of my life were winter, simply winter. Vile. But now! Here I am! And here you are, dearest Lady Calaway, the architect of my summons, the Hermes to my days, the puppet-master, indeed, upon whose strings I dangle!"

Adelia started to form an idea as to who this foppish young man was. Her many letters to family and friends on behalf of Charlie Webb's enquiries had borne fruit in the past day or so.

She had even been told of a name, a man; one surviving member of the Arbury family.

And here he was. He must have flown north by train.

She got to her feet and said, "Mr Frederick Arbury?"

He grinned as if she had won a competition, and bowed again. "I am most perfectly *delighted* to meet you, Lady Calaway. Yes. Frederick Arbury, Esquire, humble servant at your every beck and call. And I can only offer my most heartfelt apologies to you and all the ladies present for crashing in upon your little party."

He bowed to everyone in turn, and was introduced. Margaret got to her feet and stood alongside Adelia, welcoming him with a certain stiffness. That was entirely understandable. Ramon sat up a little straighter, and said, "Lady Calaway, did you invite this chap here?"

"I did not. I did ask for information, however, and my daughter Charlotte had discovered his name and where-abouts. I wrote with some general queries but received no answer..."

Mr Arbury hung his head in mock-shame. "I wrote three letters in reply and destroyed them all when I decided to simply come and answer you in person. When I arrived in Greyhaven I sent a boy here to bring you word but he scampered off as soon as I had given him a coin and he went off in the wrong direction. I gave up and decided to simply call and leave my card here. But as I came up the driveway I heard voices and so veered around to find you – not expecting to disturb such a pleasant scene."

He dug into his jacket and pulled out his card. "But here; now let me do the decent thing, and retreat. Once again, my heartfelt apologies for the intrusion – I let my excitement get the better of me, *again*, oh it is my way, I am afraid – and I hope that I might be allowed to call at a more opportune time. I am lodging at the Mason's Arms." He bowed and began to back away, his free hand on his heart like he was making a pledge of undying allegiance.

Iseult said, "But sir, you haven't eaten anything! Mama, don't we offer visitors refreshments?"

Adelia smiled. The child was bold and precocious even if she couldn't quite pronounce "refreshments" yet. Gwen giggled and Ramon rolled his eyes ever so slightly.

Margaret glanced sideways at Adelia. "Mother..."

"It's your house. It's up to you."

Margaret threw up her hands in defeat. "Please, Mr Arbury, if you would like to join us and get to know us, please do. There are chairs or you can join us scrabbling on the ground like peasants. And I will confess, I *am* intrigued to discover your history. You must be very familiar with Greyhaven." She nodded at her husband. "Ramon, do you not recognise Mr Arbury?"

Frederick perched himself carefully on the edge of a seat. He evidently took great care over his clothing and wanted to avoid stains or creases.

Ramon cocked his head. "Although this manor and these lands south of the village belong to my family, I grew up closer to the coast in one of our other seats. I am afraid not. I cannot remember much about the Arbury family at all." He furrowed his brow. "Was your father not Lord Arbury?"

Frederick nodded and adopted an air of serene sadness. "My dear late-lamented father was, indeed, Lord Arbury, and he lived in Arbury House to the north of the village part of the year. In his later years, that is the only place that he lived, as our vast estate was sold off, piece by piece. When he died, I was twelve, and the family was already utterly in ruin but I did not know that then. It was not until I was twenty-one, and in my final years of study, that I was called to the offices of Mr Zachary the solicitor, and told that nothing remained – nothing at all – not even enough to finish my studies. I found myself penniless and completely alone."

"Goodness," said Gwen, hanging on to his tale with wide eyes and a breathless manner. Indeed, everyone was fascinated. Adelia tried to work out how old the young man was. He seemed to be in his mid or late twenties.

She said, "It sounds dreadful but here you are now, and if I might say so, you do appear to have overcome those difficulties."

Everyone loved a triumph-over-adversity story and clearly, Mr Arbury knew it. He began to tell them about his reinvention as a man of taste and fashion, his careful investments, his cultivation of connections with the right sort of people, his care with money and his application to details. Everyone listened closely and smiled and nodded, and he had such a way with words that they were all soon laughing and relaxing. He could hold court like a storyteller and even Iseult was interested for a while until she wandered off to plague Nurse with a stream of questions.

The afternoon passed quickly. Before long, Mr Arbury was hearing all about Margaret and Ramon's plans, and he was intrigued, demanding to know more.

In fact, he ingratiated himself so much that Margaret impulsively invited him to dine with them that evening. A few others had been invited, and she thought it was the perfect opportunity to ease him back into the society of his ancestral home.

Theodore yawned and said he needed to stretch his legs, and he excused himself.

Mr Arbury took his leave too, promising to return for dinner that evening.

It was only as the picnic packed up and everyone drifted off that Adelia realised that the whole purpose of getting in touch with Frederick Arbury had been completely forgotten.

No one had bothered to send word to Charlie Webb.

六 6 六

Theodore stood on the bridge that led to the village. He had left the party as it was breaking up and excused himself, saying he needed to take a walk to clear his head. It was around four o'clock now and the day was still light but the warmth was quickly fading from the air.

He glanced to the right, at the mill, and then looked along the river. It flowed past the mill, towards where he was standing on the bridge, and then along to the left. Adelia had told him that there was a strange pool further along. He hadn't yet visited it, and he was wearing good shoes, so he decided to leave that for another day. Instead he wandered into the village. He had no aim or purpose save to clear his head and loosen his stiff joints.

He considered popping into the Mason's Arms to have a quick drink but as he approached the main doors, he had second thoughts. Though it was a weekday, and not yet evening, it seemed to be somewhat raucous inside. He was surprised and did pause to see what was happening; perhaps there was a wedding party or something.

As he peered through the half-open door, a man staggered

into the corridor from the public bar at the front of the building, and approached the entrance where Theodore stood. Theodore stepped to one side. The man was drunk, unsteady on his feet, and shouting wildly at the unseen men who remained in the bar.

It was, to Theodore's astonishment, a rather inebriated Beaumont Sloane.

Sloane grabbed Theodore's upper arms and yelled, "Calaway, my man! Come and have a drink with me."

"Thank you but weren't you just leaving?"

"They think they can turf me out, do they? No, no, no! Come on." He started to drag Theodore back into the public house.

"If the publican's asked you to leave, you really ought to respect him..."

"Wasn't him! Them – them lot – those blasted engineers from the mill – taking over in there – but I shan't be harried out of my own inn, no sir!"

Theodore noticed that the public bar had gone quiet again, so the cause of all the noise must have been the presence of Sloane. He leaned back, fighting against Sloane's insistence that he join the other man for a drink. Sloane let go, and flung his arms in the air in impatience, his fingers striking the wall and making him growl in sudden pain.

"I've had enough of it all, you know," Sloane said, squeezing his now-sore hand.

He leaned close to Theodore, practically pinning him against the wall of the corridor. His breath was soaked with alcohol, thick and cloying and hot. "I'll have her committed without your help. I've found a place who'll take her. Then I'm free – free to divorce her, no shame at all, in fact they'll expect it and I can finally have the future I was meant to have."

A thousand reasonable questions came to Theodore's

mind but he didn't voice any of them. Sloane was too far gone in his cups to respond rationally. Margaret and Ramon had both said that there was nothing wrong with Jane Sloane. All Theodore could do was smile and nod, appear to agree, and slide away as soon as he could.

But Sloane now had his arm up, his hand resting on the wall, effectively caging Theodore in place. Trapped, just like Sloane's poor wife Jane.

Sloane slurred, "Does she really have to come with me tonight? I'll say she's indisposed. I'll leave her at home and come alone. It's best for everyone."

Theodore was vaguely aware that the Sloanes had been invited to Griseley Manor for dinner that evening – and if Jane had been truly mad, no such invitation would have been sent – but he was surprised that Beaumont Sloane had actually agreed to come. The invitation surely had been nothing more than a courtesy one. The elite families of an area had to look as if they were on good terms whether they were or not.

But then again, Adelia often assured him that even if everyone at a dinner hated one another, they would often still attend so that they did not miss out on any gossip. And it wasn't as if anything else were happening in the village.

Apart from the usual low-level enmity, the mill, the May Day fair, the church, and so on.

Oh, and the surprise arrival of a young man in a mustard-coloured suit.

Theodore said, "Oh, do bring Mrs Sloane if she's at all well enough. And if she is taken ill during the meal, then perhaps people will see that she's not quite herself, and that will help your own cause."

Sloane looked confused, unable to understand Theodore's meaning. In truth, Theodore was simply being hideously curious. He wanted to meet Jane Sloane and find out just how "mad" she really was.

Theodore then added, "Furthermore, there will be a last-minute addition to the guest list and I think he will interest you. You might even know him as he comes, originally, from this region. A Mr Frederick Arbury?"

"A – who? Who did you say it was? What was that name?" Sloane cried, pushing himself violently away from the wall. He seemed to get larger, breathing in deeply and straightening up.

Clearly the name was familiar to Sloane and now Theodore was even more interested. He repeated the name carefully.

"That man!" thundered Sloane. "He should not have come back. Oh, what about the last time, the last time? He should have learned."

"When was he here before? What happened?"

"What happened? What happened?" Sloane roared, his eyes rolling and wide. He jabbed his thick finger into Theodore's chest, shouting with an accusatory tone as if Theodore was to blame for everything and he ought to know it. "That stupid little woodworker has stirred it all up with his questions – oh yes, I have heard, I have heard – and now he's back when he ought to have left it all well alone. The pair of them. Arbury and Webb. No good will come of this! You tell them to get gone, you tell them!"

He jabbed again with such force that Theodore had to stifle a yelp. The shouting was drawn some guests from the bar and the publican was now approaching. He was holding a large heavy tankard in his hands, and Theodore knew it was a potential weapon.

"What's happening here, gentlemen?" the landlord asked in a very gentle, easy tone, oil upon troubled waters indeed.

"I was just leaving and I am sorry for the noise," Theodore said quickly, slipping sideways out of Sloane's reach while the drunk man's attention had turned to the publican.

Sloane shouted something incomprehensible. Theodore fled.

The man was so intoxicated that Theodore doubted whether Sloane would even make it to the dinner that night. And though Theodore still wanted to meet Jane for himself, he didn't think things would go particularly well if Sloane started to argue with Mr Arbury.

He would have to warn the others. Maybe things could be put off.

❧

NOTHING COULD BE PUT OFF, APPARENTLY.

In fact, Margaret laughed when Theodore warned her that Beaumont Sloane would not be fit company for them all that night, and that he appeared to have some kind of animosity towards Mr Arbury.

"Oh, papa. He's like that all the time but he will come tonight because he can't bear the thought of being left out, and he will bring poor Jane because she's not mad at all – I promise you – it's just something that he says. We have all heard it many times before. And Mr Sloane will be on his best behaviour. I would never have invited him if I thought otherwise."

"Are you sure?"

She frowned at him and didn't bother to reply. She'd told him once, and never saw any reason to explain herself. He sighed, and went to have a lie down for an hour before he had to dress for the meal.

❧

ADELIA LISTENED TO THEODORE'S CONCERNS AND HOW they had been dismissed by Margaret. She made a huge effort to give Margaret the benefit of the doubt – after all, she knew the local people far better than Theodore did.

But it quickly became apparent that everything had been a most dreadful mistake, even before Mr Arbury arrived. Perhaps Beaumont Sloane was still too drunk. Perhaps poor Jane Sloane had been fed a little too much laudanum before being laced into a crumpled dress by an unskilled maid who had also half-attacked her hair before clearly retreating in defeat.

Perhaps it was simply an unfortunate mix of people in an unfortunately poor choice of timing.

Adelia watched Jane closely. Margaret seemed to be a little surprised at Mrs Sloane's appearance, and concerned over her strangely dull movements. From that, Adelia knew that Jane was not usually like this. She appeared to be half-asleep; drugged, definitely. She was pale, almost grey in the face, with glittering eyes and a languid manner.

While Sloane knew that Mr Arbury had been invited, Mr Arbury did not know who the other guests were. He arrived after the Sloanes, and there was a sudden awkward hush as he entered the room. Gwen was standing close to Lord Morland, and Adelia was sitting down near Theodore, trying to engage the vacant Jane Sloane in polite conversation. Adelia had noticed Theodore was asking some very leading questions as to her health, and so Adelia was trying to steer the topic back into more acceptable areas. Theodore playing doctor at a dinner party was the last thing that anyone needed, she thought.

Margaret jumped up and seized the initiative as Mr Arbury entered. She put herself in between Mr Arbury and Mr Sloane, who were now staring at one another like cats about to have a fight. If one of them had begun to hiss, Adelia would not have been surprised.

Ramon likewise waded in. He went up alongside Mr

Sloane and said, "You know, I am glad you've come tonight because I don't believe it's too late yet to stop the mill installing this engine and ruining the whole character of the place. I thought of another objection that they really do have to take seriously. Won't there be noise? And – and – and smoke? Or steam? Or something? We can object on those grounds, I am sure."

While Mr Sloane was distracted, Margaret urged Mr Arbury to come in and take a drink, but he seemed unwilling to move forward now that he had seen Sloane. He had lost all of his easy air and his words were stilted and stumbling, no longer the elegant flow that he had shown before.

Mr Arbury mumbled, "I say, I just don't think, I mean, I had no idea, and it occurs to me that really I am imposing on your kindness, and you don't know me at all, and I was rather rude really to accept your invitation for it was one of those given for politeness' sake, was it not? I should have respectfully declined. This is terribly awkward. I am most grateful. But I should go."

"No, it would be far more rude for you to leave at this point..."

Mr Sloane swivelled his head around. He snarled one word. "Go."

Ramon was furious. "Now look here, Mr Sloane..."

But it was enough. Mr Arbury spun on his heel and left the room rapidly, and everyone was stunned. Even Jane Sloane seemed to recognise that something strange had happened and she put her hand to her mouth where her fingers trembled lightly on her lips. She seemed to freeze into that position.

Margaret was as angry as Ramon but she remembered her position as society hostess, and her calm but firm handling impressed Adelia.

She put a hand on Ramon's arm to soothe him as she said,

very loudly, "Poor Mr Arbury, to have been taken unwell at such short notice! But he has had a long and trying journey today, I understand. Indeed he must have been travelling for a few days at least. We can all forgive him a little unpredictability. Now. Mr Sloane, you were telling us about the mill?"

"No, I wasn't."

"But please do. Have you met with the engineers? Have you spoken with the owners as you had promised you would?"

"I tried, madam, but he would not admit me..."

Margaret had succeeded. She had turned Mr Sloane's fury onto other matters and he was drunk enough to be redirected onto another familiar target. But the evening progressed in a tense and uncomfortable fashion and Adelia found herself eating more quickly than was seemly, just to try and hurry it over with. She was also desperate to know why Mr Arbury and Mr Sloane had such animosity towards one another but there was absolutely no way of broaching the subject and she was both frustrated and very relieved that no one else tried to ask.

After the dinner, the ladies withdrew and Adelia seized her chance to speak more privately with Jane Sloane. But the lady could barely walk by this point. She had only picked at her food but she'd downed glass after glass of wine and her eyes were red and moist. She fanned herself furiously, claimed she was having a turn, and begged leave to sit quietly and be left to herself. As soon as her bottom hit the chair in the drawing room, she sank back into the cushions, exhaled, and passed out completely.

Margaret looked puzzled. "She's not normally so ... vacant."

Gwen sat alongside the unconscious woman and stroked her hand. "Mrs Sloane? Mrs Sloane?"

"I think we should leave her. Does anyone know why her husband is so furious with Mr Arbury?" Adelia said.

The other two shook their heads. "I will find out," Margaret vowed. "The whole evening has been an utter shambles – oh! The men are coming in already. That was rather quick."

Little time might have passed but it seemed to have been long enough for Beaumont Sloane to get even more drunk. He was barely more sensible than his lightly-snoring wife. Ramon's face was like thunder now. He was slow to anger and usually very easy-going and quiet. He had obviously reached the very limits of his extensive patience.

He turned to Mr Sloane as they entered the drawing room and said, precisely and in a low voice, "Thank you so very much for coming tonight but I do believe your wife is in need of some peace and quiet. I shall arrange for your carriage to be made ready immediately."

He left the room before Mr Sloane could argue back. In company, such a dismissal would have been seen as rude and would have led to gossip. But Lord Morland, still sober, was nodding at Ramon's words, and Theodore began to steer Mr Sloane towards the door. Adelia and Margaret were ready to help the floppy Mrs Sloane to her feet as soon as the carriage was announced.

They all staggered out into the cold night air. The Sloanes' coachman was coming forward to assist with Mrs Sloane, and Mr Sloane slipped down some of the steps, righted himself, barked at nothing, and walked so determinedly and drunkenly in a circle that he ended up falling sideways into a privet hedge. The coachman simply sighed. He ignored the flailing limbs of his master and helped Mrs Sloane up into the coach before returning to scoop Mr Sloane out of the foliage.

Gwen and Lord Morland bid everyone farewell hastily and were soon gone into the night themselves. Ramon and Margaret invited Adelia and Theodore to join them for a nightcap. Indeed, it was not yet late. But Adelia declined, feeling somewhat frazzled and worn out by the events of the evening. She wanted only to get to her own room, and as quickly as possible.

Soon she was dressed for bed, though her mind was fizzing and she did not yet feel ready for sleep. So she sat up with a book, reading, while Theodore failed to read a medical journal. Neither of them had anything to say.

Adelia wondered if they really did have to stay for the May Day fair, or whether they could perhaps escape home just a little sooner.

❧

CHARLIE WEBB NEEDED TO BE TOLD THAT FREDERICK Arbury had turned up. Margaret and Adelia went to the workshop straight after breakfast the next morning. On the way, Adelia raised the issue of the May Day fair.

"It's nearly two weeks away," Adelia said. "Your father and I were wondering whether to stay that long. We don't want to become unwelcome houseguests."

"You are not guests at all. You are merely family," Margaret said with a smile. More seriously, she added, "I said it would be fine, so it is. But I will not beg and plead. You make your own mind up and do as you wish. I should like you to stay but I am not telling you what to do. I did wonder, however, about inviting some of my sisters. As you and papa are here, I thought it might make a nice reason to drag some of the others up here."

"Oh! But it's such short notice."

"That's been the problem. Charlotte cannot get away. I have not bothered to ask Mary because of her frailty nor Felicia because she ought to not travel any more in her *state*."

Adelia thought that for all Margaret's claim to be a plain

speaker, those were excuses and not reasons. Felicia was carrying a child, yes, but had been travelling across the continent until a few months ago. And Mary was no longer the delicate girl she had once been.

"What of Dido?"

Margaret sighed. "I would have loved Dido to come and she wrote to say she'd try but wrote again yesterday to say she could not. Anne, of course, took three days to reply and it was short and gloomy. You know what she's like. So that only leaves Edith and she said *yes.*"

"Marvellous! Then I must stay. Oh, Margaret dear, something's occurred to me and this might be a dreadful imposition but..."

"Mama, stop creeping around."

"I am merely being polite." Adelia was irritated but she hid it. "You remember my old friend Mrs Harriet Hobson?"

"The bishop's wife?"

"The same. Well, they are up in York at the moment, doing something ecclesiastical at the Minster. Might I invite her?"

"Of course. We have space. Write to her immediately. Now – oh, do let me tell Charlie of the news!" They reached the doors of the workshop. Only one of the pair of doors was open, and the interior was in shadow, and quiet.

"Charlie!" Margaret trilled.

"You ought to afford him the respect of his title."

"Mr Webb? Oh, I could not. He's an honest worker, a man of the soil – well, not soil, but the woods, I suppose. You can't put layers of fake modern society on someone like that."

"Have you asked him what he prefers?"

Margaret clearly didn't want her medieval fantasy to be punctured and she ignored her mother, carrying on into the workshop instead. Adelia shook her head in exasperation.

Even for a clever woman, her daughter had infuriating blind spots.

She hung back when she heard Charlie Webb replying to Margaret's enquiry. She stayed in the brighter doorway while Margaret began to explain that there had "been a development" and some "very exciting news" and even Adelia grew impatient with the way she was spinning it out.

When Margaret finally made her big reveal, Charlie Webb didn't answer at first. Adelia listened to the silence. She could only see his outline, slender against a bright window behind him, and had no idea of his facial expression.

"Aren't you pleased?" Margaret said at last.

"Yes. Yes, so very much," he said quietly and somewhat flatly. "And he's at the Mason's Arms, you say?"

"Yes. And so are you, are you not? He seems awfully nice, you know."

"Nice?"

"Pleasant. Very well bred, of course."

Charlie Webb snorted. "No doubt."

"Well-dressed, polite, educated," Margaret went on, desperate for a more enthusiastic reaction.

"Good. I've nearly finished the carving of the maypole," he said. "I'll open the rest of the shutters and you can see."

"I'm sure it's wonderful. But what about Mr Arbury?"

"Thank you for the information," said Charlie Webb as he began striding around the workshop, flinging back the wooden shutters to allow light to stream into the place. He approached the doorway last, and nodded without a smile as Adelia stepped to one side to allow him to get to the bolts that held the second door in place. He dragged the lower bolt up and began to push the door outwards.

He stopped.

Adelia turned and her heart sank as she saw Beaumont

Sloane, the most unwelcome sight in Greyhaven as far as she was concerned.

He raised his hands in the air in a conciliatory gesture. He didn't look like a man who had been so drunk he had fallen into a hedge. He was irritatingly fresh-faced and perky. He said, in a most humble tone, "My dearest Lady Calaway, I am here to apologise to every single one of you for my wife's dreadful state last night."

Her smile froze and faded. He was apologising for *Jane?* She glared at him. Margaret came up alongside her, and caught what he was saying too.

Unlike Adelia who was fully aware of her duty to be polite, especially when a guest in another's house – family or not – Margaret was more outspoken.

She said, "Mr Sloane, the sad fact is that an excess of alcohol clouds one's memory and I might therefore tell you, without hesitation, that your lovely wife has absolutely nothing about which she must apologise. I shall, however, take the apology as made on behalf of *yourself.*"

Ouch, thought Adelia.

And Mr Sloane frowned. "I have nothing to be sorry for except that I married a woman who is weak in the head. I may have shown some high spirits last night, but what man would not? Only perhaps men that were under the thumb of their women," he added, showing he had a mean streak to equal any courtly gossipmonger.

For of course, neither Lord Morland, Theodore nor Ramon had stumbled about in the undergrowth and had to be rescued by footmen.

Margaret said, "Mrs Sloane is as strong a woman as any I know, and if you were to give her a little more support, she would be the perfect wife for you."

"Failing in her duty to bear an heir."

"The best brood mare in the country would not succeed if you kept her locked in a barn and half-drugged."

"What are you suggesting? That is a foul slur, an absolute insult! She is not locked up – she came here last night, did she not! Yes, she is under the doctor but to suggest that she is my prisoner, that I am poisoning her..." He ran out of steam.

Adelia stared at him with open dislike and she didn't need to look at Margaret to know she felt exactly the same way.

He coughed and said, before either of them could remonstrate with him, "Anyway, I am not here to see you."

A moment ago he'd been suggesting he was here to apologise. "Then why are you here?" Margaret demanded.

"That woodworker you've got in there. Webb. I need to speak to the little toad."

Instinctively, Adelia and Margaret moved closer together and effectively closed off the entrance to the workshop.

A sneer twisted Mr Sloane's face but he spoke with patronising honey as he said, "Now, now, ladies, there's no need for you to be involved in any of this. I need to speak to the chap man to man, on a private matter."

"This is private land," Margaret said. "Mr Webb is busy. Good day to you, sir."

Mr Sloane completely ignored her. "Webb!" he bellowed, his hot breath brushing Adelia's cheek and making her shudder.

She couldn't stay silent. "Look here, sir, you cannot stand in front of two ladies and shout like that. It is time you left. I appeal to your manners and your status as a gentleman."

He gave her such a look of hatred that her stomach clenched. He genuinely loathed her, she realised. And not just her. He hated everyone. No – no, just women. She held his gaze. He looked away, not because she had cowed him or shamed him, but simply because he didn't rate her highly enough to be worth engaging with. He shouted Mr Webb's name again and began to actually push his way past them as if they were common women selling goods at a market.

Margaret spoke out, protesting, and Adelia gave a squeak of pain. She exaggerated it, trying to make a point. Any decent fellow would stop and apologise.

Beaumont Sloane was nothing but an ignorant lump of a country squire. He elbowed his way into the workshop. "Webb! Get yourself out here, you coward."

"I'm here." He had been there all along, standing silently next to a table. He had a hammer in his hands and he was gripping it tightly.

Mr Sloane laughed to see it. "Put that down, you little weasel. You wouldn't have the strength in those arms to lift it anywhere near me." He stopped laughing abruptly. "Right. Now you tell me what the devil you're playing at in inviting that Frederick Arbury back here."

"It's nothing to do with me. I've only just heard."

Mr Sloane swore, making Adelia hiss in warning and Margaret speak out, telling him to mind himself before she summoned the servants to have him bundled off her premises.

He ignored them both. "Nothing to do with you?" he said, advancing on Charlie Webb. "The devil it is. You're the one here, asking questions, making a nuisance of yourself in the church – the church of all places! Upsetting people, raking up the past, poking your nose into stuff that has nothing at all to do with you. Of course he's here because of you."

"No!" said Adelia loudly. "It was *I* who brought Mr Arbury here."

"I want to know what you think to gain from all of this," Beaumont Sloane went on, jabbing his finger at Charlie Webb.

"Sir!" Adelia found herself almost shouting in a most unladylike manner. "Sir! It was me."

Her words sank in at last. He twisted his head around to glare at her. "You?"

"Yes," she said defiantly.

Charlie Webb muttered something as foul as Mr Sloane had been saying, and pushed past them all. "Everyone's against me," he said under his breath, and strode off into the morning sunlight, still clutching the hammer.

"It's still his fault," Mr Sloane snarled. "You can't trust him. Get rid of him. Get him out of your house."

"He's not in my house. And he is working for me. Like many more will soon be working here."

"Oh, your bloody craftsmen. That's a waste of time and money. Give up on this village. It's dead. Let it die. I certainly intend to. Pair of..." He began to mutter a stream of insults as he, too, left, walking briskly in the direction of the main gates.

"I'm worried for Charlie," Margaret said, starting off after him.

Adelia caught her arm. "Wait. What can you do? And if Mr Webb has any sense, he will be hiding in a tree by now."

"He does have sense. Yes, you're right."

"What is going on with Mr Webb and the Arburys? And why does Mr Sloane hate it all so much?" Adelia asked.

"I don't know."

"You would tell me if you did know?"

Margaret rolled her eyes in disdain. "I said that I didn't know, didn't I?"

Theodore and Iseult rambled along the side of the river. She jumped up at the colourful rags fluttering from the branches of the hawthorn trees, trying to catch them, but only succeeded in snagging her hair in the twigs.

This was the first time that he had been along the river. He knew that Adelia had been unsettled by the fabric in the trees. To her, they hinted at dark pagan practices. Theodore was more pragmatic. A people always wanted to feel tied to their land and their ancestors. It was nothing more than that, he thought. It meant no harm and was merely a quaint super-stition.

Iseult, too, seemed unbothered and undisturbed. She grew bored of the walk, so he promised her cakes, if there could be any got in the shop in the village, and they wandered back over the bridge and onto the village green.

An ancient old lady waved at them and Iseult waved back, crying, "Nanna Black! Nanna Black!" She broke free of Theodore's grasp and ran, in that clumsy child's way, almost colliding with the old woman before a stocky man who was alongside her grabbed her and swung her high in the air, making her scream and giggle. Theodore was pleased to see his granddaughter laughing and he was also, rather uncharitably, a little resentful that if he tried to play acrobats with her in the same way, he'd put his back out.

He caught up with them as Iseult was placed back on the ground. She clung still to the man's hand, who doffed his cap with his other hand. "Jack Fletcher, sir, at your service. This is Nanna Black."

"Theodore Caxton, Lord Calaway. And I'm this little scamp's grandfather and servant," he added. Everyone gazed at Iseult with adoration in their eyes.

"She'll be running you ragged, no doubt," Fletcher said.

"She makes me feel younger while tiring me out completely," Theodore replied with a laugh. "Come on now. We're hoping for cakes, or a currant bun, are we not?"

That was temptation enough to have Iseult abandon Jack Fletcher and hurtle back to Theodore's side. They all smiled and parted on good terms. Theodore felt warm and fuzzy. Everything really was the picture of rural bliss. *What a paradise that Margaret lived in, if only one looked at it in the right way!* Even when they went into the shop, the villagers did not treat them with the same guarded deference that they had experienced in the Post Office previously. Iseult was a darling of the community, and brought out smiles in everyone around.

They were able to buy far too many sweet, sticky buns and they came out of the shop with a bag full of indulgent treats. They turned to head back to Griseley Manor, and as they left the village, they were approached from behind by a man on a huge white horse.

"Peter! Peter!" Iseult said, clapping her sticky hands.

"Lord Morland," Theodore said. "Be polite."

Lord Morland laughed as he reined in alongside them and

leaned down. "I'm Peter, of course, to my little princess. My lady, surely you must rest your weary legs!"

"May I ride?" she asked, her face shining. "May I, really?"

"You would do me a great honour indeed. Calaway, could you...?"

With a grunt, trying not to show the effort that it took, Theodore hoisted Iseult up into Lord Morland's arms. He held her securely with one arm around her waist and they walked on at a steady, sedate pace, as she chattered about what she could see from up there.

Then the little girl cried out, "And Gwen! There's Gwen and mama, come to meet us!"

"How wonderful! Goodness, though, look at your mama's face. I wonder what's wrong?" Lord Morland said.

Margaret looked mostly furious and just a little upset. But Gwen, too, had none of the welcoming smiles that she usually carried, and she nodded only perfunctorily at Theodore. Instead she focused straight in on Lord Morland.

"Peter, how lovely to see you ... *at last.*"

"Ah! Oh, my purest, sweetest Gwen. I owe you a thousand apologies."

Theodore expected him to hand Iseult down to Margaret so that he could continue his conversation in private with Gwen, but in fact, Morland continued to hold tight to the little girl.

"I ask for no apologies, but I would like an explanation," she said stiffly. "Or will this excuse be the same as last time?"

"Gwen – you know what I'm like. It's not deliberate. I get caught up in things and forget the time, or I get asked to help at the manor, or..."

"You weren't at the manor," Margaret said. "As far as I am aware, you did not stay with us last night. Did you?"

"I – I rose early and went for a ride, and got rather carried away, and lost track of the time, and when I remembered I had arranged to see you, Gwen, I hurried back as quickly as I could. I'm on my way right now. As you can see!"

"Mama, don't be angry," Iseult said with a wobble in her voice.

Margaret frowned. "Oh, I'm not. Come on. We should all go home." She spun around and began to walk decisively along the road. Lord Morland continued to carry Iseult, and Gwen fell into step alongside them. Theodore half-ran to catch up with Margaret and to give the quarrelling lovebirds some space.

"Margaret, is something wrong?"

"Yes. Apart from Peter performing his usual music hall vanishing act, someone else has also gone missing."

"Who?"

"Charlie Webb has just upped and left without a word."

"Has he? When? And why?"

"The maypole was finished and he always said he was going to go but I was surprised he went so soon and so quickly and without saying anything. It's rude, frankly. Mind you, he always had a sullen and mulish streak to him. So I ought to not be quite so surprised."

"I thought he'd wait to see the pole up on the village green though," Theodore said.

"So did we. And to go like that – without even a thank you!"

"Was he paid?"

"Yes, of course."

"Well, there you have it. The working man is a different breed, you know, however much you have this ideal of how things ought to be."

"I know that. I'm no dreamer."

He tried not to let his amusement show on his face. Of course she was a dreamer, the biggest dreamer of all his daughters. She just wouldn't admit it to herself.

He said, "Did he take all of his stuff?"

"He didn't come with much and he's taken nothing from here that wasn't his. Don't imply he was a thief."

"I wasn't. I was wondering if some accident had befallen him, actually."

"Oh."

Theodore said, "What about all his obsession with the Arburys? Do you know what that was about? Did he get to speak to Mr Arbury in the end?"

"I think so. Maybe that's why he left so abruptly too. Perhaps he got what he really wanted. It's all a bit odd but mostly it's infuriating."

"You've lost your little craftsman," Theodore said, reaching out for her hand.

She pulled away. She didn't want comfort and she certainly didn't want insight like that. She half looked over her shoulder. "Gwen, have you told him about Charlie?"

Gwen nodded, but Lord Morland was already speaking. "She has. And good riddance."

"What had he done to offend you, Morland?" Theodore asked.

Lord Morland's mouth pursed briefly. "Oh, I didn't care for the fellow at all. I'm sorry, Margaret, but I have to be honest. He was shifty, if you ask me. He was always where he ought not to be."

"Unlike you," said Margaret pointedly. "You are never where you *should* be."

They passed the last few hundred yards to Griseley Manor in an awkward silence.

☙❧

ADELIA WAS VERY EXCITED. HARRIET HAD WRITTEN TO SAY she would arrive in a few days' time. Nearly a week had passed since the abscondment of Charlie Webb and Margaret's irritation had died down. Gwen and Lord Morland seemed to be on good terms once more, though she seemed to watch him closely. Adelia had heard from Theodore first about the lovers' tiff, and later she had spoken with Gwen herself.

Something about the matter had piqued her interest. Gwen was convinced that Lord Morland was hiding something from her, but Adelia was also convinced that Gwen herself was holding something back. She asked Margaret about it, who dismissed it with her usual curtness. Adelia let the matter drop. She was not here to interfere in other people's love lives – unless she was asked to get involved, of course. She did hope that they would.

But they did not.

Mr Frederick Arbury surprised everyone by remaining lodged at the Mason's Arms. He didn't seem in a hurry to return to London. Margaret was able to persuade him to join them at a dinner, this time without Beaumont Sloane, and they all got on swimmingly. After a few more meetings, Margaret and Ramon impulsively invited him to stay at the manor rather than "slum it" at the inn, and he accepted.

Indeed, he was very good company and brought a touch of light-hearted London glamour and fun to proceedings. He was also very interested in their plans for bringing together artists and craftsmen in a kind of pure rural community, though the more that they talked about it, the more unlikely it seemed to Adelia.

Still, they had plenty of wealth, and pretty much anything was possible in life if you could throw the cash at it.

Almost anything.

They had not been able to prevent the installation of the Corliss engine at the woollen mill.

The owners of the mill were a group of wealthy investors

from Newcastle. They had bought it from a local owner who was retiring and they felt no need to listen to the pleas of people like Ramon and Margaret, or the derision of Beaumont Sloane. There was nothing in law to stop them improving their mill and the workers, for the most part, supported it. Adelia bit her tongue whenever the matter came up. However she had spoken about it privately with Theodore and they both felt that the engine would be a good thing, and that the plans for it to be installed must have been agreed on many months ago; the protests of Margaret and Ramon were but token noises.

And, naturally, on the day that the engine was to be set into motion for the first time, absolutely everyone wanted to see it – and that included all the inhabitants of Griseley Manor.

Adelia and Theodore dressed warmly. The weather had turned slightly cooler and there was the threat of rain in the air, making Adelia's hair turn to frizz at the edges. Lord Morland and Mr Arbury were both still happily ensconced at the manor and neither showed any signs of leaving, and nor did Margaret hint that their welcome had run out. Adelia began to recognise that Margaret *needed* a busy household. She might have kept herself to herself as a child, but she had been surrounded by constant noise and activity nonetheless.

Even some of the servants from the manor came along with them. Everyone from the village had had the same idea, and the enterprising souls from the shops had closed up and brought trays of food to sell at the mill instead. The landlord of the Mason's Arms had sent one of his members of staff to the mill with a barrel of ale and some tankards.

But not everyone was getting swept away in the party atmosphere. Adelia spotted Reverend Talfourd standing by the edge of the crowd. It was impossible for everyone to get up close to the great horizontal pistons and flywheels and pumps and pulleys, and rather than push his way forward, he hung back. The new engine was housed partly in the original stone building of the mill and partly in a newly-built wooden extension to one side, and it had large doors that had been thrown open to allow as many people to see the spectacle as possible. From where he was standing, the Reverend could not see a thing. There was no sign of his mother.

Adelia left Theodore. He wanted to elbow his way through for a better view so she left him to his fight and instead she approached the Reverend to say hello. Before she got to him, she was waylaid by Gwen.

"I'm looking for Lord Morland," she said. "Did he not come with you from the manor this morning?"

Adelia immediately noticed his name change from the more casual "Peter." Another argument had happened, then. This didn't bode well for the marriage though it could all be put down to cold feet. Adelia smiled sympathetically and said, "He did come with us, yes. I think he will be trying to get closer to the engine and you might be better waiting until the crush is over. Miss Fitzroy-Harris, might I ask if anything is the matter and if there is anything that I can possibly help you with?"

Gwen's face clouded. She was young and had not learned the art of hiding her emotions. "I don't know what the matter is," she said, a little sulkily. "But thank you." She turned away, still looking for Lord Morland.

Now Adelia was too late to get to Reverend Talfourd. He had already been buttonholed by Beaumont Sloane. She wandered closer anyway, curious about Mr Sloane's rather threatening manner. He was looming over the churchman, and as she got within earshot, she could hear that he was demanding to know why the church had "let this happen."

"We support the provision of honest work for the poor," Reverend Talfourd was saying in reply.

"That's all very well," Mr Sloane thundered, his raised voice turning heads their way. "But what about the Holy Pool?"

"What Holy Pool?"

"What Holy Pool?" Mr Sloane repeated in a mocking tone, adding a high-pitched whine to his voice. "You know very well which blasted Holy Pool I'm talking about. It's not like we've got hundreds of the things scattered about. There's only one pool and it's the holy one."

"If you are referred to the water feature marked on the maps as 'Wilson's Pond' then I know the one, but I cannot see why that is of any concern," Reverend Talfourd said formally. His voice barely held a trace of the local accent and he was getting increasingly rigid.

"It's the Holy Pool and always has been. Isn't water sacred in the Bible? Baptisms and all of that?"

"Water which has been blessed is holy, of course, but it does not follow that all water is somehow imbued with power, which is what I can only really call a pagan superstition. And what is that to the mill?"

Lots of people were paying them attention now. If they could not see the engine, which was now thudding away with hisses and squeaks, they would watch this growing entertainment instead.

"Ha!" said Mr Sloane. "How do you think this steam engine works? It takes water into the workings of it – somehow – I don't even profess to know the details myself but I clearly know more than you do. It uses water, a great deal of water. Why do you think they had to extend the mill outwards? It was to bring the engine closer to the river."

"Very interesting," said the Reverend, backing away from Mr Sloane's rolling eyes and spittle-flecked mouth.

"Interesting? Interesting? Can't you see it, you dense block of wood? God, no wonder the church is on its knees these days, if you're the calibre of man that's running things. It's already taking too much water from the river!"

Reverend Talfourd shrugged. "The village gets its water from the pump on the green. I may be dense, sir, but I know it's fed from an underground aquifer, and has nothing to do with the river. No one will go without water because of the installation of this thing here."

Adelia felt a tall presence alongside her, standing with a familiar closeness. She glanced up to see Mr Frederick Arbury, all decked out in his finest London frippery, leaning on his cane and listening intently. He was frowning.

"I don't give a fig for how the village gets its water," Mr Sloane said. "But it's going to drain your Holy Pool in the end, isn't it? The engine will take the water from the river. The pool will dry up. Now do you see?"

The Reverend Talfourd shook his head with incomprehension. "I do see," he said, "but I fail to understand why I should be remotely bothered about the destruction of a pagan relic. Indeed, I welcome it. Let the pool be drained, and filled in, and completely forgotten about." His total unconcern was understandable, as far as Adelia could see.

Beaumont Sloane, on the other hand, was red in the face and had entirely run out of logical arguments, and was instead relying on obscene language and insults. Adelia turned away in disgust.

And to her side, Mr Arbury had gone very pale indeed.

❧ 8 ❧

By the next morning, Theodore could see that Adelia was already bored of talking about the Corliss engine and the more complicated developments in the world of steam power, but Ramon was quietly fascinated and they dominated the discussion at the breakfast table. Ramon had brought books to back up his insights.

Lord Morland was silent, sunk into some gloomy introspection of his own. Adelia had told Theodore there was already strife in the lovers' relationship. Mr Arbury, too, was not remotely interested in speaking about the mill. He muttered something about having to leave, and then immediately contradicted himself. Margaret pressed him to consider staying until the May Day fair. He didn't look willing to do so, but could not say what was dragging him back to London.

Everyone drifted away from the table but Theodore and Ramon remained, drinking a little more tea and talking about what might be next in the unstoppable march of progress. Ramon was just making some predictions about the possibilities of gas and maybe even electrical power when he stopped and cocked his head, listening. There was a shouted ruckus coming from the corridor outside. They went to look.

"The pool!" said one of the gardeners. He was standing at the far end of the corridor that led back to the servants' area, clutching his brown hat in his hands. He couldn't come in any further with his boots in the state that they were. The hallway was a cluster of family and servants, all listening. "The pool's draining, they say, the Holy Pool. It's already half gone and sinking like it's had the bung pulled out!"

"Oh, what a shame," said Margaret. "It was a lovely place to walk."

"It can't be permanent, can it?" Adelia said. "That would be dreadful."

"I expect so," said Ramon. "I say, shall we go and have a look? We could all walk down and see for ourselves."

Mr Arbury shook his head. "It will just be a temporary effect from the engine," he said. "All you'll see is a mass of mud. And it will smell. Such things are not for ladies or the well-bred."

"Well, I am a lady and well-bred and I still want to see," Margaret said. She nodded at Adelia. "Mama, let's dress and go together, even if the men are too dull to want to see new things."

Ramon laughed, Theodore nodded, Lord Morland shrugged and sighed. Mr Arbury threw his hands in the air. "Very well, though I too will need to change. I cannot risk *these* trousers."

THEY LEFT HALF AN HOUR LATER AND MADE A SEDATE progress along the road. Many of the servants had already gone to see, with or without express permission from the household, but no one seemed to mind. Adelia walked with

Margaret, ahead of the men who were lagging behind to discuss the optimal geographical sites of mills and such like.

"Goodness, what do you think has happened?" Adelia said. "Look!"

"What do you mean? Oh, mama, stop being a detective."

"I cannot help it. There's trouble up ahead." She speeded up.

Theodore called from behind and she waved her arm to get him to catch her up. She wasn't going to slow down for him, dodgy knees or not. They reached the grassy slope that led down to the pool. The willows and the hawthorns were just as before, and they could see the tall waving reeds making a waist-high fence around the pool; later in the season they would be higher than a man's head.

And there was a chain of men from the village, holding on to one another's belts, making a snake out into the soggy dregs of mud that was once the Holy Pool. They were sinking up to their knees but they were trying to get further and further out into the treacherous swamp.

They were trying to reach the body.

"No! It cannot be!" cried Margaret in alarm, her hands flying to cover her mouth. "That hair, that jacket..."

The figure was slight and slender, and lying on their side, their arms outstretched in an unnatural way. Their face was buried in the mud, as was the lower half of their body.

But it was almost certainly Charlie Webb.

Theodore went ahead and then spun around. "Adelia, take Margaret away from here. No one needs to see this. I'll handle it."

Ramon stepped up too. Lord Morland was turning away, frowning. Mr Arbury had taken one look at the scene and turned on his heel. He strode away, holding a handkerchief to his face, his foppish sensibilities quite overwhelmed.

Margaret let out a small sob and Ramon went to comfort

her. Adelia could not help her curiosity, however, and she inched forward to take in the whole view. A few other things had also come to light, lodged to varying depths in the mud. There was nothing near to Charlie Webb except a small brown bag from which spilled a cloth and some tools. Given that it had not been buried very far, Adelia guessed that this was his everyday bag. So he had intended on leaving, then.

But there was one other thing around ten feet away from the body that looked unusual. It was a much larger thing, like a brown box, though whether that was just the mud was hard to tell. It was wedged against a stone which had stopped it sinking. It was closed, and had a chain wrapped around it.

"Adelia!" Theodore said again, urgently.

She shook herself, apologised, and put her hand out to lead Margaret away from the terrible scene.

MARGARET PULLED FREE OF ADELIA'S ARM QUICKLY. THEY walked up the path back towards where it joined the road over the bridge but Margaret kept glancing back at the crowd around the pool.

"It was Charlie, wasn't it?" she said.

"I believe so," said Adelia. "I am so sorry."

"But what could have happened?"

"He was a troubled young man."

"Do you think so? Oh – mama – what are you implying? Do you mean to suggest that he could have possibly taken his own life? No! Never!"

"I don't suggest a thing and actually, that had not occurred to me. I meant only that he was a man with a strange way about him, and such people have secrets. And secrets can lead to arguments and terrible deeds."

"You assume murder then?"

"I wonder. It hardly looks accidental."

The thunder of carriage wheels made them stop. The police had arrived, and two coaches shot past with one of the village boys riding up top with a coachman, directing them to the pool.

Margaret said, "Mama, I don't want to go home. I want to know what's happening. Let's go to the inn and wait there. And I could do with a drink. Couldn't you?"

"It's a little early. And it is a public inn."

"It's medicinal. My nerves..."

"Margaret, you've never suffered from weak nerves for a single moment in your life. But very well; let's find a room there, if possible, and you think it acceptable. You know this area better than I do, and I shall be guided by you."

"We shall be welcome in the back bar. There are booths, all screened off. They call it the snug and ladies are admitted with discretion. You can be assured of our name being unaffected."

"I *hardly* think so. A booth in a bar? Oh, Margaret. We must take a room."

"Mother, this is not London. This is not the south."

It *was* rather thrilling to consider sitting in an inn, although Adelia couldn't shake the feeling that she still ought to set an example for her daughter even if her daughter was fully grown, married and a mother herself.

"Oh, there's Gwen!" Margaret cried.

Gwen hurried to them. She must have walked down from the Old Tollhouse on the hill, for her boots were dusty and her face flushed.

"Hodges came up talking about the most terrible thing," she gasped. "Is it true?"

"Come to the Mason's Arms and we shall tell you everything," said Margaret.

So the three of them ended up in a small room – Adelia

won that one – with frosted glass in the windows, paying twice the price for the same poor sherry that they would have got far cheaper out in the tap room with the everyday drinkers. Before they had even got settled, Margaret had told Gwen everything that they had seen.

Gwen was shocked, naturally. "How had it happened? Why was he there? What about the other thing you mentioned – the box? Was it a chest? How large was it?"

"It was like a small travelling trunk. He could have been carrying it," Adelia said. "Indeed, my immediate thought is that he could have stolen it. Margaret, has anything gone missing from your house?"

"Absolutely not! And this is exactly the kind of snobbery that I loathe," Margaret said with some passion. "You were casting aspersions upon him earlier, suggesting that if he has met a violent end, that it must be his own fault due to his concealment of secrets. And now, *now*, you want to brand him as a thief too! And all because he was a working man, and sometimes quiet, and perhaps did not feel the need to pay you all the respect that you think you are entitled to receive."

"Oh, for goodness' sake," Adelia snapped back. She was no longer walking on eggshells around Margaret, as promised. "That is not what I meant and if you choose to read such nonsense into my words then I suggest that it reflects more deeply on your own prejudices."

Margaret's mouth dropped open. "I have no prejudices at all."

"There are other ways to be a snob. You don't look down on working men like Charlie Webb, this is true. Instead you idolise them and raise them higher than they are, putting them on pedestals and unable to see them as real people who may do right, but who also may do wrong."

"Like Tess in Mr Hardy's book," Gwen said.

Adelia had read it recently; it was very new and somewhat

modern in some of its themes. Indeed, it was talked of in hushed tones in certain of the better types of drawing rooms.

She said, "Almost like that."

Margaret, to Adelia's surprise, nodded. "Very well. You do make some points which I will reflect upon later, mama. But for now, whatever are we to do about Charlie?"

"Do?"

"Has he any family? A sweetheart? People will need to be informed."

"That is down to the police," Adelia said.

"And papa. He'll sort things out, won't he?"

"He'll certainly try to. Margaret, do you mean that you don't know anything about Charlie Webb's circumstances?"

"Not a thing, though I asked and asked. He just appeared one day, and was asking for work here in the inn. Someone sent him to us and I saw his potential immediately."

"What a mystery. Do such things happen here in Grey-haven?" Adelia asked, half-jokingly.

But Gwen took it seriously. She said, "There's been nothing recently but I grew up here, don't forget, and there were so many strange tales when I was a child."

Margaret smiled indulgently. "Dear Gwen, that's very sweet, but not exactly what we're talking about."

"Don't treat me as a child just because I am younger than you. I know things, too. You're as bad as Peter."

"What's the matter between you two?" Margaret said.

"Nothing."

"You can speak in front of my mother."

"I would but there is nothing to say."

"There must be."

Gwen remained obstinately silent until Margaret relented and said, "Very well. Tell us about these strange events from the past."

"It's about the Arburys, you see. And I know that Charlie was asking about the Arbury family, wasn't he?"

"Oh! Yes, he was."

"See! Perhaps it is relevant."

"What is? You haven't told us anything yet."

"The secret tunnel!" Gwen said triumphantly.

"What secret tunnel? I am losing patience. It's been a trying day already."

But clearly such bickering was a normal part of their friendship because Gwen took no offence at Margaret's harsh words, and simply stuck her tongue out, like a small child. After indulging in a moment of superiority, she finally told them about the tunnel.

"They say that there is a secret way that goes under the stone wall between Arbury House and the church!"

"For what purpose?"

"Nobody knows!"

"Have you seen it with your own eyes?"

"No but Mary Jenkins said that her sister said that their family's maid had actually been in it."

"And Mary Jenkins is...?"

"Ah, she's a disgraced woman now and won't be ever coming back here and no one speaks of her, but this was before she fell."

Adelia was smiling by this point. "And how might this secret tunnel be connected with the tragic death of Charlie Webb?"

"Well – that's for you as a detective to discover, isn't it?" Gwen said. "But surely it's a clue!"

"We will bear it in mind."

Margaret said, "Are you really going to investigate?"

"As to that, it will be up to your father. Or rather, up to how well he can persuade the local police..."

❧ 9 ❧

The main police station house in the nearest town was entirely under the thumb of a capable and professional inspector called Tompkins. There was a superintendent somewhere; Theodore heard his name mentioned. There was a small bevvy of constables and a few sergeants, all going about their business in a quietly ordered fashion. Inspector Tompkins had been on the force for more than half of his life and he struck Theodore as clever, efficient and perfectly willing to allow "the celebrated gentleman detective" to share in the initial investigations.

"Anyway," said Inspector Tompkins as he whisked along the beige corridors of the station house, "You are a witness to the discovery of the body, and you had met the deceased I understand, so it would be useful to have you here both as an eyewitness and as a professional sort of man in your own right."

"Marvellous. And I do appreciate your concessions."

"Not at all. Here we are – I shall leave you in the capable hands of our doctor. Klein, this is Lord Calaway. I expect the usual from you. Thank you. Good day."

Theodore was left in the well-scrubbed mortuary. The walls were painted pale green with white tiles extending halfway up to the ceiling, and the fittings and furniture were all clean wood.

Doctor Klein was standing by a sink, laying out some knives. He was a short man, very lean, with tanned skin suggesting he spent all his free time engaged in healthy outdoor pursuits. He had a neatly trimmed pale orange-blond beard and he nodded without smiling, though his eyes creased in welcome.

"Other inspectors would be breathing down my neck by this point, insisting on my first impressions, demanding to know how they died, pressing for answers so they could make a hasty arrest and move on. But not Inspector Tompkins."

"He seems a very capable man."

Doctor Klein laughed. "He's capable of very neat paper-work and not much else. He doesn't want to be bothered with all ... all of this." He waved a hand that was holding a scalpel, and Theodore suddenly noticed that the edge of the blade did not shine like it ought to have done.

Klein wasn't washing his implements. He was just using the space to spread them out. Theodore's confidence in the local police was already beginning to wane.

"And that suits us," Doctor Klein went on, strolling over to the body on the table. He used the tip of the blade to lift the lower corner of Charlie Webb's jacket and flip it away from his body, revealing a sodden white shirt that clung to his body. "Hmm. He's been in the water a few days, wouldn't you say?"

"It was fresh water. I don't believe there is the same bloating that occurs as in sea water?" Theodore suggested. "Or at least, it occurs at a different rate."

"Oh, it fluctuates. It's impossible to give a precise time.

But see, I'm thinking anywhere between two and ten days, looking at the finger-ends and so on."

But Klein wasn't really looking at the finger-ends at all. He was standing at a little distance and merely glancing at the body as a whole. Theodore's hands itched. He wanted to get in there, examine every inch of the clothing while it was still on the corpse, then strip it down carefully and methodically.

While Theodore fought his inclination to seize the dead body, Klein turned away and picked up a large notebook, still holding the scalpel in the same hand, a rather dangerous arrangement of paper and blade. In his other hand he picked up a pencil and sucked the end which made Theodore cringe. It was generally unwise to put anything to one's mouth when one was in a mortuary.

"Drowning," said Klein to himself as he juggled the paper, blade and pencil between his hands and then began to write.

"Not necessarily, surely?" Theodore said, going to the head of the body. "Ought we not to check whether they were dead before they entered the water?"

Klein looked up and smiled. "I suppose we could, but it's obvious, don't you think?" He waved the pencil in the air vaguely. "But I am not bothered either way. I know who you are; I've heard a little of your exploits in London. I'm not possessive about my little kingdom down here and if you would like to perform your investigations, you can go right ahead."

Klein put the notepad down. "Here, we do tend to prefer the easier life. This person – well, look at him. Do we even know his name?"

"Yes. He was called Charles Webb."

"Oh. Is that so?"

"Yes. He had a name, and a past, and a skill – he was a craftsman, working in wood. And he did have a future until all of this happened. He was known to me, at least slightly.

And even if none of this was the case, even if this was a poor nameless tramp from the streets, he is still – he was still – a human being and deserving of some respect!"

Klein nodded. He didn't appear particularly moved, however. He simply said, "You make good points, of course. And I suppose you are bored, and need to keep your hand in, even if this isn't your usual sort of investigation. Don't you usually deal with the problems of wealthy families?"

"It hardly ever comes down to such a neat distinction," Theodore said. "The more I stumble between the worlds of the rich and the poor, the fewer differences I find."

"Nonsense," said Klein with the first flash of any strong emotion that Theodore had seen in him. "If we were all the same, we wouldn't *have* rich and poor at all, would we?" But then he grinned for the first time. "But enough of this philosophy. You want to get stuck into some everyday policing, and the inspector has told me to do what is necessary, so let us waste an hour or two down here. I don't mind."

He spoke as if he were doing Theodore a massive favour in condescending to actually do the job he was paid to do. Now Theodore could see why the police station seemed so quiet, ordered and efficient. Everyone understood that they were to do the bare minimum but to ensure that the paperwork was excellent; everything else could be brushed aside.

It certainly meant they'd have a quiet life.

But it was wrong, Theodore thought in a simmering fury, and he stalked over to the body of Charlie Webb. *This man deserves better.*

He began to make his observations, completely ignoring Doctor Klein now.

All men deserve better, he thought, as he worked his way methodically along the clothing, peeling back layer after layer.

All deserve *justice*, he thought at last.

"Right," he said, once he was done with his exterior observations. "A little tearing on his clothing, suggestive of a fight perhaps, but nothing conclusive. No blood stains that have remained visible but we can test for residue if marks on the body indicate that we should. Have you a sharp knife? Good. Let us now see how he really died."

❦

SMITH WAS WAITING FOR THEODORE OUTSIDE THE STATION-house. He rushed into the street, jamming his hat on his head, looking up and down in a state of excitement and astonishment. He spotted Smith and seized her until the look of absolute disdain on her face made him hastily drop his hands.

"I do apologise! But have you seen Inspector Tompkins?"

"I do not know, my lord. Might you describe him?"

Theodore took of his hat and raked his hand over his rapidly-balding head. "The desk sergeant said they'd all gone for lunch and not to expect them back any time soon. But this is intolerable!" He suddenly paused. "Smith? Why are you here? Has something else happened? Oh, no..."

She shook her head. "Do not worry, my lord. My ladies are all in a private room at the Mason's Arms back in Greyhaven. That is all I've come to tell you. I thought you would worry if you returned to Griseley Manor and found it deserted. Indeed, the whole village is at the inn, in one way or another, trying to make sense of what has happened."

"Sense? Sense? I can tell you now, Smith, that this all makes far less sense than anyone could have predicted. And now the inspector is *at lunch?* By heaven, Smith, I should hurl a firecracker into his dining room. Now what do I do?" He paced up and down, utterly at a loss.

Smith watched him silently. She didn't move and eventually it was as if her implacable calm had some kind of effect on him. He circled round her one more time, slowly, then stopped.

He made a decision.

"If they will not step up and sort this out, then I will. I can see that they will not act on what I have discovered unless I shame them into it. I will go to the inn and make the announcements that they ought to be making, and that will shake them into starting the investigation. Smith, let's go!"

❦

THE TOWN WITH THE POLICE STATION-HOUSE WAS NOT FAR from the village of Greyhaven, at least not by the crow's flight. There was a well-used flagstone path that cut up and across one of the hills and in pleasant weather it was a good walk of only a few miles. Carriages and horses had to use the lower road, however, which snaked along the valley bottoms and covered a distance that was twice as far.

Theodore would have been happy to walk but he could hardly ask his wife's lady's maid, a pristine woman of high standards and advancing age, to trek over a hillside. So they found a willing coachman, one of the sort of odd-job-men that you found in rural towns, who might be chopping wood in the morning, hiring out his shabby carriage at lunchtime, cleaning windows in the afternoon and serving in a bar that night.

As soon as Theodore stepped into the public bar at the front of the inn in Greyhaven, he was beset on all sides by people who seemed to know exactly where he had been and what he had been doing. They clamoured for information and that was what he wanted. He could, in truth, barely grasp the revelations he had just encountered and he was not even sure how to speak about it. The public bar or tap toom was where most of the working population drank, almost all male. But the door to the saloon bar at the back opened up and women peered in, pushing their way through to the tap room to hear what Theodore was about to say. Even Adelia, Margaret and Gwen appeared from their private closet, keeping their distance, but standing on the tips of their toes to see what was happening.

Everyone was there.

And everyone was staring at him.

So he told them. He started to speak but the landlord stopped him, grabbing a wooden chair and urging him up onto it. Theodore gripped the publican's shoulder as he stepped up onto his makeshift platform, and began again.

"Charles Webb—" His voice broke on the name. He coughed. "Charlie Webb did not die by drowning in the pool."

Everyone went "ooh!" as he knew that they would.

"Charlie Webb was dead before he hit the water."

"Ooh!" and also "How?"

"He was hit over the head and may well have been in a fight or an altercation of some sort. It is not easy to say. He might have been randomly attacked and his injuries were sustained in self-defence. There are certain signs, some clues I could look for, but he's been in the water which has unfortunately obscured some evidence."

"But it's still murder!" someone shouted.

Theodore nodded. "Yes. You are right. It *is* still murder."

"When?" some people said, and there was a shouted discussion about the last time they'd seen the craftsman.

"Not more than a week," Theodore said. "I'd like to do more tests."

"Then go and do them!" a man cried.

Theodore didn't think he had any links with Charlie Webb, but it was the principle of the thing. He was pleased and also angry that this rough working man had more concern for justice and morals than the whole of the rather dismissive local police force.

"I intend to," Theodore replied grimly. "But there is one more thing I need to ask you all."

"Ask us?" There was confusion. The assembly wanted to be told things, not questioned.

Questions implied suspicion, of course.

"Yes," said Theodore.

He faltered. There were women present, including his own wife and daughter. This was a very delicate matter. Not that he thought he'd shock Adelia, but he still had to look as if he were preserving her innocence in public.

Nevertheless, he ploughed on. "Is there anyone here, anyone at all, who knew Charlie Webb? He was originally from this area, he claimed; does anyone know of his family?" He scanned the crowd, his gaze alighting first on Frederick Arbury and then on Beaumont Sloane. But both men shook their heads. Mr Arbury looked worried, as did most people; Mr Sloane was his usual perpetually-angry self.

And no one else spoke up. They looked at one another sideways, shaking their heads. Eventually an old woman's voice made itself heard over the mutterings. Of course, it was Nanna Black.

She said, "I remember the May family, but they didn't live in Greyhaven so I didn't know them. None of us did. There was a row of cottages to the north of here, a nothing sort of place with no name and nothing there to speak of. They're all fallen down now. But his family lived there and then they left."

"And did you know Charlie Webb when he was a child?"

"No, not really. I saw him from time to time, but he never went to the school and he never played much with the other boys in the village. And then they moved away when he got to the age that he had to start work." She raised her voice. "Bob, didn't you play kickabout with him?"

A man answered. "Sometimes but he was pretty quiet and not into all that rough and tumble. He was all right, don't get me wrong, but not into what we were into."

That was all the information the village had. All eyes turned back to Theodore, wondering where this was leading.

He took a deep breath. "The body in the pool was not Charles Webb," he said.

There was an immediate outcry. "Who? Then why were you asking about him? But you said..."

Theodore waited for silence.

Then he said, "That is, I should say: Charles May was a woman."

❧ 10 ❧

There was absolute uproar, naturally. And Theodore just didn't know what else to say or how he could have expressed it in any other way. He scanned the faces of the people pressing around him, hunting for any clue, any sign, that it wasn't a surprise to even one person. But everyone, even Nanna Black, who could surely have been relied upon to know everything about everyone, was open-mouthed with astonishment.

She kept shaking her head. "No," she said. "No. You are ... mistaken?"

As if someone could be mistaken on such a point. But he had no stomach for explaining the finer details of what he saw and how he saw it. He jumped down from the chair. As he backed away, the villagers advanced. He continued to inch backwards, batting away the slew of questions with non-committal answers: *I don't know, I don't know*, was all that he could say.

Adelia elbowed her way through, followed by Margaret and Gwen. The crowds parted a little for them, out of old respect, and he was able to escape out of the front door.

Everyone else remained inside, talking loudly at one another, their speculative theories bursting into flower immediately.

Smith appeared from wherever she had been lurking, ready and poised to attend to Adelia's every need. She stood close to her mistress, eyeing everyone else with suspicion.

"Theodore!" Adelia cried. "So was it Charlie or was it not?"

"It was the person that we have known as Charles Webb, yes. It simply seems that the person we knew was not the person that they really were."

She blinked, frowned, shook her head, looked sideways at Margaret. "Can you truly believe it?"

Margaret was logical. She pursed her lips. "Well, I have to believe it as papa has said so, and I do not think he could possibly be wrong in this matter. But how and why did he – she – do this? His arms – her arms, her hands, were thin, slight. But isn't that how the poor folk look? They are shorter, more delicate if they have been badly fed. But this! How, how did he – did she do this? From childhood?"

"That suggests it might not have been her original desire," Adelia said. "Don't you think, Theodore? If a girl-child is dressed as a boy, which has happened from time to time, then it's the parents' doing. I wonder why? And obviously she stuck with it. Maybe it became habit, maybe it was something more."

"Well, yes," said Margaret. "If she had been a boy and treated as a boy, why on earth would she then step down to being a girl again?"

Gwen was appalled. "Margaret! How could she even think of staying as a man once she knew it was wrong? It even tells us in the Bible that we are not to take on the clothing of the other. It's just ... well, isn't it an actual sin?"

"Felicity wrote to me when she was in Egypt. She met Christians there, you know, but they did not dress as we dress. The men wore garments that here we would call female accoutrements – robes, long gowns. So, there, those articles are considered to be male attire. What, then, can the Bible really mean?" Margaret said. "We've seen the old paintings. I could wear what Abraham himself once wore, don't you think?"

"I think it's rather obvious what the Bible really means," Gwen pouted.

"Ladies, please," said Theodore. "I am not sure this is the main question here. Now, I cannot believe that no one knew of his – her – true nature. And if we can find out who knew, then I am sure we will find the murderer. It is obvious and it is simple."

Adelia spluttered a short and inelegant laugh. "It cannot possibly be so simple."

"It is," he replied stubbornly. "Did you observe any particular reactions from anyone in the inn?"

She grew serious again. "We were all shocked. Everyone seemed angry and upset that she was murdered. As to the second revelation ... it's hard to say. I think people are going to feel betrayed or repelled. Or intrigued. Or all three. But no one looked afraid, as a murderer might."

He nodded. "Do please keep listening and watching."

"But what of the police?" she asked.

"Ha! What, indeed! I am going back to the town now. I hope the inspector has concluded his long lunch. I am going to speak very firmly to the man and remind him of his duties. He will have word, now, of what we discovered. I hope to hear what he intends on doing next."

"We will go back to the manor," Adelia said. "Good luck."

He knew, already, that he was going to need it.

MARGARET AND GWEN KEPT CLOSE TOGETHER ALL THE WAY back to the manor. Adelia walked with Smith, feeling pleased all over again that Margaret had finally found a close confidante but also strangely excluded from their easy intimacy, which was wrong of her, and added to her emotional unease.

I am a mature woman and ought to be far beyond petty jealousies, she told herself. *And a jealousy of my own daughter is deeply wrong.*

Well, if getting rid of a feeling was as easy as telling oneself to do so, then no one would ever be unhappy.

When they got back to the manor, Adelia went up to her room. She was feeling tired. The day had started early and she had been buffeted by events ever since; she wanted to sit quietly and think things through. In the end, she didn't do any thinking at all. She fell asleep. She was awoken out of the slumber she'd slipped into when Theodore came back from town.

She knew, as soon as she saw his face, that he had had no luck with the police.

"I hadn't really expected to," he said angrily. "But I had dared to *hope* that they might show a tiny bit of backbone. But no! All they want is a quiet life and anyway, as they kept repeating to me, *who cares about the accidental death of an unnatural woman?*"

"Is that how they referred to her?"

"It is. And it is as if they want to hush this death up and pretend it never happened. Perhaps they think that any hint of publicity about the case will bring shame upon the whole area. But this is the bigger shame, is it not? To ignore a murder, to write off a death, to look the other way! I am sick to my stomach, Adelia."

He threw himself into a chair and noticed that there was a small dish of nuts and fruit. He wasn't too sick, then, as he began to pick at the food while he ranted.

But she thoroughly understood his feelings. She said, "Then we will investigate. This is what we do, after all."

"Are you sure?"

She felt affronted that he would even question that. "Good gracious, Theodore, what sort of person do you take me for? Of course we will do this. If the police cannot or will not, then we shall. We will do it for justice, naturally, but more importantly, we will do it for our daughter. She was Charlie's friend, after all, if Charlie had any friends at all."

"How has Margaret taken it, this revelation?"

"She is stunned and not a little upset but she's hiding it well. Have the police forbidden you from investigating?" she asked.

"No, because I have not asked for permission," he replied.

"Ah, good. What are they intending to do with the ... with her body?"

"I think some enquiries will be made about family and so on. Otherwise, she'll have a pauper's grave. The Reverend Talfourd has been noticeably absent, you know."

"Are we to put him as a suspect?"

He wrinkled his nose. "No, just as a silly spineless sort of fellow. As to suspects, what do you think? Charlie seemed quiet, but you spoke with ... her ... more than I did. Could you imagine her getting into a brawl? Could this be an accidental tavern fight?"

"Perhaps. But you saw the size of her." Adelia was finding it easier than Theodore to switch pronouns now she knew the truth of the matter.

"Small. Slight," he agreed.

"And she didn't seem to be the sort of person to socialise with anyone so it's hard to see how a fight could have broken out. There's another matter, though, Theodore. What of the other things that have come to light at the bottom of the pool? Did the police take the leather case that was also there?

I know it was found a little distance from the body but there were currents and all manner of things moving in the water, I am sure."

"Yes, it was taken to the police station but it doesn't seem to be related. The leather was quite rotten and pitted, and there were markings on it that I didn't recognise. It had been underwater for a lot longer than Charlie had been. You know what really sickens me?" he said, picking at some more nuts.

"Go on."

"The police were actually far more interested in the contents of the case. They had them all spread out on a table next to the body and no one looked at Charlie Webb. Instead they were examining the objects from the case. They were things of some considerable value. There was a pocket watch that I am sure was silver, and various other things."

"Who did they belong to? Was there any clue?"

"Yes." Theodore smiled and prolonged the tension until she threatened to throw something at him. His smile faded. "Yes," he said again. "They have sent for an old family solicitor to confirm the provenance of these articles."

"What? Whose family?"

"The Arburys," he said.

She sat in silence for a while before clicking her fingers. "Very well, then. I suppose we must begin a list of suspects."

"Frederick Arbury, then, will be at the top?"

"He will certainly be on it, yes," she replied. "We *must* discover the connection between him and her. What did he know? But another person springs to my mind. Did you know there is a secret tunnel between Arbury House and the church?"

"You cannot suspect that wet blanket of a vicar!"

"Not at all," she said. "But what of his mother? Remember how she chased us out of the church when Charlie was asking questions? She is a woman of considerable determination. Her past is proof of that."

"That's true. And didn't Beaumont Sloane have a violent reaction to Webb too?"

"He did, though he has a violent reaction to anything that displeases him. He probably shouts at rain," she said. "That said, he came looking for her, demanding to know why she'd invited Frederick Arbury here."

"But she hadn't. That was you."

Adelia winced. She hoped that her letters of enquiry hadn't sparked off this whole sorry chain of affairs.

And as soon as she had let that thought into her head, she was consumed by shame, and she could not let it go.

THEY ALL DISCUSSED THE MATTER THAT NIGHT AT THE dinner table. Lord Peter Morland was there, still outstaying his welcome, but there was no sign of Gwen. Theodore thought that it surely could not be long now before Lord Morland left and Gwen called off the engagement.

Also present was Frederick Arbury, who had been informed that certain objects that might or might not belong to his family had been found. He squirmed in his chair, utterly beside himself. Theodore could barely imagine what he was experiencing. After all, he'd told everyone the family history of how they had lost everything but he had rebuilt himself as a gentleman against all the odds. To now hear that he might have a few relics from his past was surely disorienting. And they weren't just links with his family; they could be items of considerable worth.

Ramon was fascinated by Charlie's ongoing deception, and so was Margaret. The talk ranged from why Charlie had done it to who else could have known but they didn't come up with anything concrete.

Everyone was intrigued to learn that Theodore was to investigate, but he had already discussed the matter with Adelia and they decided not to let on any details of the investigation to anyone else – including Ramon and Margaret. They were simply too close to the potential suspects. As well as Mr Arbury and Mr Sloane, Theodore had begun to wonder, too, about Lord Morland.

After all, he was definitely hiding something. Could it be more than simply a waning of his passion for Gwen? She had hinted that he was unreliable; that he missed pre-arranged meetings and he never had a truly convincing explanation about it. He didn't seem to have any links with Charlie Webb, but that didn't mean there weren't any. Adelia told Theodore that Lord Morland had said that Charlie Webb was "shifty" and he didn't like them. So he, too, had been added to the list, making four suspects in total although Adelia had been keen to point out that absolutely everyone in the village was a suspect in one way or another. After all, if this had not been a targeted attack, but was the product of an impulsive fight, it could be anyone.

But in that case, Theodore had countered, it would be easier to solve; fights like that could not happen in secret. And he agreed with her, too. It had to be considered. They would speak to everyone in the village and soon discover if anyone had seen anything. While he'd talk to the working men, Adelia would speak to women and children.

The children, in particular, would have very useful observations, if it were possible to speak with them.

But they kept all of these plans to themselves that night at dinner and instead let the others take the lead on the conversation.

ॐ

THE NEXT DAY, A MESSAGE CAME TO THE MANOR FROM THE police station. It was requesting the presence of Mr Arbury as the family solicitor had been brought in to verify the potential Arbury heirlooms which had been cleaned up and laid out for inspection. Mr Arbury dressed in his very finest London clothes, looking very swell and dapper. He was also strangely nervous. Adelia said quietly to Theodore, "Why don't you offer to go with him?"

"I had not intended on being left behind," he replied.

Mr Arbury seemed unwilling to accept his presence, arguing that there was no need for Theodore to trouble himself, but all of a sudden, he agreed. He was overwrought, he confessed, and not thinking straight at all.

"Please, I would welcome a steady man at my side," he said.

They didn't converse in the carriage at all, and Theodore bit on his tongue. He didn't want to upset Mr Arbury any further before he set eyes on the family heirlooms. Mr Arbury's reaction was surely going to be telling.

They were shown into Inspector Tompkins' office, which was a relief, as Theodore wasn't sure how Mr Arbury would cope with being in the mortuary, which was where the items had been laid out previously. Indeed, Mr Arbury was pale and almost shaky as he entered the office, and he stopped dead when he caught sight of the ancient, grey-faced man hunched in a chair.

"Mr Zachary!" he breathed. "Oh my goodness me. How good it is, how *good*, to see you, sir!" He threw himself to his knees, paying no heed to the state of his clothes, and took the old gentleman's gnarled hands in his own, looking for all the world as if he were praying before a venerable saint. "Oh, Mr

Zachary! What a beacon of hope you have always been for me!"

The old man patted Mr Arbury's hands. "Frederick, dear boy, I am delighted to see you. You're keeping well? Well, yes, I know that you are. I confess that I did keep my eye on you, you know, after ... after it all went wrong. We felt so very dreadfully helpless, you see. I was so sorry that it happened like it did. And I am so very happy that you have managed to make a success of yourself, in spite of it all. You had a penniless start and yet here you are, now, a fine figure of a man! And look here – perhaps at last, some things might be restored to you."

Mr Arbury bowed his head for a moment as he mastered his emotions. Then he got to his feet and brushed himself down. "I hope so too," he said, very quietly. "But under what dreadful circumstances!"

Inspector Tompkins shrugged that aside. "Now, sir, here is all that was recovered from the pool."

Mr Arbury went to the desk and stared at the objects. Theodore remained where he was, not wanting to crowd the man, but he could see quite clearly that there was a watch on a chain, a cigar case, a closed locket, a silver tankard with an ornately fashioned handle, and a brass telescope which had not been affected by the water very much; even the wood had survived well. From his seat by the desk, Mr Zachary was nodding.

"I remember all of this, all of this quite well," he said. "But I do not understand how it came to be at the bottom of the pool. We passed it all onto you, Frederick. I remember that day quite clearly for I went home and I will not mind admitting to you that I shed a tear."

"Mr Zachary..."

"I did, lad, I did! I am not ashamed of it!" He then became

aware that no one else knew what they were talking about. He cleared his throat and said, "When Frederick attained the age of twenty-one, it fell to me as the senior partner at the firm, to tell him of his inheritance. But this was it. This was all that was left. I had been forbidden to tell him before his birthday and he came to my office all eager and fresh, and left as a crushed and broken man, carrying nothing with him but these scant items. Not a single other thing remained of his inheritance."

Mr Arbury nodded, tipping his chin up high proudly. "I was not broken for long," he said.

"You were not! I am so proud! But what happened...?"

With an effort, Mr Arbury said, "I was set upon and ... it was all taken from me."

"On the way from my office?"

"No, no. Later. I took it all back to ... where I was staying ... and thought about my future. I had but one year left at the university and no means of funding my remaining time there. I resolved that I should sell all of these things, and thus fund my education. I might be a penniless man of little name, but if I had a degree, I could make my way."

"Where were you staying?" Theodore asked, noting his omission.

"I – I had come back here. But nothing was as it had been. The house was not fit for living in so I stayed at the inn and spoke to a few old acquaintances, asking where I might sell this sort of stuff to get the best price for it. It was strange to be back. Once I had decided on my course of action, I set to it immediately."

Mr Zachary smiled. "You were never one to sit and feel sorry for yourself."

"Absolutely not. I learned, early on, that the world will never drop its riches into my lap if I sit and wait. One must go out and forge a future to suit. So I did. I was full of enthusiasm. I remember not feeling a moment of sadness that I was selling my last links to my poor late father. Instead, I was excited for my future. And then..."

"Then you were robbed."

"I was. The man came from nowhere, just one I believe though I cannot be sure. Before I knew what was happening, I had been struck a blinding blow across the back of my head." His hand went up to this brow as if he could still feel it. "I fell, calling out, and was kicked most viciously. I am not a fighter," he added, almost in apology.

"To your credit, to your credit," cried Mr Zachary.

"Well, perhaps if I had been, things would have gone differently. But here we are. I lost it all. And had to start again, from an even lower point than before."

"I always wondered why you did not finish your studies," Mr Zachary said. "Lad, my Frederick, with the love our firm has always had for your family, I must ask ... oh, why did you not come back to me? I would have helped you."

"I was too proud," Mr Arbury said, smiling kindly, and speaking simply for once. His words were from his heart. "And I made myself a success in the end, did I not?"

"I would have sent money. I watched you, got word of you whenever I could, but if I had known..."

Theodore and the Inspector looked away in growing embarrassment as the two men embraced, Mr Arbury leaning over the old man in his chair to tell him how much he had missed him all those years. While they reassured one another, Theodore distracted himself by paying another look at the case that the items had been found in.

"These objects were in another bag, weren't they?" he said in a low voice to the inspector.

Inspector Tompkins seemed grateful to have something else to occupy his attention. "Yes. They were all packed in this cloth, and it was the Arbury name inscribed on the back of them that alerted us to their original owners. But curiously, the cloth is in this leather case." He poked at it and flipped it over.

"There's a crest on it," Theodore said, peering more closely.

"We wondered about that," said Tompkins in a bored voice that spoke of very little actual wonder and certainly none of the curiosity he'd mentioned.

"I have seen it before," Theodore said.

"Whose it is?"

"I cannot be sure. But I shall let you know if it comes back to me."

"Of course," said Tompkins, and Theodore immediately decided not to tell him a thing. The inspector would do nothing with the information, that much was clear.

Later, when they walked back out into the street, Theodore remembered where he had seen the crest. They climbed back into the carriage that Ramon had loaned them for the day, and the coachman set off at a sedate pace.

Mr Arbury was restless. He sat forward in his seat, staring out of the blurred window. The bag of heirlooms was at his feet.

"What will you do now?" Theodore asked.

"I have no idea. Why on earth would they be thrown into the pool? I cannot understand it."

"Nor I. But there is one other thing that I did not mention," Theodore said.

Mr Arbury went still, his eyes widening. "What?"

"I know whose crest was on the leather case. It was indistinct but the police had cleaned it up. They are local men, mostly, and ought to have spotted it for themselves. It was the sign of Beaumont Sloane."

"What?"

"Yes. I am sure of it."

Mr Arbury sat up straight, the colour draining from his face. "After all this time," he said in a whisper.

"What do you mean?"

Suddenly he stared at Theodore with such intensity that Theodore was afraid for Mr Arbury's heart. "After all this time!" he repeated, and grabbed the handle of the door. Before Theodore could stop him, he had leaped from the rolling carriage, and ran off across the hill, leaving all the heirlooms behind, his hat falling to the ground, and his mustard jacket flapping in the wind.

The coachman pulled up. "Shall we go after him, my lord?"

Theodore stood on the step, hanging on to the side of the carriage, and watched the figure disappear. "No. He's heading for the manor, not for Sloane's house. Let's carry on. If he's not there when we arrive, then we'll turn around and go straight to Beaumont Sloane."

While Theodore was in town to discover the origin of the heirlooms with Frederick Arbury, Adelia could not simply settle down in a corner and await his return. She shook off Margaret's solicitations and instead went for a walk. She dressed warmly but decided to stay within the considerable grounds of the manor. She walked slowly and deliberately, looking at small things, trying to force her attention onto the often overlooked wonders of creation – insects, weeds, indistinct brown birds that hopped in the undergrowth rather than the more impressive and showy ones that wheeled high above.

She wasn't sure why, at first, she had this compulsion to look at insignificant things. But as she gazed upon a small fly struggling to free itself from a dew-jewelled web that was strung between the dead foliage of last year's delphiniums, she had an insight. The fly twisted and spun and suddenly, gloriously, broke free. It reminded her of the verse in the Bible about sparrows falling yet not being unnoticed and so on; and she tried to let it bring her some comfort.

Because what was gnawing at her, deep inside, so deep

that she could not yet bear to bring it to the light to really examine it, was this: she thought that somehow, she was responsible for the death of Charlie Webb.

But her mind spun away from that thought, just as the fly had fought its way free from the web. No. She was not, could not be, remotely connected. Yes, she had brought Frederick Arbury here; yes, that had caused problems within the area. Charlie had reacted strangely and not at all with the joy and gratitude that she'd expected. Mr Arbury had upset Beaumont Sloane, true.

But it was Charlie *herself* – Adelia forced herself to rewrite her memories of the young man to show the truth of it, as a young woman – who had acted and reacted in the ways that she had. Charlie had upset Dorothy Talfourd. Or Dorothy Talfourd had been upset by Charlie. But either way, none of that was attributable to Adelia, was it?

Her feet ached and she realised she'd been standing in one place for too long, staring at nothing.

Charlie Webb had been a difficult, reticent and abrasive young man. Young woman. A person of layers. A person with secrets. Of *course* they had upset some random drinker in the Mason's Arms where they had been lodging. That was the easiest and most likely explanation.

As soon as Theodore returned, Adelia decided, they would both head into the village and begin the necessary interviews.

⚘

SHE HAD CHANGED HER CLOTHES TO SOMETHING MORE suitable for walking around the village and talking to people, and was standing in the hallway, feeling a little at a loose end, when the front door slammed open. She started forward, expecting to greet Theodore returning from his meeting with the solicitor at the police station, but it was Mr Arbury who burst into the entrance hall. He was in utter disarray. She was shocked to see the London swell appeared to have fallen into a ditch, rolled down a hill, and climbed a tree, at the very least. Bears might have been involved.

"What's happened?" she asked, searching him for signs of injury.

"What?"

"What's happened – I thought you might have been attacked – where is Theodore?" A million terrible possibilities now flooded her mind.

He put his hand to his head and seemed only then to realise that he had lost his hat. His palm patted his hair with a loose and confused motion. He was breathing heavily but he shook his head. "No, no. He is coming in the coach. I wanted to walk."

"Walk? Mr Arbury, you look as if you were pursued by wolves."

"I – had some news."

"Please, sit down before you fall down." It might have been more polite, she thought, to call for a servant and have him taken upstairs for a wash and a change of clothes, but she simply couldn't bear not knowing what had happened. She led him to some ornate chairs that stood against the wall, tall carved things that looked straight out of a Druidic Eisteddfod. He sank down and let all the air out of his lungs in a long whistle.

His head lolled back though the carvings were not comfortable, and he closed his eyes. "The stuff in that bag was mine," he said. "Just as we all thought it was."

"Have the police allowed you to reclaim it?"

"Yes, yes, it's in the coach with your husband. But..."

She waited.

Unfortunately the expectant silence was broken by the

doors being flung open again and this time it was Theodore who thundered into the hallway. He saw them immediately, and slowed down. He looked relieved to see Mr Arbury.

"Your hat, sir," he said, handing over a thoroughly battered specimen that ought to have been burnt immediately.

Mr Arbury took it automatically. "Beaumont Sloane," he croaked.

Adelia stiffened and looked at Theodore, trying to ask silent questions with her eyes. He tried to answer them. Neither had any idea what the other was communicating, however, and she gave up before they attracted attention and were carted off to be sedated.

"Gentlemen, do forgive me, but I still have no idea how those objects came to be at the bottom of the pool."

Mr Arbury said, "It was him, all along, was it not? Oh my poor, poor Jane."

The mention of Beaumont Sloane's wife stunned Adelia and seemed to be news to Theodore too. He perched himself on a nearby chair and leaned forward.

"Mr Arbury, what do you think happened?"

"I ... I had been given those things, those fripperies, as the last of my birth-right, just as Mr Zachary said. I was a youth. I was called to the offices and told that this was all that remained of the once great family of Arbury. There was no money, nothing to inherit, no more to our name than a cigar case and a few odd bits of silver. I took it, all wrapped up in that cloth, and stumbled out into the streets, friendless and alone."

"How terrible."

"But I do *not* stay low for long," he said fiercely. "My fire will always burn brighter! I came back here. Arbury House had been my home when I had been very small, but I was soon sent away to school. As my family declined, so my visits home became fewer and indeed I was often sent to stay with distant cousins, where I was relegated to small attic rooms and told to be grateful – I was never sure for what I ought to show gratitude. I did not know, then, how much I was living on the charity of others. I *am* grateful for it," he added.

Adelia nodded sympathetically.

"But at twenty-one," he went on, "when I learned my family had been lost many years previously, I could think of no other place to come than to Arbury House. Seat of my ancestors. Roots of my soul."

"But Arbury House..." Adelia said.

"Is derelict. I did not know. I had not seen it for many, many years. No one had told me and it was another blow. I stood at the gates and gazed upon utter ruin, and thought that I beheld my future. For a while, I was lost, and not myself at all."

"Goodness. It was blow after blow."

"Worse was to come. I had pawned one of my heirlooms which paid for my travel and for a stay at the inn. And while I went around the village, speaking to anyone who remembered me, trying to find out what had happened to the house, I met upon one person who had always treated me kindly. Well," he added with a cough, "she had always been rather more than merely *kind*."

"Who?"

With a smile that suggested the fondest of memories, he said, "The incomparable and heavenly Miss Jane Walker-Andrews. A jewel amongst women." Then his tone changed. "But you know her now as Mrs Beaumont Sloane."

"Oh no," said Adelia as a fear began to prickle the skin on her neck.

"Oh yes. We had been close as children and when I left, we had continued to correspond. The boys at school mocked me when they found out, at first; later, as we grew older, it was something of a badge of honour. Our letters matured and so did our feelings. But when I went to university, our letters cooled."

Adelia wanted to reach out and pat his shoulder. She restrained herself and waited for him to go on.

"Perhaps she had been advised to withdraw, and I understand why. I have always had a gentleman's sensibilities even if that has not been reflected in my outward appearance at times. And, oh, the joy of seeing her again! We quickly found that we could pick up where we left off – the years meant nothing. She was mine and I was hers. But there was one problem." He sighed heavily. "I was as yet still a penniless nobody."

Adelia bit her lip.

He continued. "So I resolved that I had to complete my studies. If I had an education, it would open doors to me – maybe not the highest doors, but it would let me into a world that would give me opportunities to work, to rise. I could be worthy of her. And to do that, I needed to sell everything. *Everything.* I could allow no sentimentality to get in the way of my aims. For her, I would give up everything – and gain, in the end, her hand in marriage, which to me was a gain beyond compare."

"You are a noble man!" Adelia said in true admiration.

He snorted sadly. "If only that were true. For I took evil counsel. I did not know how to obtain the best price for these things and I was concerned that I would be seen as a green young man, and tricked out of the items' true values. Therefore I asked for advice from an older man. Mr Zachary was too close to my family and it would have broken his heart if I had suggested to him that I wanted to sell these things. Therefore I went to another local man of great respect and influence."

"Beaumont Sloane!"

"Indeed. And he welcomed me into his house, that wolf, that snake; he gave me the name and address of a trusted man in the town. He asked me my intentions and I unburdened myself. I cannot tell you how long I had been without true male company! I told him what I could not tell Jane; I could not tell Mr Zachary. I told him of my longings and my desires and I thought that I had found wise counsel in a man of authority. I told him of my plan to leave early the next morning, sell the items and go straight back to university. And he encouraged me and told me that I was doing the very best thing."

"And then?" Adelia said.

"Ha. Lord Calaway knows this part. I did exactly as I had told Sloane, and I set out the next day, on foot, and was attacked from behind by a man who beat me and robbed me and took my last few possessions."

Silence gripped them as they tried to make sense of it.

Eventually Theodore said, "And you never suspected that it could have been the work of Beaumont Sloane?"

"Not at the time, no! Why would I? He was older than me and I respected him. I could never have suspected *him*. I left here in disgrace. I never returned to Greyhaven. I went to London and do not ask me how I rebuilt myself but you can see that I did, by luck, by hard work, by the help of others too. I am grateful every minute for the kindnesses that others showed to me. And then I heard that you were asking for me, Lady Calaway, and I thought that if I ever were to come back here, then at least I could come back as a success."

"But you found your sweetheart married to Beaumont Sloane."

"Yes, and even then, though I was sick to my stomach, I did not suspect him. Of course she had married someone. I was glad of it, at first, until Sloane's reaction to me made me realise that I was not welcome. And I didn't question that, either, because of course, what man would want a reminder of his wife's first love? I took care, then, to stay out of his way."

"Naturally and that does you credit."

"Does it? I ought to have called him out and knocked his head off." Then he laughed. "As if I could, though. I am not a fighter and never have been. If I were, I would have already ridden up to Sloane's house and rescued poor Jane from his clutches."

Adelia said, "But I am still confused. What has made you think that it was Sloane who robbed you?"

Theodore explained. "The leather case that the objects were found in carried Sloane's crest."

Adelia nearly gasped. "Are you sure?"

"Indeed. And now it all makes sense to me. By taking the things from you, he prevented you from making a success of your life – so he thought – and certainly delayed you. He was able, then, to marry Jane. I suspect he had held a candle for her for a long time. And your return was unwelcome. So he got rid of you, but had no need for the things that he stole – indeed, they were as good as worthless to him, being marked with inscriptions and engravings."

"That's true."

"He could have taken them to a city, I suppose, and had a clever artisan remove those things, but why bother? He hid them in a case and threw them into the pool, never to be seen again. He took your sweetheart and made himself a life."

Mr Arbury nodded. Adelia felt her heart break for him. He had done all that he could, behaved well, worked hard: and for what? He had made money and bought fancy clothing but he had lost the love of his life, and now he had discovered she had been actually stolen from him.

She jumped to her feet. "I have half a mind to go and have this out with Beaumont Sloane," she said fiercely.

Theodore stood up and put a hand on her arm. "Dear heart, I would suggest we don't interfere."

She sank down but something had been triggered in Mr Arbury. Before they could stop him, he had run to the door and left, hatless and distraught.

THEY CAUGHT UP WITH HIM AS HE SLOWED DOWN THROUGH Greyhaven. He had been running but he couldn't sustain it. Theodore and Adelia went after him on foot but they both agreed they knew where he was going, and they were correct: he was heading to Beaumont Sloane's house to challenge him. They tried to persuade him that it was a bad idea, but he would not be dissuaded and shook off any attempt to stop him. He was wheezing slightly, red in the face and utterly determined to somehow rescue his long-lost love from the grasp of the ogre that was Sloane.

Short of physically throwing him to the ground, they were powerless but they continued along with him in case they could prevent anything bad happening – or at least be witnesses to whatever *did* happen.

It was an uncomfortable thought.

Adelia had not been to the house before but it matched very much what she had imagined it would look like, with its Greek-style new statuary and overdone ornamentation. As they approached, still trying to convince Mr Arbury to turn around, she spotted movement in one of the upstairs windows. Someone had been looking out and now they stood up, opening the casement.

Mr Arbury saw the window open and he began to shout. "Jane! Jane, my love! I have come back for you! He lied, he lied, he lied!"

"Frederick! Freddy!" Jane Beaumont leaned out of the

upper window, her hair hanging loose like a young girl. She seemed to be dressed in a silk wrapper, not at all fit for receiving mixed company like this, her red and gold sleeves flapping as she reached her hands out into the air.

Adelia stifled a scream of terror. "Mrs Beaumont, be careful! You'll fall!"

But before the woman could tumble from the window, she was abruptly and roughly dragged back into the house. They heard a high-pitched keening sound, which was cut off with the slam of the window closing.

Mr Arbury growled through his tears. "I shall call him out!"

He headed for the doors but they were opened with a slow, sinister squeak before he got three steps closer.

Beaumont Sloane stood there, filling the space with his bulk, and he had a shotgun in his hands.

He raised it very slowly and deliberately.

"Oh – bother," said Theodore.

Mr Arbury's language was less restrained. He took a step forward, in spite of the weapon now pointing straight at them all. Theodore grabbed his arm.

"Get – yourselves – away from here!" Beaumont Sloane yelled, keeping the shotgun steady. Adelia could not help but be impressed. It was difficult to hold a heavy weapon very still like that for any length of time. He was strong.

And he was armed. She began to back away.

"Mr Arbury, Theodore, let's go," she said, and was not surprised to hear a wobble in her voice.

Sloane's finger moved over the trigger.

"Come on!" Theodore cried, dragging at Mr Arbury. "Yes, yes, we're going, we're leaving," he shouted to Sloane.

Mr Arbury broke free of Theodore's grasp and ran forward two more paces, waving his fists. Sloane moved the shotgun suddenly and sharp bang ricocheted through the air.

Adelia was frozen to the spot, her ears ringing while her eyes filled with tears. *No, no!*

Mr Arbury danced backwards as a cloud of dust rose around his feet. Theodore grabbed him again and this time Mr Arbury did not resist.

Sloane shouted, "Take that as a warning! I will aim to hit you next time!"

Whether it was a deliberate aim to miss or an accident did not matter. They fled.

12

They all went back to Griseley Manor in shocked silence. As soon as they got back there, Ramon and Margaret met them. They had heard that something had happened and wanted to be updated on what Mr Arbury had discovered at the police station. That all seemed very long ago now to Theodore, but it had only been that very morning.

Mr Arbury brushed off the endless questions and went to his room to settle down. He joined them later for luncheon. There was no sign of Lord Morland. No one had any idea where he had gone.

After luncheon, Theodore and Adelia left Mr Arbury telling the others what had happened. They decided that they ought to carry on with the investigation. The trouble surrounding Mr Arbury was compelling but Theodore was not convinced that there was any link to Charlie Webb's death.

Adelia said she was not sure if she agreed.

But they both were of the same accord regarding the next stage of the investigation: they had to speak to everyone in the village who might have seen Charlie Webb before she was killed.

They quickly found that most people were still calling Charlie "him" so it made for a strange and confusing conversation at times. Together, they spoke to the landlord at the Mason's Arms and found him to be keen to help.

"He paid up per week in advance, and kept in his room most of the time. He never came down and drank with the others. I suppose we know why, now. He wouldn't have been able to keep up and they would have soon rumbled he was not as he said he was."

Theodore nodded but Adelia said, "It surprises me that you have not encountered a woman who can drink as much as a man."

The landlord looked taken aback for a moment. "Well, now that you mention it, Old Bet was notorious for having the lads under the table. But generally, you know. You *know*. Anyway, so he paid up for the last few days and then he left."

"Did he say that he was leaving?"

"He did not. And he left a few things behind but maybe he meant to."

"May we see?"

"Aye, you can. I am surprised the police didn't ask, if I'm honest. Step this way."

But there was nothing in the room that struck Theodore as being of use, and he could see that Adelia felt the same way. He poked around the tiny space while she peered in from the corridor; the room was barely big enough for one person. There was a narrow gap where you could stand, alongside the bed which was rammed up against the other wall. The ceiling sloped down over the bed and a small window, barely more than a hand-size of thick mottled glass, let in milky light. The bed was made up neatly and there was a long cream shirt folded on the flat pillow. At the foot of the bed, on the floor, was a pair of leather gloves.

But that was all. Theodore even flipped the mattress to check for stashed notes or clues but there was nothing.

They thanked the landlord and went back to stand in the street. The sun was out and there were children playing on the village green.

Theodore said, "What do you think?"

"It's hard to say. She was not wealthy and not the sort of person to leave valuable things behind. The shirt was folded as if she expected to return and wear it in bed that night. And the gloves were not damaged. You wouldn't simply throw them away. However, she must have been carrying everything else she owned with her."

"There were a few clothes in the bag that was found on her person."

Adelia was distracted for a moment. "Look," she said. "That man there is carrying a bundle. I would wager there's a washerwoman or two in this village who will do for the single men. For all we know, Charlie was taking her clothes to be washed. So we cannot say one way or the other if she was definitely leaving."

"But she said that she was going to go once the pole was done, and it was."

"True," said Adelia. "But she was also keen to find out about the Arbury family and as far as we know, she never did talk to Mr Arbury."

"We need to confirm that – once he is in a state to be spoken to. The poor man has had some shocks today."

"I do admire him."

"So do I. And I have hope that his future will be bright. He has proven, over and over, that he can overcome all manner of obstacles which would fell a lesser man. I will confess that when I first saw him, I dismissed him as a shallow fashion plate, but he's a much stronger man than I had ever imagined."

"There's a lesson for you," Adelia said. "Theodore, do you think I did right in making enquiries and bringing him here? It's been devastation upon devastation for him."

"Oh, dear heart," he said, taking her hand but tucking it carefully out of sight behind them both. "You acted out of honesty and therefore cannot be blamed for anything. And he does have his rightful inheritance back again, for whatever it's worth."

"That is true." She sighed heavily.

"You don't sound convinced. What is bothering you?" he asked in concern.

"Nothing."

He knew that she wasn't being entirely honest but he let the matter drop. "Come," he said. "We have more people to speak to. And I know where we must start – Nanna Black, of course."

"Of course."

⊶❦⊷

But it was Nanna Black who found them first. She came stumping her way across the green, leaning on the arm of a younger woman who had a face like she had licked a stinging nettle. "There you are," she said with no formalities or courtesies. "I heard you were asking questions and I ken a few folk who'll be willing to speak to you."

"That's marvellous," said Theodore. "Do you happen to know anything yourself?"

"Oh, many things, many things!" she said with a laugh. "But naught that you want to hear. No – you need to speak to Jeremy Box who's out in yon fields at the moment. I heard that he saw something."

So after getting directions to "yon fields" they tracked down a plump and overfed young man with a red face, the unlikeliest field hand they had ever seen. He was grateful for the chance to pause in his repair of the stone wall.

"Aye, it's true, I saw him in a fight. Well, no, it wasn't a fight as such. No fists. Call it an argument. A disagreement." He nodded and leaned back on the wall. Some of his carefully-placed stones shifted.

"With whom?" Theodore asked.

The answer surprised them all. "That fancy toff on the big white horse. The one that's courting our Miss Gwendolen from up at the Old Tollhouse there."

"Lord Peter Morland?"

"Aye, him, whatever he's called."

"Charlie Webb was arguing with Lord Morland?" Theodore asked again.

Jeremy Box nodded vehemently. "Aye, aye, he was!"

"What about?"

Now he looked shifty. "I wasn't eavesdropping."

"Of course you weren't," said Adelia. "But it's natural that you can't help overhearing what people say if you accidentally happen to be close by."

"Aye, that's it, right enough. So the chap, Charlie, or I suppose he's not a chap, but anyway, him, he was saying to the fancy lord, *I know who you are, I saw you before when you were in York.* And the toff says that everyone knows who he is. And Charlie says, *but I know the sort of man that you are and the sort of place you were in and you aren't right for her, you must break it off.* And then the lord gets all angry and says that Charlie knows nothing. And Charlie says, he goes, *well I'll tell Miss Gwen myself if you won't. She doesn't deserve a man like you.* And he says that nothing would come of it, like no one would believe it or something, I suppose. And then Charlie goes forward like he's going to fetch him a crack about the head and says the lord is to *watch himself* and the lord just laughed and walked away and that Charlie were left stood there all helpless-like. And that's what I saw," Jeremy finished.

"Goodness me," said Adelia. "That's fascinating."

Jeremy beamed. "So what I thought was, I thought, well, that Charlie fancies Miss Gwen for himself, like, as if she'd ever look at a man like him!" But then his face fell. "But that can't be true now, can it?"

Theodore reached into his pocket and gave the man a coin for his trouble. "Leave the interpretation to us," he said, and thanked him for his information.

As they walked away, Adelia said, "So what is our interpretation?"

"I really don't have a clue," he replied.

It appeared that Adelia and Theodore were not the only people out and about in the village that day. The Reverend Talfourd was walking down the street with his elderly mother on his arm, inching their way along, which gave everyone else plenty of time to get out of their way and avoid them.

Theodore tried to steer Adelia out of sight, too, but she stubbornly slowed down and he was too late to evade them. Reverend Talfourd hailed them from some distance, though he was immediately and obviously reprimanded by his mother who elbowed him sharply. One did not call out like a street hawker in public. He was somewhat pink in the face, Theodore noticed.

Reverend Talfourd began to say, "Good afternoon, Lord Calaway, Lady Calaway, and what a pleasure it is to..."

He was interrupted by his mother. "We're collecting for the repair of the church roof," she said.

"Oh? I am sorry to hear that it has been allowed to fall into disrepair," replied Adelia, and Theodore curled his toes in embarrassment. It was a sentence worthy of the waspishness of his own mother.

"We have, of course, been spending what little we have on providing as much assistance as we can to this poor flock," Reverend Talfourd said. "As you can see, we..."

Again, Dorothy Talfourd spoke over him. "We have opened a subscription but there are very few people of any means in this area. We held a garden party a few weeks ago but that, too, was sadly ill-attended." She grew breathless and stopped for a moment. Her son had more sense than to try to jump in and speak in her gaps, Theodore noted. She said, "And those that did come were ... well, the adults could not pay for the food and the children simply robbed us."

Reverend Talfourd went red in the face again. "I have spoken at length about stealing in my latest sermons."

"They would not know anything about the content of your sermons as they have not attended church *at all*," Mrs Talfourd said.

Theodore was about to defend his wife, reminding them that Mrs Talfourd had ejected Adelia from the church. But before he could speak, Adelia got in.

"I suppose it's easy to notice one or two missing if the congregation is already somewhat thin," Adelia said and once more Theodore could have died on the spot. Was his wife actually enjoying this game of words? It certainly seemed so.

"Anyway, anyone of any reasonable standing in the village is contributing to the fund," Mrs Talfourd said firmly.

She turned her gaze quite deliberately away from Adelia and fixed Theodore with a watery stare. His fingers twitched as his hand moved, almost of its own volition, to his jacket pocket. If this wasn't witchcraft, it was something close.

Adelia slipped her arm through his, stopping his hand.

She said, with a smile, "That is most excellent news and I wish you all the best in your endeavours." She made it sound as if she hoped they both fell down a well. She tugged on Theodore's arm and began to walk away. He had no choice but to follow along.

When they were definitely out of earshot, he said, "You were very rude!"

"Yes," she replied, with something of an air of pride. "I was, wasn't I?"

"But that was ... well, she will be dreadfully upset with us. And in other places, you have been most concerned about making a good impression for the sake of our daughters. After all, Margaret has to live here. You could make things difficult for her."

"Margaret has nothing to do with either of the Talfourds nor the church in general," she replied. "And I am growing increasingly aware that Margaret can certainly deal with most things herself. Speaking of church matters, Harriet is arriving tomorrow."

"Oh. From York?" he said, dully. Harriet Hobson, with her loud voice, predilection for alcohol, and tendency to always make him feel like he didn't know half enough scripture, was not his favourite person.

"Yes, from York. Don't look like that. She knows to stay out of your way."

"I don't mean that."

"Yes, you do. Well. Shall we speak to more people?"

"We should try. Are you ready?"

"Yes."

They headed into each shop in turn, accosted as many passers-by as possible, tried the bribe the children with sweets, and then went to the mill. Adelia would not come in. She continued on back to the manor, and Theodore hung around outside the mill, waiting for the shift to end. He looked gloomily at the now-dry river.

They had not learned anything else useful from their interviews so far.

Lord Peter Morland, however, certainly had some explaining to do.

❧ 13 ❧

Adelia and Theodore could not agree on what they ought to do next. Their interviews with the villagers and mill workers had brought up no more new information. The village children, once their hope of good information, had proved to be as wily and slippery as the basest urchin of the rookeries of London.

The only person Charlie had publicly threatened was Lord Peter Morland, and he had also been heard to call her "shifty". She had also been at loggerheads with Dorothy Talfourd who clearly hated her, and Beaumont Sloane who had sought her out to tell her to leave. She was connected, somehow, to Frederick Arbury who himself was at odds with Beaumont Sloane but that seemed to be a different matter entirely.

"It all comes back to Sloane, don't you think?" Adelia said, as she sat in a comfortable chair in their sitting room that adjoined their bedrooms. Griseley Manor had many guest suites and of course they had been given the very best. This room caught the morning sun and had a fine view of the hills.

On a bad day, it was dark and oppressive, but this spring morning was light and full of promise.

"Maybe it all comes back to Jane Sloane."

"Maybe. But thinking of women and their complicated love affairs, what about Lord Morland and poor Gwen? She knows something, now, I am sure of it, which could explain not only their arguments but also what Charlie knew about him, too."

Then a horrible realisation struck Adelia. "If it is something bad enough for Lord Morland to kill Charlie for, then isn't Gwen in danger too? Lord Morland seems pleasant enough but he is up to something. What does he *do* all day? Who is he? Oh, Theodore..."

He was pacing the room. He stopped and gazed out of the window.

"The problem is that I do not wish to alert any of our suspects to our suspicions. Nothing is keeping Lord Morland here, now, except I suppose his courting of Gwen. I confess that when I awoke this morning, the first thing that I wanted to do was to seize Morland and drag the truth out of him. But all that would do would be to scare him away. I have no authority to keep him here; this isn't like some of our previous cases. We must be very careful, very circumspect."

"I agree *but...*"

"But?"

"I don't know. I am worried that we could be in danger of letting them all slip away. Furthermore, if we do not speak to everyone, they will find that even more strange because everyone knows that we are looking into the death. Ought we not treat everyone in the same way? Perhaps there is a way of us speaking to each person in an informal, light sort of way, as if we are asking for help rather than buttonholing them for information."

Theodore grimaced. "You mean we should be tactful and sensitive..."

She winced too. "Yes. Please don't actually try it."

"Leave it to you, then?"

"Yes. No. Perhaps not so directly..."

He resumed his pacing. She wanted, desperately, to be able to leap up and declare that she was to investigate – that she would call everyone into a small room, one by one, and by careful degrees, subtly extract the truth from each individual.

In her head it worked wonderfully.

But the reality would not shake out so neatly, and she knew it.

ALL THEY COULD DEFINITELY AGREE ON, IN THE END, WAS that they would listen and watch as much as they could. Adelia would try to tease the truth from Gwen, without letting her know that Morland was any kind of suspect. Theodore would stick closely to Mr Arbury and attempt, if at all possible, to find out more about Sloane and Charlie Webb – although the fact that they had been chased off the Sloane property at the wrong end of a gun didn't offer much hope.

And then Harriet arrived and she brought with her energy, enthusiasm and a fresh pair of eyes.

She came in the afternoon, just after luncheon. Adelia thought that it was lucky for Theodore he had already disappeared off on his investigations, though quite what form that investigation was going to take was a mystery. He was also still interested in finding out about Charlie's background when her family had left the area, and what she'd been doing the past few years so she imagined he'd go back to the police station. In spite of the authorities' disgraceful lack of concern for the dead woman, they would surely seek out her next of kin.

That was the absolute minimum respect they could show, Adelia thought. If not, she herself would march down there and create a scene.

It was funny, she reflected, as she stood on the step and watched the coach rumble up, how people assumed that her involvement in death and murder would harden her – shocking, they thought, for a woman to risk degrading her finer feelings in such a way! Yet the reality was that she was even more emotionally concerned about the dead these days, and had not become hardened or blasé at all. She was adamant in her insistence that they all be treated with the utmost dignity. No matter a person's station in life, all had to be acknowledged as *people*. She did not shy away from it.

And Harriet, she knew, was someone who shared her views.

Harriet Hobson stepped down from the coach, scattering bags and books and shawls and half-eaten sandwiches in her wake. The two old friends embraced, although this meant that Adelia got a mint humbug stuck to her sleeve, and Harriet laughed fit to burst. She hadn't brought a maid or any servant with her; Harriet was a whirling mixture of high ideals and everyday practicality. She was intensely religious, as befitted the wife of a well-respected bishop, but that faith was rooted very firmly in her personal revelations and understanding of Christ as a man, on his knees, washing feet and feeding the poor and throwing tables around in temples. She'd sell her last Bible if it would feed a child.

Such morals made many others rather uncomfortable. She was not a friend of the establishment, bishop for a husband or not.

Margaret came out to greet her too; Harriet had been close to the family throughout the daughters' childhood, and she was treated much as a favourite aunt might be. The three of them went into the house, and spent a happy few hours talking, eating, and catching up on one another's lives.

AROUND FOUR O'CLOCK, MARGARET WENT TO SEE ISEULT for her daily update from the nurse on her daughter's progress. Adelia got up too, assuming that Harriet would want a few hours of peace and rest before dinner.

But Harriet leaped to her feet. "Now, you must tell me all about the murder!"

"I told you everything."

"No. Sit down. You only told me what you wanted Margaret to know."

"There isn't very much more..."

Adelia was dragged back to her seat, nevertheless, and outlined the facts of the case to Harriet. Harriet listened very closely. She said, "I want to meet absolutely everyone."

"The suspects?"

"Yes, them, and all the people of the village too. We shall have this solved in hours, I am sure of it."

Adelia grimaced. "As for the people of the village ... well, Theodore and I differ in our opinions generally. I say, as a woman of faith, what do you think about country folk and their pagan ways?"

"Depends on the substance of those ways. Are we talking unspeakable sacrifices to ancient deities or the harvest festival?"

"The harvest festival isn't ... oh."

"Indeed," said Harriet. "So tell me – are there to be some unspeakable sacrifices?"

"No."

Harriet sniffed in disappointment. "So what is bothering you?"

Adelia thought carefully. "In truth, I think I can overlook or accept everything – almost everything – save for the insinuations that the village 'protect' Iseult in some way."

"Witchcraft? What exactly have they said and done?"

Adelia shrugged. "Now that you ask me for an example, simply nothing. There are some scraps of fabric tied into a tree, and an old lady said that everyone 'looked after' Iseult." She shook her head. "I cannot describe to you the *feeling* of wrongness."

"And this old lady, she is trustworthy, do you think?"

"Not at all. I think she says things for sport, just to rile up her betters."

Harriet laughed and cast her eyes dramatically to heaven. She didn't have to say anything else. Adelia laughed too, and let the matter drop.

It *was* all in her imagination.

"As for strange old ladies, though, I don't like the sound of this Dorothy Talfourd," Harriet said, returning to the subject of the murder. Adelia had spoken in broad terms about it in front of Margaret. Margaret, indeed, had described Dorothy Talfourd with great relish. "Let's look at her. And Sloane! What a repellent article. We can pin it on one or the other, no doubt."

"There is to be no *pinning* of anything upon anyone. That's not how it works. We must be objective."

"There is no such thing. Not a single human alive can be objective, though of course we may *strive* to be without judgment."

"You don't even bother to strive."

"This is true. Anyway, I'll come tomorrow."

Adelia was confused. "Harriet, you are moving too fast and I have lost track. You'll come where tomorrow?"

"To the planning meeting for the May Day fair. Margaret mentioned it."

"She did, but it's not for us. It's in the Mason's Arms, for a start, and it's just the committee deciding on what will happen and how. I don't know why they bother because it will be the same as every year, according to Ramon. Margaret thinks she can change things but she's up against the Talfourds. And they still don't know about the maypole."

"They have to accept it now. It's the work of a dead woman so they have to show respect. Isn't that marvellous that she made it?"

"I think the fact she was a woman, not a man, will count against her. They will burn the pole as being the pagan work of a witch, surely, not the generations-long culmination of skill by a talented artisan. There, that's your witchcraft, right under your nose," she added.

"Huh. But if Margaret is going to this meeting, I can go too. And you."

"I really hadn't planned to."

"You have other plans?"

"No."

"And now?"

"What?"

Harriet stood up again. "Do you have any plans for right at this moment? If not, let us go for a walk. I fancy seeing this village, this hotbed of intrigue and murder."

"That is not respectful."

"I shall be the absolute *model* of propriety. Watch me. Come, let me prove to you how good I can be..."

HARRIET SOON REVEALED SHE HAD A VERY CLEAR IDEA OF exactly where in the village she wanted to go. She scanned the

THE COUNTESS'S DEADLY DISCOVERY

green and the shops until she spotted the church and the curved wall around the vicarage. She set off across the grass and Adelia had to hurry to keep up.

"I know you said you thought you could 'pin' it on her, but although Mrs Talfourd behaved very rudely towards Charlie, we have no other reason to suspect her of any foul play," Adelia said. "And honestly, she's totally incapable of any violence. She struggles to catch her breath if she tries to speak an overly-long sentence. I don't know much about her past but I get the impression that she has come from a poor background and worked hard to better herself and provide opportunities for her son. That is something to be admired."

"But you also mentioned before that this son is a weak-willed article and completely under her thumb."

"Yes, but I do not believe he is so completely at her mercy that he would kill on her command."

"People are surprising."

"I know they are – you do not need to lecture me."

Yet Harriet merely smiled in a supercilious way, and continued on her path.

Infuriated, Adelia could do nothing about her friend's stubbornness. She caught her up again and said, "So what are you planning to do? For I must warn you that I told you all about our investigation in the strictest confidence. If you speak out and ruin everything, I shall never have anything to do with you ever again."

"Have no fear. I merely wish to call upon the local representative of the Church of England as befits my own status. They will understand." She shot Adelia a sidelong glance and added, with a wicked smile, "Even if you do not."

"You are *so rude*."

"And you so faithless! Now, here we are. Where is he likely to be? Is he a cakes-with-parishioners sort of clergyman, or one that likes a bit of a pray-and-protestation? Do we go into the church first, do you think?"

Adelia replied, "You're the one who knows this sort of stuff."

"Now you are being rude."

"I am not sure he is either of those things."

"Very well." Harriet veered to the right and headed around the church to enter by its cool porch.

They were lucky. Reverend Talfourd was sitting in the pews at the back, his head bowed, but he heard them come in and he jumped up to welcome them. Well, "welcome" was perhaps too strong a word. Like before, he froze and stared at them.

Adelia hailed him with a warm greeting. He quivered as he recognised her, but Harriet took over. She grabbed his hand and pumped it as if they were old friends, introducing herself, apologising for introducing herself, talking about the Bishop, sending warmest regards from various mutual friends, and name-dropping shamelessly until poor Reverend Talfourd was quite overwhelmed.

Well, thought Adelia, *I might as well make the most of this opportunity, especially as we are currently free of his mother's pernicious influence*. She said, "More information has come to light about Charlie Webb."

His eyes widened and he glanced towards the door as if he were afraid someone was about to come in. "Oh?" he said.

"About her background. She said that her family came from this area – not Greyhaven itself, but hereabouts at least, as you know. I imagine there might be records about them in the parish registers."

"Oh, yes, I mean no, um, that's already been checked. She asked questions before, you see."

"But your mother wasn't willing to let them be checked."

"No, I mean, prior to that."

"Did she? When? And what did she find?"

"I cannot remember exactly when. Somewhen. The days, you know, do run together. Except Sundays, obviously." He laughed nervously. "But she found nothing."

"Nothing at all?" Adelia thought it odd that Charlie had not mentioned that. And surely a churchman would not lie?

"No, sorry. What a dreadful shame." He took a step towards the door and looked back at them, expecting them to take the hint.

They didn't, of course, and deliberately so.

"The police, too, will want to know," Harriet said. Adelia wanted to kick her.

Reverend Talfourd was still looking around with a hunted air. "But what, why?"

"Her family needs to be traced, does it not? They need to be informed."

"Yes – yes – of course! But maybe they already know, through other means, for the police have not been here, at least as far as I know."

Adelia tried to imagine the average sort of policeman coming up against Dorothy Talfourd. The scenario ended with a battered constable limping away in shame.

And she wouldn't have necessarily told her son about the police making a visit, one way or the other.

Then Harriet appalled Adelia even further by sidling closer to the vicar and saying, "And who do you think killed the poor, innocent lost soul? Your heart, like any decent person's, must be crying out for justice; the Bishop himself specifically asked me to send you his regards as he appreciates what a toll such events take on the leader of the flock in difficult times."

It was too much, all in one go, and Reverend Talfourd could only gasp for air like a fish thrown onto dry land. "I do

– indeed – for justice – but the – but Charlie was – I mean, not entirely *local*."

Oh, the implications, the accusations, contained in that one word. Not *local*. Not one of us. Other, somehow. Not quite *right*. A woman, dressed like a man. A woman, working with her hands, hedged with secrets, plagued by the past – if such a woman came to a bad end, then could she really be entirely blameless? Adelia read all of this and more in the vicar's miserable impression, and knew, with a sinking feeling, that she could only read it in his face because she felt it in her own heart. She tried not to feel such things, but the years and generations of society's teachings were very, very clear on the matter.

But, she told herself sternly, even *if* Charlie was utterly to blame in every single way, she was still *dead* and that was *wrong* and a culprit had to be found.

This same passion had fired Harriet's ire too. She said, "But she was here, and you are here, and the murderer must be here too. Did you see anything? Has anyone spoken of any particular antipathy towards her?"

"No, no; she was barely known and did not attract anyone's notice. She worked and she slept."

"Commendable."

"Er..." Suddenly he seemed to think of something in his desperation to get them both out of his church. "Maybe there is one person you could speak to."

Adelia assumed that he was going to suggest Nanna Black.

But he did not. "I'll take you to see her now." He raced off out of the church. Harriet grinned at Adelia, and they took off after him.

❧ 14 ❧

He led them across the green and towards the row of shops that ranged in a terrace either side of the Mason's Arms in the middle.

Adelia said, "But we have already spoken with every shop-keeper." Then she cursed herself for making it sound like they really were investigating.

But how could they truly keep it a secret? Everyone knew that Adelia and Theodore investigated crimes and they had already spoken with too many people. The best they could hope for was to be very discreet and not let any of their suspects know they were getting too close.

Unless Theodore decided to revive one of his previous mad ideas and deliberately let the principle suspect know they were under suspicion in the hope that they could be provoked into action. It *had* worked previously, just about ... although it always seemed to end with someone in great danger. She would rather avoid the whole threat of kidnap-pings and so on, this time.

"Have you been introduced to Mrs Lacey?" Reverend Talfourd asked.

"I don't believe so."

"Very well."

He stopped at a narrow door to the side of the main entrance to the grocer's shop, and knocked very loudly. It was opened by a slender young woman of around seventeen, with large dark eyes and crooked teeth.

"May we pay a call upon your aunt?"

"Oh, yes! She'll be delighted. You know how it is – people say they'll visit again but they never do come back. Except you, of course. If you'll wait here as usual..." The girl darted away up a tight set of steep stairs.

While she was gone, Reverend Talfourd explained.

"Mrs Lacey has been bed-ridden for a decade or more. It's an unusual wasting disease, but I don't understand the details. Her trials have been shouldered with great fortitude. I visit her as often as I can. And her bed is set up so that she can see all the comings and goings of the village. She loves market day and gets much joy from watching the children playing on the green. If anything happened involving Charlie Webb, she will have either seen it, or heard from someone else who saw it; sometimes the villagers visit her to talk. Well, as you heard her devoted niece say, they don't come as often as they *ought* to. Nevertheless, she devotes herself to the study of good works."

"She sounds like a perfect angel," said Adelia.

"She is. She is a marvellous example to us all. So very, very brave."

"Brave? Did she choose to be confined to bed?" Harriet asked, and there was a waspish tone in her voice.

"No, of course not."

"Then how is she an example?"

"It is her bravery in enduring."

"She cannot be brave. Her only option is to endure.

Bravery is a *choice* in the face of fear and one can always walk away from the choice; that is what makes it bravery."

"No, you misunderstand."

"I don't think that I do."

"You'll understand when you meet her," the Reverend finished lamely.

Adelia was not following her friend's argument at all, but clearly something had annoyed her. They were prevented from going any further by the niece returning.

She beckoned them upstairs, saying merrily, "My aunt cannot wait to meet new people!"

Maybe it was something in the Reverend's description that made Adelia expect to meet the very opposite of the person he had described, but in fact, Mrs Lacey was everything he had said she was. She was barely there, just a hollowed wisp of a person, nestled in so many plump cushions that it made one yawn and long to burrow into the bed. Her skin was blue-white and papery, and her high bed was set so that she could not only see out of the window which had been enlarged, but a mirror was angled to give her even more of a view. She smiled in greeting. She had no teeth.

Revered Talfourd made the barest of polite introductions and then, to Adelia's astonishment and relief, he took his leave and departed.

Mrs Lacey seemed disappointed at his absence. "I do like to talk with our Thomas," she said. "He is constant in his visits unlike ... But still! Here *you* are! Lady Calaway, what an honour! And Mrs Hobson! I know your name. I have read some of your husband's writings. You are both very much admired. Please do take a seat."

The room was full of a variety of newspapers, periodicals, magazines, and books. Mrs Lacey was clearly keeping her mind sharp and up to date.

She proved that by going on to say, "And Lady Calaway,

you and your husband are well known in certain circles for the careful and clever assistance you give to the police. Yet I cannot imagine you have been asked to look into the death of this poor unfortunate ... *woman*. This would be beneath you, surely?"

"No death is beneath us," Adelia said. "Everyone is worthy of notice. And you, sitting here, are able to notice everything..."

"Ah!" Mrs Lacey said, wiggling in glee. "I was going to send a note, you know, to the police about what I saw, but then people said that the police weren't too bothered, on account of, you know ... her *situation*."

"Her poverty?" Harriet said.

"Yes, that. And the *other* thing. You know. So I thought I'd best let the matter drop. I do understand how a person like that ought not to be talked about. Ha! I see an awful lot through this window, you know, and I have quickly learned that most of what I see is actually no concern of mine. The moment one speaks, that is when you set in motion a wind that often becomes a storm. So I watch and I learn but I keep it all inside. I store up knowledge like others collect stamps."

"Is it knowledge? Or just information?" Harriet said.

She didn't sound very impressed with Mrs Lacey. Adelia herself didn't enjoy the almost cultish worship that had grown up around those who were bed-ridden but she understood why people needed to reassure themselves that there could be some good out of a bad situation.

Mrs Lacey ignored Harriet completely. She focused her attention entirely on Adelia, and said, "Would you like to know what I saw?"

"Yes please, if it is relevant."

"I am not sure."

"Not sure if it's relevant?"

"Not sure if I ought to break a confidence. As I say, I see a lot but I know to keep my own counsel."

Harriet sighed and Adelia realised that Mrs Lacey wanted them to beg for her help. What other power did she have, indeed, from her bed in this room?

Adelia began to summon up some pleasantly persuasive argument but Harriet took a different tack. She simply turned on her heel and made for the door. "Thank you for your time, Mrs Lacey, and we wish you all the best. Good day."

Mrs Lacey worked her toothless mouth and her gnarled, stick-like fingers gripped the sheets. "But Mrs Hobson ... oh, Lady Calaway, you do understand?"

Adelia realised what Harriet was up to. She nodded and said to Mrs Lacey, "Yes, we do understand completely. We would never ask you to gossip or break a confidence. We are so very sorry to have troubled you."

She followed Harriet to the door. Harriet was already out of the room now and standing on the landing.

Adelia had got one foot over the threshold when Mrs Lacey crumbled. "It's not breaking a confidence if I only tell you what I saw happen in public!"

Harriet, unseen by Mrs Lacey, was grinning in triumph. Adelia composed her face a little more politely and turned to face the old lady.

"Perhaps," she said with doubt in her voice. "But you must be absolutely sure. Why don't we leave you to think about it?"

"No, no, stay. Do come back in." Her desperate pleading became a wheedle. "After all, what I saw was in public view so it's not a secret, and I didn't hear anything, and maybe it's not important at all..."

Now she wanted to be told that it was important. Once again, Harriet rose to it. "If it is not important, then I agree with Adelia – let us leave you alone and if you decide it was important, let us know by note perhaps?"

"I don't know if it is important or not! Come back and let me tell you everything."

Finally they re-entered the room and arranged themselves at the side of the bed, patiently waiting for Mrs Lacey to speak. She waited, too, presumably to be persuaded and cajoled into speaking out. When she realised that neither Adelia nor Harriet were going to do so, she told them what she'd been longing to spill all along.

"I saw him! Her, that person – Charles Webb. I had seen her a few times, of course, crossing the green early in the morning, a bag of tools with her like any common workman and I can tell you that I thought *then* that something was wrong with her. Yes, I did. I have watched many people and I have long years of experience. I can *tell* when someone's not *right*."

She tipped her small and rounded chin up in a challenge to them, eyeballing them as if she were judging Harriet and Adelia on their *rightness*.

Adelia merely nodded.

Mrs Lacey went on. "I never saw her talking with anyone. Anyone! Ever! That's another sign, isn't it?"

They both nodded without speaking. Mrs Lacey frowned very fleetingly, and Adelia knew that she was annoyed that no one was playing her game.

"Do go on," Adelia said.

"Well. Well! So then, just over a week ago, I did see her. I might have been the last person to ever see her!"

"What day was it?"

Mrs Lacey shrugged. "I have no idea. I am more concerned with my soul and my death than the everyday passage of time. But it was before she died, and she was not alone."

"Who was she with?"

"I don't know."

Adelia did not move or speak. Internally, she was screaming. No doubt Harriet felt the same way. She tried to remind herself that poor Mrs Lacey was all along most of the time, and deserved their sympathy and patience.

The lack of reaction from either of them prompted Mrs Lacey to give them a description.

"He was a tall man but awfully well-dressed, far too fancy for our little village, and I did not know him. I know everyone here, you know. Mr Sloane. Lord Morland. Reverend Talfourd. Mr Alfoxden. But I did not know him and so I was immediately suspicious."

"Did he have a cane, and a mustard-coloured jacket?"

"He did!" Mrs Lacey straightened up. "Do you know who it was?"

"It sounds very much like Mr Frederick Arbury. But he and his family used to live here, Mrs Lacey. Do you know anything about them?"

"Of course I do!" she said indignantly. "The Arburys from Arbury House. Oh, they were so rich and so fine. But they all went away, many years ago, and as you can see, here I am, unable to leave the house..."

"Did you know that Charlie Webb's family was from around here, too?"

"No, no, they weren't."

"They lived in the old cottages just out of Greyhaven."

"Exactly. They weren't from *here*."

Adelia realised that the boundaries of the village were very small, and very fixed. She moved on and said, "So what were they doing together?"

"Arguing! It was early in the morning, as was usual for her. She must have left the inn. I can't see the door from here, of course, but she was heading across towards the bridge so I assumed she was going to work at the manor. And then he appeared, on foot, strolling along like he was taking an early morning constitutional. I watched but only because he was a stranger to me and I have a duty to the village to keep an eye on who comes and goes. One cannot be too careful, living up here in the wilds."

"Indeed. So who spoke first?"

"She spotted him and changed her route to go towards him. He lifted his hat in greeting so I wondered if they knew one another – why would a rich man pay such respect to a worker like that? There is no need. But he did, and she stopped, and they began to speak."

"You wouldn't have heard what was said, I imagine," Adelia said.

"No, not a word, but it quickly grew heated. They waved their arms around, and he stepped towards her, his fist clenched and raised in the air; she stepped back."

"He threatened her?"

"That's what it looked like. She went backwards and then reached into her bag and pulled out some kind of tool – don't ask me what – and waved it at him, forcing him away. He looked furiously angry. And I don't know how things would have ended, but they were interrupted by the workers heading for the mill and the start of their shift."

"Which way did they go?"

"She carried on to the bridge, swept up out of sight with the others, and he stamped into the village and on."

"Could he have been going to Arbury House?"

"He could have, or the church, or to see Reverend Talfourd. It's impossible to tell. I just know he headed up the track that leads to all of those places."

They thanked Mrs Lacey for her time and left at last, and promised to send her some sweet things in a basket for her trouble. She wanted to continue talking, and tried to think of more things that would interest them, but she clearly had no more information. Adelia felt sorry for her, all alone up her room, and made a little polite conversation with her until Harriet's sighing grew too loud to bear.

As soon as they were out in the street, and barely a few strides away from the house, Harriet exploded. "I cannot tell you how many people I have met in that position!"

"Yet you had no sympathy at all. Harriet, I am not jesting with you now – I want to say that I do think you were unforgivably cold and rude to that poor invalid."

Harriet kicked at the ground as they walked back towards the manor.

"You saw how she was. So manipulative, so controlling. Those women, they are like spiders in the centre of webs, playing the part of a poor weak invalid. Everyone around them is powerless. They have to dance to their tune, be at their beck and call. Every transgression that the invalid makes is instantly explained by their illness and forgiven. They can do no wrong. No one can have a life because it revolves around them. That niece will never marry, never have children, never be anything more than a skivvy to a dried-up woman who has no business lying there in bed. None at all. I bet she gets up in the night and dances while she laughs."

Adelia stopped dead. The hate and vitriol in Harriet's voice was so unlike her that Adelia was almost scared.

"Harriet, my oldest, best friend in all the world – Harriet, what has made you like this? What of your Christian mercy and charity, qualities that I so admire in you?"

Harriet gazed away from her, tilting her face to the sky, and her throat bobbed. "I told you my mother was dead, didn't I?"

"Yes. Harriet, you came to stay after her funeral. I remember those weeks distinctly. We had been acquaintances prior to that – after the funeral, you stayed, and that was when we became close."

"Then let me tell you that I am nothing but a repellent and seething mass of lies, Adelia. I am sorry. There was a funeral, but it was for my father. My mother still lives. And I have not seen her since that very day."

Adelia let that new information sit with her for a few moments.

Before she could speak, Harriet said, "Oh, Adelia, I am sorry. Sorry for you, and me, and her, and my own mother. I took it out on Mrs Lacey but it wasn't about her." Her tone hardened briefly. "I stand by what I said, though. Mrs Lacey was trying to control us."

"Yes, she was, and that is understandable in her situation. Can we not let her do that, for a few moments in a day?"

Harriet looked up at the sky. Perhaps she was looking for her dead father.

She said, "You are right. I can offer no excuse, only explanations that do not absolve me of blame. She sparked something in me, some reaction that took me straight back to my childhood days...I will tell you all about it, dear Adelia, one day. Not now, not today."

"Whenever you are ready."

"Thank you. Because in truth, I am shocked at my own behaviour. I had thought I was all past it until just now. She has unearthed a feeling in me that I thought long buried. Now I see that it is not the case and I am ... shamed."

Adelia reached out to her friend. Harriet let her shoulder be caressed before she sighed deeply and set off walking again.

❧ 15 ❧

They didn't speak all the way back to Griseley Manor but they didn't need to. Adelia could tell, from Harriet's words and reactions, the gist of what had happened. The lies stung, a little, but were entirely understandable; society would destroy a daughter who openly confessed to turning her back on her own mother, no matter how unpleasant that mother might have been.

Harriet and Adelia had not been close then, and the lie had not been significant until they grew more secure in their friendship – and Adelia, of all people, knew how hard it was to correct a lie as time went on. Her own lie had nearly wrecked her marriage but they'd overcome it. Theodore had forgiven her, and now she had to forgive and understand Harriet.

And she knew that soon, they would sit down and talk it all out. The seeds were being laid.

Harriet went off to her room. There was a little bit of time to spare before dinner. Adelia went to look for Theodore, and to give him the news that Frederick Arbury could well be a more significant suspect than they had previously thought.

But then she remembered Reverend Talfourd's evasiveness too, and her confusion grew.

MARGARET AND RAMON WERE MORE THAN HAPPY TO allow Harriet to come to the May Day fair meeting in the Mason's Arms. That meant Adelia felt obliged to go, too, and Theodore said he'd come along. "You are like reinforcements," Margaret said as they headed into the village the next day. "You can stand up to the Talfourds with us."

But in the event, the Talfourds were not the problem.

Beaumont Sloane dominated the proceedings. He was loud, blustering and boorish. Many of the villagers were present, too, mostly men; not even Nanna Black was present from the village side of things. The only other woman present was Dorothy Talfourd, who sat in a comfortable chair specially brought in by the landlord. To her utter fury, she was not able to be heard. Sloane spoke loudly over her, and she could not seem to stop him.

Sloane was in a furious rage from the very beginning. When he saw them all arrive in a group from Griseley Manor he raked his eyes over them, each in turn, but they looked back defiantly. He snarled and turned away.

Adelia was glad that Mr Arbury had declined the invitation to come along. He had things to do, he said regretfully, and he recognised that in spite of his heritage, he did not have a place in the village. That had made Margaret frown and nudge her husband, but nothing more was said. Adelia suspected something was being planned, but she didn't ask.

Someone mentioned the mill to Sloane and suggested he was still smarting about his views on the installation of the engine being overlooked. He dismissed it with a grunt and Adelia realised that he had never opposed the new Corliss engine at all – he had only ever been worried about the draining of the Holy Pool. Someone then tried to make a joke about the robbing of "that young daft Arbury" and Sloane roared at them. An awkward silence fell.

Sloane then seized the silence to run the meeting in his own way.

He unrolled a large sheet of paper and began to explain whose stalls would be where, what they would cost, and why he was not allowing certain people to sell certain things. This caused an outcry all over again which came from the village men.

"David Bell has always come over from Grafton and sharpened knives..."

"People will expect Old Nell to play at telling fortunes here..."

Even when Dorothy Talfourd spoke up in favour of excluding the fortune teller, she was overlooked and ignored. Sloane ran the meeting and he ran it his way. Clearly, he was expecting to run the whole fair.

Ramon, usually so quiet and reserved, finally spoke up. "The show-ring for the dogs cannot be in the centre. That is for the maypole."

Sloane swivelled his head very slowly to look at Ramon with utter disdain on his face. "The what?"

"We have had a maypole carved. It is to be the centre-piece. The village used to have one years ago but..."

He was cut off by a violent hissing sound from Dorothy Talfourd.

"We will not have pagan relics here!"

Sloane laughed rudely and completely ignored her. Perhaps to spite her, he said then to Ramon, "No one cares one way or the other about some maypole so just shove it wherever you can find space."

"It has to be central, with an area around for the girls to dance."

Dorothy was wheezing now. "Dancing? There will be no dancing!"

"You'll find somewhere, I am sure. Keep it away from the hog roast." Sloane tapped the map and began to talk about the kind "donation" of a pig which, judging from the expression on the particular farmer's face, had not been a donation that was freely given.

There was nothing more for anyone to say about the maypole, and the meeting rumbled on. It was, in fact, rather less of a meeting and more of a lecture given by Sloane about the way things would work.

❀

AFTERWARDS, THEODORE LEFT THE INN WITH ADELIA AND Harriet. Margaret and Ramon strode past them to look at the village green and plan where they were going to put the maypole.

Theodore heard Margaret mutter to Ramon, "If we set it up the night before, it will go wherever we please..."

Adelia lifted her hand and pressed the back of it to Theodore's chest. He stopped and listened to what had just caught her attention.

They could hear Dorothy Talfourd speaking. The inn had an archway in the centre which led through to the coachyard behind, and they all drew into its sheltered darkness to be out of sight as the Talfourds left the inn. He heard the clack of her cane on the cobbles, and the grating wheeze of her voice as she spoke in complete fury to her son.

"You left me, abandoned me to the savage attack by that – that – that man! Barely a man! Evildoer, sinner, worm!"

"Mother, what was anyone to say?"

"You were to leap up and defend me, you worthless, spineless boy. I have been humiliated, quite destroyed, and how could you possibly bear it? How could you witness it? How can you live with yourself? Oh, if I were able to, I'd ..."

"Mother, calm yourself. You are struggling to breathe. Stop and take a moment."

"Calm! Calm! When I am beset on all sides by fools and idiots, people who think they know best, people who think they know the past and what's good for the future of the village – well let me tell you, son of mine, that I know what's what and I can tell you that no good will come of this. Of any of this!"

"Mother!" There was a sad urgency in Reverend Talfourd's voice. "Please do calm yourself. Please wait – there's no need to rush home." His voice grew fainter.

"Why would I linger here in this nest of vipers?" Her croaking was likewise muffled now.

They heard nothing more.

Theodore looked at Adelia. "She said that she knows *what's what*. Have you any idea what she might mean?"

"None but I am very suspicious of the pair of them."

Harriet was bouncing on the balls of her feet. She said, with glee, "She told him to kill and so he did!"

Theodore didn't dignify such idle ramblings with an answer. They headed back to the manor.

"THEODORE, MY DARLING, COME TO THE WINDOW," SAID Adelia that night after an early dinner.

He crossed the sitting room of their suite and leaned on

the windowsill. She had the leaded casement flung open and was thrusting her head out into the cool night air.

"Are we to recreate Romeo and Juliet?" he asked. "I could pop outside and serenade you perhaps."

"I wouldn't bother. There are roses with some vicious thorns just below us. But can you smell smoke?"

"Of course. People will have their fires lit."

"It's not the usual smell. I would expect coal or even wood perhaps and I know as you get further north, they use peat and that smell is rather unmistakable."

"I cannot see a fire," he said, now sniffing frantically like a dog on a mission to root out where his master had hidden the treats.

"No, nor I." Impulsively, she said, "It's a pleasant evening and I don't feel inclined to join the others. Margaret and Ramon are speaking at interminable length about this May Day fair, and Mr Arbury is gloomy and Harriet is bundled up in her rooms with books and gin. Shall we take a walk?"

He agreed immediately. They wrapped up well and sallied out into the grounds of the manor. He brought a lantern with him, pilfered from the kitchens, and the moon was half-full. There were high thin clouds which reflected a certain amount of strangely flat grey light so that they could just about see the lighter parts of the path unless they were in the shadows of trees. Once their eyes had adjusted, things got easier. Adelia clung close to Theodore, nevertheless.

"Did you discover anything new at the police station?" she asked.

"I've told you everything," he said glumly. "They seem to be hushing the whole thing up. They wouldn't tell me if they had found her family now but one constable winked at me and suggested to me, in private, when he was able to speak, that the family had been informed but wanted nothing to do with the matter. So it'll be a pauper's grave and that's it. They don't want it in the papers."

"They cannot keep it out of the press!"

"Apparently they can, or that's the way it works up here. You're right that in London, this would be on pamphlets and broadsides by now if there were no other news of interest. It could be dressed up into a very thrilling tale. But here, everyone seems to owe everyone else something, and if the powers-that-be don't want a thing to be known, then it won't be known."

Something in his words tugged at Adelia.

"Don't you find it awfully strange," she said, "that the Arburys were an old and significant family in this area for years, but no one would really speak about them and no one admits to knowing of Mr Arbury? And Charlie Webb's family was likewise rooted here for generations as far as I can tell but because they were slightly outside the boundaries, again everyone is using it as an excuse to deny all knowledge of her or them? I cannot quite believe it, you know."

"You are right. There are people here who *do* know what's going on. Do you think..."

"Theodore, what's wrong?"

He had stopped walking. He shook his head. "No, it's silly. I just thought that surely Ramon would know more than he is saying. His family, the Alfoxdens, have branches and scions everywhere and they are as settled here as the Arburys ever were."

"Was there rivalry between them, do you think?"

"Possibly. Yet he does *seem* to be the most honest and helpful chap. Rather quiet, but I like that about him. Unless ..."

"Theodore?"

"Unless he is quiet not because he is naturally reserved, but because he is hiding something."

Adelia rubbed at Theodore's hand. "Let us not jump to conclusions, dear heart. After all, we have a sizeable list of more obvious suspects at the moment. Each of these people have been seen arguing with Charlie, although we are yet to establish any real motives for them."

Theodore resumed walking. He went through the list at her prompting.

"Now we know that Frederick Arbury argued with her just before she died. It appears that she approached him, which makes sense, as she was the one asking about him."

"And I was the one who brought him here," Adelia added, a little glumly.

"An act done out of the goodness of your heart, and unlikely to be connected. Do not fret about it. Next, we have the Talfourds. I am struggling to see how either Dorothy or her son Thomas could be involved; the only evidence we have is the fact that Mrs Talfourd refused to let Charlie see the records, and the reverend himself is evasive about allowing access. That suggests to me one of two things: either she hates *anyone* seeing the records because they are destroyed or inaccurate or she likes the control of it and it's spite – or, there is something incriminating contained in them."

"We must find out!"

"Indeed we must. For that will surely point the finger at someone, even if it is not the Talfourds themselves. So we will gain access to the parish registers by fair means or foul as soon as we can."

"We cannot break into a church, Theodore..."

"We will do whatever is necessary for justice."

She didn't feel happy about it, but she knew he was right.

He went on. "But there are yet two other suspects. Beaumont Sloane came to the manor specifically to seek Charlie Webb out and threaten her, telling her not to ask questions."

"Wait," said Adelia. "Was that simply because he didn't

want Frederick Arbury to come back, because he knew it would expose the things that he had done? The way he had robbed Mr Arbury, taken his things, taken his sweetheart in fact, and made her his wife?"

Theodore slowed his pace again. "All very good points, and very true, and I suggest that slides Sloane down the list of suspects. Finally, then ... Lord Peter Morland."

"I hate to agree with you but yes, that man is certainly hiding something. My heart breaks for poor Gwen. There must be some way of speaking to him to find out the truth," she said. "The witness said that Charlie told Lord Morland he was not good enough for Gwen and that she'd expose him."

"He's a young lord. The secret could be *anything*," Theodore said. "But I shall make some discreet enquiries of my own amongst the less salubrious sorts of folk that run with his crowd."

They reached the northern edge of the manor grounds. They turned right and followed the wall which had grey stone almost glowing in the pale moonlight. They wandered on, unwilling by mutual consent to head back to the manor yet.

But as they stood on the green, its edges fading into darkness, Adelia said, "I can definitely smell smoke."

She looked around. Along one side of the green were the lights of the houses and the inn itself, which was lit up joyfully. People moved around outside, and she could hear voices, laughter, jesting, and shouts.

Theodore licked his finger and held it up. The night wind was very gentle and it was difficult to tell from what direction it was coming, but after turning in a slow circle three times, he nodded towards the church itself.

"It can only be coming from there," he said.

"The church?" Adelia felt immediately uneasy. They walked to the track that led from the village towards the church. Their footsteps crunched loudly and the sounds of merriment soon faded behind them. The church rose up on their left now, with the Talfourds' house lying behind it. The church was all in darkness, which was what they expected and indeed hoped for.

Theodore sniffed. "I can definitely smell something," he said. "You were right all along."

"But it's not coming from the church." Adelia tugged his hand and they went onwards, approaching now the ruined house of the Arbury family.

Theodore moved sideways, drawing them both from the noisy stony track and onto the softer grass at the side. He shuttered the lantern and they relied on instinct, memory and dark looming shapes to navigate their way towards the derelict house. Things rustled in the undergrowth. Adelia heard a high-pitched squeaking which ended abruptly. Something hooted in the trees that lay between the house and the churchyard. She'd been in the countryside at night many times, of course – and it never got less unsettling.

The smell grew fainter. Adelia was about to pull on Theodore's arm and tell him that they were wrong when they reached the gates and peered through the twisted metal and clogging ivy to see something – what? Movement? No – *flames!*

There was a red glow to the left of the tumbled stones that marked the edge of the house. Theodore passed the lantern to Adelia and wrestled with the damaged gates, trying to drag them open enough to let them pass through. Metal scraped on metal and she cursed silently – but there was no way he could do any better than he was doing. They slipped through, her cloak snagging on the ironwork, and headed towards the fire.

It was going out. Any flames that she thought she'd seen were dying now. The smell rose up but was fading already. They were twenty yards away and suddenly she thought she saw movement beyond the fire. She cocked her head, using her peripheral vision, the edges of her sight which always seemed to be better at night.

A figure was hurrying away.

"Theodore!" she hissed. "Do you see them?"

"I do!" And then, because surely the noise of the gate and their footsteps and their whispers were carrying, he abandoned all stealth.

He leaped forward, leaving her behind, shouting, "Ho! Stop there!"

He disappeared into the shadows.

She went after him, her heart hammering, but when she reached him, he was standing quite alone. "There's no one here," he said.

"Are you sure?"

"They must have scaled the wall."

He took the lantern from her and pulled back the panel to let its light be directed around them. He raked the area in a circle and all they saw were brambles, hedges, weeds, stones, and a high wall that encircled them. The wall was in better condition than the house itself.

"They didn't go past me so they didn't go into the remains of the house, and they could not have gone past you to the gate. Either they flew over that wall or they are hiding under a pile of last year's leaves."

"Or they used the secret tunnel," Adelia said.

"The tunnel to the churchyard! Well, this is interesting..."

She felt that there was nothing more to be done in the darkness but he had to get it out of his system so she waited patiently while he combed over the area, hunting for any access to a tunnel. He fell in a few holes, and nearly turned his ankle. By the time he came back to her, she could see from the reflected light of the lantern that he was bleeding from the thorns hitting his face, had torn his shirt, and she didn't dare imagine the state of his jacket.

The fire was completely out by now.

"Tomorrow," she told him. "We will come back."

"At first light."

"Yes. At the crack of dawn."

She led him home and thought that neither of them would find sleep easy.

Who was burning things so secretly at night?

Her first thought was the most obvious one.

The Talfourds. Parish records.

Evidence. Had they foolishly missed their chance?

❧ 16 ❧

Theodore was dressed and ready and sitting by the window when Adelia awoke. He smiled at her and tried to be patient but he was itching to get out to explore the site of last night's fire, and while she got dressed, he went off to find some breakfast that they could eat on the way.

"Everyone must surely know what we are up to," she said to him as they walked through the village. It was to be an overcast day with the threat of rain in the low dark clouds, and the workers were streaming to the mill with their heads down and their hats pulled low.

"I am sure that they have known since the very first moment," he replied. "Nothing is truly private here. They all know what we are doing but they don't know what we know."

"We know very little."

"We are soon to know more."

He strode quickly in fits and bursts, remembering from time to time to slow down and allow his wife to catch up. But she didn't grumble at him. She was as keen as he was, he knew. He thought about Charlie Webb. If Adelia could have worn trousers for active days like this, he thought, it would make it all a lot easier. But the thought of Adelia in men's clothing made him feel a bit funny; and anyway, it wasn't done. It was wrong. He had seen such things in music halls, of course, and the associations were unsavoury. He put it all out of his mind and concentrated instead on getting to Arbury House as quickly as possible.

They went first to the blackened spot where the fire had been lit. The centre was just a heap of ashes and charred wood which must have been laid to help the fire burn steadily, but around the edges there were scraps of paper with blackened edges. Adelia gathered up as many as she could, with her bare hands so as not to spoil her gloves, and dropped them in a linen bag she'd brought for the purpose.

"Is there any writing on any of them?" he asked anxiously.

"A few words. And I think I have found the spines of some ledgers so I'll take those. The leather does not burn as well but the glue that has held them together seems to have melted into a mess."

"Any clues from the words?"

"No. But we will spread it all out when we get back to the manor – I don't want to risk damaging anything here, or have a gust of wind lift a piece of evidence and spirit it away."

Soon she had gathered up anything of worth and they moved on to explore the area that the figure had seemed to disappear into.

By daylight it was far easier to find the tunnel's entrance. It was simply a matter of following the trail of flattened grass and broken vegetation. Theodore examined the brambles carefully and whooped with joy when he found a scrap of fabric on a branch, but Adelia punctured him immediately by pointing out it was the same colour as the jacket he'd been wearing the night before; the same jacket that Smith was now bent over back at the manor, cursing and muttering as she darned the rents and tears.

The rough path led downwards between two stands of briars which curved up and over, making a natural tunnel itself as the ground level sank below it. The tunnel entrance was marked by two uprights of hewn stone and a thick wooden lintel lay over the top, about five feet high. Theodore lit the lantern he'd brought.

"You do not have to come with me," he said. "Indeed, I'd advise against it. Smith will give notice if you come back covered in dirt and weeds."

"She will, but it will be a temporary fit, and I shall help her to clean up once she has decided to come back. Of course I am coming with you. Who would turn up the chance to explore a secret tunnel?" she said.

He laughed. "Just about every other society lady I've ever met. Oh, I am a lucky man indeed. Come on then. Keep close."

"Close? I shall not let go of your coat-tail."

The air quickly grew foetid and the darkness was all-consuming. It seemed to eat the edges of the light that was cast from their feeble lantern. The ground was damp and their feet slipped into pools of water. He heard Adelia squeak in surprise and disgust more than once, but she stifled herself as much as she could.

He inched forward, his shoulders and back aching almost from the start as they had to hunch over while they walked. He made the mistake of putting out his hand to the wall to steady himself. His fingers touched something soft and he recoiled hastily.

"Did you know," he said, to distract himself as much as Adelia, "that cave-dwelling spiders are the largest sort of native spider in Britain?"

She hit him on the back of his head without a word and

he decided he might have made a mistake, and remained silent after that.

The darkness pressed in on them. He was beginning to feel that it had all been a dreadful mistake when he saw something up ahead. He tried to work out what it was and then realised it was simply light. "We're nearly there," he said.

Adelia muttered a shocking word that he pretended he hadn't heard, and then said, "Good."

Yet it seemed to take an interminable time to get to the end of the tunnel and by the time they tumbled out into the churchyard, his back was on fire and his knees were screaming. He leaned on a gravestone, stretching and wincing for a good few minutes before he was able to assess where he was.

The tunnel had grown very small by the end and the entrance at this side was only just large enough to crawl through. It came up in a disused far corner of the graveyard and he shuddered to think how close to the graves they must have been passing. Stones and broken bits of masonry made a natural screen to their inelegant exit.

Adelia was sucking in deep breaths. "You were lucky," she muttered. "You didn't have to do that in a corset. I may have punctured a lung."

"You haven't," he told her cheerfully. "You would sound quite different if you had done so. But do let me know if you get any sharp stomach pains as I often worry about your spleen."

"Do you?"

"Yes, I do."

"How romantic." She didn't seem to be as grateful as he'd expected she might be.

They walked home, heads held high, trying to ignore the stares of the villagers. They were in something of a state of disarray, and Smith's reaction was exactly the one that they'd predicted.

It was an hour or so before they were washed, redressed, and ready to examine the things that they had found.

❦

RAMON AND MARGARET WERE KEEN TO LEARN WHAT THEY had found. Adelia and Theodore were prepared for this. They didn't want to lie to their daughter and her husband, but they were mindful of some questions regarding their loyalties. So Theodore remained in their suite, examining the scraps of paper they had found with his forensic eye while Adelia took tea with her in-laws and told them all about the discovery of the secret tunnel.

Harriet was also present, as was Mr Arbury. Everyone was delighted by Adelia's adventure and it sparked much chatter about other local legends that might also be true. Mr Arbury was particularly taken by the tunnel.

"I wish I'd known about it when I was a small child there," he said, wistfully. "How was this knowledge kept from me? I would have hidden down there a lot."

"What would you be hiding from?" Adelia asked.

"Oh – you know, the usual things."

"Such as?"

But he was not to be drawn any further on the topic.

When Gwen was announced, Ramon and Mr Arbury left so that the women could talk undisturbed. Margaret leaped to her feet as her friend was shown in.

"Gwen! What's happened? Oh – the cad – what has he done to you? Is it all broken off for good?"

"It might be," Gwen said with a sniff.

Her eyes were pink and she'd clearly been crying. She was led to the best chair by the low fire, and the bell was rung for more food and drink. Almost all emotional crises could be tackled with a good cup of tea, after all.

As soon as all the servants had been dismissed, Gwen burst into floods of tears. "Margaret, I think he's the murderer!"

Instantly, the three other women closed in around her.

Adelia said, "What makes you think that? Do you have evidence?"

Harriet tutted at her. "Let us show some sympathy first – and then start the investigation. Can you not be a woman first and a detective second, at least for a few moments?"

"No, no, it's all right. Anyway, I've brought the evidence," Gwen said.

She was holding her fists tightly balled up and Adelia had initially taken that to be simply a symptom of her emotional state. But Gwen extended her right hand and opened it. There was a very crumpled piece of paper on her palm. Margaret picked it up and spread it on her skirts, flattening it down carefully.

"Dear Miss Fitzroy-Harris, I need to warn you that he is not what he seems to be. Lord Morland... oh, that's spelled wrong, but never mind ... Lord Morland has lied to you. Leave him. Do not marry him. He will rue – run – oh, ruin! He will ruin you." Margaret looked up at Gwen in horror. "And it's unsigned, of course. What a coward! Who sent this to you, and when? You poor, poor thing."

"I got it three weeks ago," Gwen confessed in a small voice.

Everyone gasped at that, even Harriet, who had not seen the emotional ups and downs between Gwen and Lord Morland.

"Why did you not tell me?" Margaret demanded, almost harshly.

Gwen hung her head. "We were having disagreements and I had already begun to see that he was hiding something from me, but I was embarrassed and I wondered if it were my fault, because if I were a proper sort of sophisticated woman like from London, he wouldn't try to keep secrets from me, and I thought maybe he wasn't telling me everything because he thought that I wouldn't understand."

"How on earth could you think this was your fault?" Margaret demanded. "You silly goose. And have you any idea who sent it? How did it get to you?"

"I found it in my bag after I had been here."

"Who could have put it there? Only a servant, surely."

"I thought ..."

Adelia knew exactly what she thought. She said, "Had you been in the workshop that day?"

Gwen nodded.

"You cannot think this was the work of Charlie?" Margaret said.

"I can and I do," Adelia said. She had to reveal a little of what they already knew. "After all, I am afraid that there is an eyewitness who saw Charlie and Lord Morland arguing. He overheard some of their conversation too. This note matches what was said. Once again, she was warning him off."

"Why would she try to split us up? Oh, but then again, what if it is true? He has been acting so very strangely. In fact..." Gwen cried harder and it took a few moments to calm her down again. "In fact, that's why I came here today. It's all got worse, very suddenly."

"What's happened?" They all clamoured together for information.

"He's panicking. I don't know what's going on. He won't talk to me. He was supposed to come to tea yesterday and my parents do adore him, you know. But he didn't turn up. Father was so upset. I made excuses for him, again, as I do."

Everyone cooed in a mixture of sympathy and exasperation.

Gwen sniffed. "And then I was angry, not upset. I went

out and I thought maybe I'd come and find him. I took my father's man with me to light the way and I came down here into the village. I was going to come to the manor to look for him. But on the way, we met him in the village itself, riding out of the inn. He didn't expect to see me but he was looking all around, his eyes were wild, and he had a pistol at his hip, I am sure of it!"

"What did he say?"

"He said he'd forgotten about the arrangement for tea and he had been called away on business. But what business? What has he said? Is he even still here?"

Adelia stared open mouthed at Margaret. "*Is* he still here?" she demanded.

Margaret, too, was looking shocked. "He didn't come to breakfast this morning but he often doesn't. I don't know. But he didn't mention leaving to go anywhere and surely he would have said something?"

"Go and ask," Harriet said.

Margaret rang the bell and got to her feet, intercepting a maid as she came to the door. They had a hurried conversation and then Margaret turned back to the room.

"He came back very late last night, and took bread rolls in his room this morning," she said. "But he has gone out again now, and he didn't mention where he was going. He was on foot and not carrying anything to suggest that he was leaving."

Adelia said, "We must find out what he is up to. Even if it is not connected to the death, it's for Gwen's sake, isn't it?" Everyone nodded in agreement.

Gwen said, "Whatever you find out, though, I think I need to forget him utterly, don't I? No more wedding planning. No more dreams. Oh, I am broken, lost, alone..."

"You are much better off than being shackled to a liar and a charlatan," Margaret said very firmly. "And you are right to drop him, drop him *completely*. Mama is awfully good at finding husbands." She looked at Adelia and said, "You will, won't you?"

"Of course. Leave it with me. But now, about this note. I would like to check the handwriting against something of Charlie's, if possible."

Margaret handed her the paper. "I don't think we have anything but I will search the workshop. I am not sure what else we can do."

"I will go to the inn, and around the village generally," Adelia said.

Harriet stood up alongside her. They left Margaret to console her best friend, and headed out into the village.

❧ 17 ❧

"This is complicated now," Harriet said with a slightly petulant tone.

"You just wanted the guilty party to be Dorothy Talfourd, didn't you?"

"Yes, I did, because there is something wrong with her and I don't think her son reflects well on the church. I have a professional interest in the matter," Harriet said. "But now we must look at this business between that lovely girl Gwen and the evil bounder Lord Morland. I don't like the sound of him at all. I didn't like him when I met him at dinner."

"You got on splendidly with him."

"I was lulling him into a false sense of security."

"You were not."

They bickered lightly all the way to the inn. Adelia had never set foot inside such an establishment before she had become an investigator and even now, she felt a flicker of hesitancy before she stepped over the threshold. She remembered how she had insisted on taking a private room even though Margaret had assured her they were accepted in the booths in the back room.

Harriet, however, seemed to consider that she had a ticket to any manner of place. She could say that she was there on "charitable Christian business" and assume entry by dint of her overwhelming middle class do-gooding. She surged right in without a moment of consideration, and Adelia followed her, trying to walk with absolute confidence.

Harriet did still have enough decorum not to attempt to walk into the tap-room, however. They met a serving maid in the corridor who showed them to one of the snugs in the back room and asked the landlord to come and speak to them. Adelia perched on the wooden bench, feeling out of place but a little bit thrilled.

Harriet lolled like she had been born in a bar.

The landlord recognised Adelia from their earlier visit and greeted them warmly but with an apologetic shake of the head.

"I haven't heard nothing more. What do you think I should do with the things that were left behind? We've got them stored."

"Oh! I am sure the police won't want to be troubled with it so why don't you send it all to the manor and when her family come forward, we can pass them on," Adelia said straight away. It might only be the matter of a shirt or two, but it was something. She then added, "And I was wondering if she left behind a book or any letters, or notebooks with her drawings and things in, anything we didn't see when we came to look before."

"Not as far as I can recall," he said. "She wasn't one for writing things down. We get them, sometimes, working men who has been at the institute and circulating libraries and all that, and they sit themselves in the corner of the bar with a notebook, making out like they know stuff. But generally people don't do things like that. She didn't."

"We just need to see a sample of her handwriting."

"Oh, well, as to that, just wait here."

He went off and returned quickly with a small scrap of torn paper. "My Maisie fished this out of the bowl of washing up water. It had fallen in from the shelf above it, and it was only there because there was another note on the back."

He handed it over. On one side was a list of prices, like a tally of someone's purchases. But on the other was a printed sentence: *"sorry I will have the muney tomoro"*.

"What money?" Adelia said in alarm.

The landlord laughed at her expression. "The rent for her lodgings, that's all. She was a day late but she paid. She left the note for us and we thought nothing of it, and it would have been thrown out but then Maisie was noting the milk money on it, and then it got stuck on the shelf, and then when it fell in the water a few days ago she got all sentimental or superstitious or something on account of how Charlie died, see. Drowning, you know."

Adelia had to ask: "Are most people superstitious around here?"

He snorted with derision. "No."

"I apologise. So do go on."

"Well, most of us are not superstitious but our Maisie is a special case. She said we had to look after the paper." He smiled and lowered his voice. "So I put it on the shelf again to humour her and all but I was going to throw it out as soon as she had forgotten."

"May we keep it?"

He shrugged. "You can if you like."

They thanked him and went out thoughtfully.

"Does it look the same?" Harriet said, trying to peer at the two pieces of paper now held in Adelia's hands. They headed towards the post office so they could pick up some stamps and other letter-writing supplies.

"I am not sure," Adelia said. "It is possible that the writer of the note was disguising their handwriting because look, some of these letters are written in different ways. People do stick to the same sort of loops and so on if they are writing naturally." She tucked them into her bag as they entered the post office. "Of course, now we have Charlie's writing..."

She stopped as soon as she saw Dorothy Talfourd.

"What do you have?" the old woman demanded instantly.

Adelia looked down her nose at the woman, and summoned up her inner countess. "Excuse me?" she said as icily as she could. "What can I help you with, Mrs Talfourd?"

"You just mentioned writing. Something of that – that one who died. What did they write? A notebook? It has to go to the police really, you know that. Hand it to me and I shall ensure my son takes it directly to the station house."

"That won't be necessary. Thank you." Adelia let her gaze slide over the top of Mrs Talfourd's head as she spoke, dismissing her.

She stepped around the old woman but she was fast with her cane, shooting it out to stop Adelia taking another step.

That was intolerable and Adelia did not have to pretend to be outraged. "Excuse *me!*"

Mrs Talfourd said, "You can trust us. Why won't you trust us? What are you hiding?"

"Allow me to pass so that I might conduct my business with the postmaster," Adelia said loudly.

There was a woman ahead of her at the counter whose head turned around, and the postmaster himself moved to the side so he could see what was going on.

Mrs Talfourd raised her cane and began to wheeze. "Don't you dare threaten an old lady! Where is your respect? Your..."

Harriet, who had been silent all the while and probably laughing, nudged Adelia's side with her elbow. "Let's step outside for a moment. I think something's happening."

It was certainly easier than trying to press forward and

run the risk of toppling the elderly woman to the floor, which would not have looked good, regardless of who had started it. And Adelia realised that Harriet was right. Behind them, out in the street, they could hear shouts and threats.

They left immediately.

⊗⊙⊗

THERE WAS AN ALTERCATION HAPPENING.

And Lord Peter Morland seemed to be at the centre of it.

He was standing as tall as he was able to, with his left hand holding a cane and raised up slightly. He didn't usually carry such a thing and Adelia wondered if he had borrowed it from Mr Arbury. His right hand, more worryingly, was resting on his hip and hidden by the curve of his jacket. She remembered that Gwen had warned them that he'd taken to carrying a pistol there.

He looked defiant and confident. He had a boxer's stance and a upturned head, ready for anything. He wasn't someone that you'd pick a fight with. The width of his shoulders, the lack of any fat on his body, his youth and his energy: he was a formidable opponent and could clearly best any man.

But he wasn't facing just one man.

Two men were up against him. One was seated on a big black horse with rolling eyes and foam on its bridle, and though he was a whip-thin, slender sort of man, he was thoroughly and openly armed with a long-muzzled pistol and some sort of military-looking sword. He looked down at Lord Morland with absolute disgust on his lean, angular face.

The other man was every inch a hired heavy, paid to do the work that would sully the mounted man's fine hands. He was well-dressed which merely meant he was good at what he did, and paid accordingly. And when he advanced upon Lord

Morland, he towered over the aristocrat, who still resolutely refused to show a single tremor of uncertainty.

Lord Morland's stubborn idiocy in the face of such a show of force was almost admirable. Terribly misjudged, but certainly something to behold.

Harriet and Adelia were not the only ones gathering to watch the show. Adelia felt that she ought to step up and do something, but what? At best she'd be ignored.

"You've had your chances, Morland. Do you have what we want?" the man on the horse was saying. He spoke casually, in the mild manner of a man who was playing the part of a reasonable person. Everyone watching knew that this was not going to go reasonably at all.

"I've paid back everything," Morland spat out.

"Oh, yes, you paid back the initial sum. There is the matter of the interest. My bosses don't lend out their hard-earned cash for free. That was *always* in the agreement."

"Usury is a sin!"

"And so is gambling away every last shred of one's money and then borrowing money to gamble some more. You know why we are here. You know what you owe. You've ignored or evaded all the other attempts to have you face up to your obligations." His tone shifted from idleness to a sneer. "You rich toffs are all the same. You think you can run from your responsibilities and hide in the big houses of your wealthy friends. But we will always find you. And here we are. You may have given Cruncher a bash the other day, but you shan't manage it a second time. Not here, not now, not with *us*. Give it up. Put down your cane. Let's have the money."

"And if I don't give you the money?"

"Then we take you."

A thrill rippled through the crowd and Adelia began to feel sick.

"We ought to tell Ramon and Theodore," she whispered to Harriet.

Suddenly there was no time for either of them to do anything. The hefty man on the ground advanced upon Lord Morland, saying, "You or the cash, mate? What's it going to be?"

Lord Morland pulled out his pistol but before he could even lift it, the heavy had smacked it clean out of his hands. It tumbled to the feet of a small boy who gazed at it with wonder until an older boy picked it up and was boxed on the ears by a man who made him put it down again.

Meanwhile the thug grabbed the cane from Lord Morland's other hand and dramatically snapped it over his knee. A woman in the crowd said "Ooh!" in an impressed sort of way.

"How dare you!" Lord Morland cried as the thug threw the two pieces of wood away.

Suddenly the hired heavy made a lunge for the aristocrat. Lord Morland jumped back two paces, lightly, but the thug kept on coming for him. He was surprisingly deft on his feet for his size, and amazed them all by suddenly dancing around Lord Morland and grabbing him from behind in an unexpected bear-hug, leaning back as he did so to lift Morland right off his feet. With his arms pinned to his sides, he was utterly helpless.

He roared in indignation and the sight was too much for some of the onlookers. Adelia recognised Jack, who she'd met with Nanna Black, and a few other men from the mill. They strode out of the crowd and as soon as they got involved, the small private matter turned into a large affray. Harriet stepped backwards, pulling Adelia with her, as others surged forward to throw stones, shout encouragement, or try to land random punches themselves.

"We must send for help!" Adelia said.

A woman alongside her, a thin and poor-looking sallow-skinned woman, nodded. "Someone's already gone for the police, or Mr Sloane, or Mr Alfoxden already. It doesn't matter who comes as long as they have a gun."

"That's hardly the answer..." Adelia began but then she heard the hoofbeats.

Three riders were coming over the bridge from the direction of the manor, and from behind she heard another horse and the now-familiar bellows of Beaumont Sloane. Within moments, the seething mass of brawlers were surrounded by Sloane, Ramon, Mr Arbury and even Theodore who was trying to look comfortable on a rather feisty hunter which seemed to want to go sideways rather than forwards.

The threatening man on the horse cursed. He rode around the fighters, shouting for his man to leave off and come away now; there was no response so he simply turned and rode off.

Sloane was carrying a long shotgun. He let off two blasts in quick succession, aimed at the feet of the brawlers, or at least Adelia hoped they were always supposed to be merely warning shots. The big debt-collector in the centre of the fray was being pinned down by two village men but at the sounds of the firearm, one of them let go and that was enough for the thug to break free. He stumbled to his feet, his arms wildly flailing out around him to keep everyone away as he pushed his way to the edge of the crowd and went off at a limping half-run in the direction the horseman had gone.

"Go after him!" Harriet screamed, but she went unheeded. Sloane rode around the group of men, roaring at them, as they realised that the objects of their fight had now left. No doubt a few of them had taken the chance of chaos to settle a few scores with their fellows, as rather too many people were slightly injured than was strictly necessary.

Theodore slithered down from his horse and ran to get to

Lord Morland, who was lying on the ground. Adelia grabbed Harriet's hand in fear, but as they watched, they could see that Morland was still conscious. Theodore helped him to sit up and then, with Ramon at his other side while Mr Arbury held their horses, they got Morland to his feet.

One or two of the villagers went forward to offer assistance but were rebuffed. Sloane stayed up on his horse, watching proceedings with a now-distant expression on his face. Ramon and Theodore helped the unsteady Lord Morland walk away while Mr Arbury came up behind with the horses. Harriet and Adelia followed.

"You know what's particularly strange?" Harriet said as they went. "All the village came out to watch, didn't they?"

"That's not very strange."

"Didn't you notice who was not here? Dorothy Talfourd did not stay around and her son did not appear at all."

❧ 18 ❧

Lord Peter Morland slumped in a wooden chair at the table in the dining room. Theodore and Ramon had steered him there by an unspoken agreement, even though Adelia had run up the steps ahead of them when they reached the manor, and headed initially towards a more comfortable sitting room.

Theodore did not want Morland to be comfortable.

Margaret came in, followed by maids with hot water and cloths, but Theodore told her to put them on the table for the moment.

"He's not about to die," he said, somewhat snappily.

"You sound as if you wish that I were," Morland said. There was blood in his mouth and his speech was thick. He put a hand up to his jaw and pressed, wincing.

A broken tooth, perhaps, Theodore thought. Again, that was nothing too serious and it could certainly wait.

Theodore sat down and leaned back, his arms folded, signalling that he was not about to do any medical things at all. Ramon stood at the head of the table, resting against it slightly. Adelia, Margaret and Harriet stayed by the door, clearly aching with curiosity.

Mr Arbury was nowhere to be seen.

"You *were* about to be beaten to a pulp or dragged away, possibly both," Theodore said. He glanced up at Ramon, suddenly aware that he was taking charge in another man's house. But the mild-mannered Ramon nodded at him, and remained silent.

Theodore went on. "I don't ask for thanks for saving your life, and neither do the others, I am sure. But what we do demand is the truth."

And then he waited.

Morland shifted in the chair, pain flitting across his face.

The silence lengthened.

Theodore said, "Or we can, of course, call those fellows back and hand you over. Anyway, they know where you are, now. It's only a matter of time before they turn up here."

"Endangering us," Margaret hissed.

"I'll leave..." Morland said, starting to get up.

Ramon was there in a flash, and dropped one hand onto Morland's shoulder, pressing him easily back down to his seat. "You will not," he said. He remained there, pinning him down.

"Good grief!" Morland said in a burst of anger. "You know very well what the truth is! Wasn't it obvious? I've got myself into a little difficulty with cash – you know how it is – a few late nights at a gaming table here and there have brought me to a sticky spot, but I only need a little more time to straighten it all out, that's all. Those men have over-reacted, I'm telling you."

"Yes," said Theodore. "I myself have found myself occasionally embarrassed by a temporary interruption in the flow of finances while I've been indulging in a little entertainment. It's not unusual, as you say."

He could feel Margaret's eyes upon him but didn't look her way.

He went on. "But even in my wildest days, in my youth of excess and debauchery, never did I find myself in such a position that hired thugs were sent after me to extract what was owed with threats and violence. Never. That, sir, is a step too far. That, sir, is far beyond what is usual. And that, sir, suggests to me that you are still not telling the truth."

"I don't owe you any more explanations than I've given. We're gentlemen, and upon my honour, I've told you more than I am obliged to."

"Honour! You make me laugh."

Theodore would have said more but Adelia came forward and he realised, from her warning glance, that he was letting his anger get the better of him. He wasn't usually so prone to such unguarded emotion and he wondered what had really needled him about the situation. It was the betrayal, he decided, a betrayal of his daughter's hospitality – and the lies that had been told to Margaret's friend, the sweetly innocent Gwen.

She deserved better than this low seducer.

Adelia pulled up a chair on the other side of Morland. He turned towards her, hoping perhaps to find an ally.

Theodore knew Morland was badly, *badly* mistaken.

Adelia said, "So what happened in York, Lord Morland?"

"I – what? York? Nothing. I barely visit York."

"Yet you were there and you were in some low places, Lord Morland, gambling and gaming and goodness knows what else besides. Newcastle, too, I hear."

Theodore watched him closely. Morland was uncomfortable. He flared his nostrils and obviously didn't have a quick answer for them.

Adelia said, "We do, of course, have a witness."

"To – what?"

And then he broke. He hung his head and sighed and all the fight went out of him. He couldn't bring himself to be angry and defiant to Adelia – he was too well-bred and nicely-mannered for that, at least. And he was in pain, injured, pursued and broken. He had nothing left to lose.

Lord Morland could not meet anyone's eyes as he spoke. "It's worse than you can imagine. I'm being harried from London to Glasgow. You have seen how I do not drink – here it is. I simply cannot. If I take one drink, even the smallest, then I must have another and another. And I pick up the cards or the dice, go to the wheel or the table, and I gamble and I think, at that moment, that I am having the most brilliant time."

"But you're not."

"No. No, I never am. The stakes rise, the wine flows, and I wake the next morning – no, if I am honest, I wake late the next afternoon – and realise I have been an utter fool. I resolve to change my ways, each and every time that this happens. I do not harm anyone, I tell myself. The only true victim is myself, so I am not a bad person. Not like those who fight and brawl, who seduce and go with low women. I am not *really* bad, just ... lively. And I can stop all of that. So I do stop, for a day or two, and prove to myself that it's not an issue, I'm young and doing what all young bachelors do. Then a friend will call me up and invite me out and it all starts again."

"You have not been like that here!" Margaret said.

"That is precisely *why* I am here," he confessed. "Ramon is such a rock, so steady and solid. He is like a lighthouse for me, a beacon in the dark. He does not drink and gamble. The worst thing I've ever seen him do was when he spent rather too many guineas on that copy of the *Morte D'Arthur*."

"How many guineas?" Margaret asked, shooting her

husband a very familiar look. For that brief moment, she was the very spit of Adelia and Theodore felt a rush of warm pride. Then she shook her head and let Morland carry on.

"And," he said ruefully, "It was also an advantage to be out here in a remote sort of place, many miles from anywhere where people might find me."

"Except someone did see you, didn't they?" Adelia said.

He clenched his fist. "I ... look, I know this makes me look guilty, doesn't it? Why do you think I've wanted to keep this to myself? Quite apart from everything else, yes – yes, Charlie Webb had seen me in a very large, well-known gambling hall in York. Things were particularly bad for me at that time. Well, I thought they were particularly *good* so you can imagine what I was like. He was there with a small team of carpenters. He!"

"She."

"Yes. But it feels strange to think of him as anything other than what he seemed to be. So, there he was, working on some new bar area and I think they were paid in drink as much as cash. That's how he saw me. That was some time ago. I didn't recognise him, of course. Why would I? But he certainly knew me. No doubt I made something of an ... *impression.*" He winced.

"And he spoke to you here, when he saw you in Greyhaven."

"He threatened me. He knew I was sweet on Gwen, my poor dear Gwendolen. And he was furious about it. Quite rightly so, I suppose, but I will not be spoken to like that by any common workman. It's not on."

Harriet snorted. "You'll hear the truth from someone else but not one whose status is lower than yours? The truth is the truth ... *sir.*"

"It's about honour. You don't understand."

"Worse than that. I understand *perfectly*." Disdain dripped from every syllable that Harriet spoke. Even Theodore curled his toes in embarrassment as he recognised his own feelings of snobbery reflected in Morland's pitiful excuses. "Honour is supposed to be the preserve of the rich man, and it galled to have decency spelled out to you by a commoner, did it not?"

Adelia had something in her hand and she spread it out on the table in front of him. "Charlie Webb didn't just speak to you, though. She also tried to warn Gwen."

He read the note while shaking his head. "This was sent to Gwen? It's all over between us, isn't it?"

"Yes. I think it's all over for you in many, many ways."

Lord Morland put the note down on the table. He said, a sneer entering his voice once more, "I know where this is leading, now. I can admit I am a gambler, a drinker and perhaps – sometimes – a fool. But I am not a murderer in spite of the motive this appears to give me."

Theodore bit his tongue. No one else spoke either. The silence lengthened.

But Lord Morland would not break again. He did not protest his innocence. He had spoken and he left it at that.

Theodore was not sure what to make of it all.

ADELIA WAS IMPRESSED TO SEE THAT LORD MORLAND showed his face at the dinner that night. But then, it was characteristic of the confidence he had shown so far. Perhaps, she thought, such confidence might also be called "brazen stubbornness" but such unassailable self-belief had been a feature of the English upper classes for generations and had not failed them yet as they bestrode the globe and dominated the world. As long as one glossed over certain facts of history, particularly involving the Americas or rumblings in India, that sort of thing, it was hard to imagine how that solid self-confidence could ever be really shaken permanently.

Lord Morland was a perfect example. He'd seem contrite for a while, then he'd surely bounce back.

Nevertheless, he was somewhat subdued in his manner at the moment. He must have been aware that suspicion still hung over him. He had the perfect reason to have killed Charles Webb, after all and if he left now, he would simply add to the suspicions around him. He remained quiet while Margaret did exceptionally well as a hostess and kept the conversation flowing around the table, steering it into light and uncomplicated waters.

She didn't even let the topics settle on the matter of the May Day fair, which was something of a relief. Adelia still wasn't sure that the whole maypole issue had been resolved, and she was now regretting ever saying she was going to stay for the event, let alone inviting Harriet to come along.

Furthermore, one of her other daughters, Edith, was even now travelling north to pay a visit.

It was only once they retired to the fire that had been lit in the drawing room later, to chat idly about nothing very much, that Margaret alarmed Adelia with her proposal.

It was aimed at the somewhat startled Mr Arbury, who clearly had not been expecting it at all.

In fact, it came on this back of his declaration that he was considering heading back to London. He was thanking Margaret and Ramon profusely for their hospitality, and for the chance to explore his childhood home once more, but it was time, he felt, to move on. Certain things from his past had been revealed – he was alluding to the sad business with Beaumont Sloane, Jane, and the robbery – but now he had to reinvent himself all over again. Adelia admired his tenacity and was just saying that she wished him all the best, when Margaret spoke over her.

"Oh, please do wait, Mr Arbury! You must stay. We have plans."

"The May Day fair does not really concern me, and it would be supremely more awkward as it is so very dominated by ... that man. I do not wish to speak of him."

"I don't mean the fair. I mean you, and us, here, and our dream."

Everyone except Ramon stared quite blankly at her. Ramon was gazing at her with unashamed adoration.

Margaret said, "No, our plans for a centre for the growth of artisanal crafts. I have been so inspired by what Mr Morris has done, and what Mr Ruskin writes about, oh and Mr Mackintosh in Glasgow. Can't you feel the world is changing? This is our chance, at last!"

Mr Arbury smiled politely. He said, "I am sure it will all be a roaring success but perhaps you are mistaken in what you see in me. I do like fine clothes and I have an eye, I do admit, for flattering fabrics and so on – but none of this qualifies me, in any way, for the sort of craftsmanship that you are speaking of. I am neither a maker nor a true connoisseur. I am, at best, a merely superficial consumer of pretty things."

"You do yourself a disservice but it is irrelevant. No, Mr Arbury, we don't seek to persuade you to stay for any of those reasons. We want you here because you are *Mr Arbury*. You do still own Arbury House, of course."

He laughed. "Have you seen that pile of rubble lately? There is barely a roof on the place. I own a derelict pile of dust and memories. I cannot look at it without seeing, in my mind's eye, money leaking away. It is worthless."

"But isn't that sad?"

"It was a shock but I have learned to accept it. I think of the future."

"And so do we! Ramon, isn't it true that we have the capital to invest in the renovation of Arbury House?" Margaret looked at Ramon who nodded. "So you see, Mr Arbury, this is our plan. We would like to have Arbury House restored as a centre for craft and learning, for the making of fine things, for the discussion of high ideals, for the return to the values of the past, indeed, a new Avalon to be built right here! Honest production on a small scale, not soulless factory things!"

A new Avalon was certainly pushing it a bit, Adelia thought with a smile, but that sort of talk would attract exactly the sort of rosy-glowed nostalgic mediaevalists that Margaret was so enamoured with.

Mr Arbury was still laughing indulgently but it soon became apparent that Margaret and Ramon were deadly serious. The laughter stopped when Ramon pulled out some sketches that he had prepared; he had drawn up rough plans of what currently remained of Arbury House, with suggestions as to what might be done to it. There were guest bedrooms, a lecture area in what was now to be called The Great Hall, workshops, and an outdoor exercise area for group callisthenics.

"But this is all too expensive," Mr Arbury protested at last.

"It is our money. And if we wish to gamble it on this, well, this is our choice."

He shook his head. He was now looking increasingly miserable as he realised that they were determined in their plan.

"No," he said. "I cannot stay..."

"Don't decide yet! Sleep on it, walk and think. You will soon see that this is perfect. You will remain the owner and in charge, and of course you will then begin to get a rental income. We will draw up a legal agreement to take a small percentage, and in this way we will recover our investment. So we will not be out of pocket in the future, and this guarantees you a home and an income too! Why would you ever think of saying no?"

It was a compelling offer, Adelia thought.

So why did Mr Arbury look so upset?

❧ 19 ❧

Adelia and Theodore were not able to make much sense of the burned papers they had recovered from the grounds of Arbury House.

Adelia made a few careful enquiries of Margaret, trying to ascertain whether Mr Arbury and Lord Morland had been at the manor at the time of the secret bonfire. Mr Arbury had a perfect alibi as he had been gloomily reading in a corner of the room where Margaret and Ramon had been making their plans. Lord Morland was unaccounted for, however.

Still, Adelia felt that some suspicion had to fall upon the Talfourds simply because of the use of the tunnel. And surely it made sense that the fuel for the fire, indeed the purpose of it, was to burn the parish records that related to Charlie Webb?

But why?

"It has to be linked to Mr Arbury and the inheritance," she said to Theodore the next day as they walked into the village. They were hoping to make yet another plea for access to the records. Harriet had promised to write to the bishop if necessary. "He'll put a firecracker up their trouser legs," she had said, adding hastily, "Ecclesiastically speaking, of course."

But the church was empty and the curtains all drawn at the windows of the vicarage behind it. Adelia rang the bell anyway, and a maid answered promptly, saying that no one was at home. It was impossible to prise from her whether the house was actually empty or whether the occupants were simply not receiving visitors.

They lingered for a while. Adelia had hoped to see how the Talfourds lived. The vicarage was a fine one, but of course the incumbents did not have to pay for it. But was his living enough for them to dine on fine food, or did they struggle, as many rural parish priests did? Those with family money fared better. The curtains at the windows seemed fine enough, especially in comparison to the rags that many of the cottages had.

But there was nothing more to be gleaned from what they could see from the outside.

They returned to the village feeling frustrated. They had interviewed everyone that they could. If anyone knew of any more links between Charlie Webb and the Arbury family, they weren't saying. The suspects remained Mr Arbury, Beaumont Sloane, Lord Morland and possibly the Talfourds. Yet all were the most tenuous of links.

"We have discovered the secret behind Charlie Webb's life," Adelia said. "But what if there is more? We must look deeper."

"I agree, but unless we can discover where her family now lives, we are stuck. The police refuse to tell me anything. The villagers are being evasive in that irritatingly respectful way that only a rural yokel can manage. We could spend the next month visiting every hamlet, village and settlement in the north asking for word of her family but it is clear they do not want to know, and will easily evade us if they try."

"We are not giving up."

"No," he said. "We certainly are not. We must get access to the records and we must discover what was burned. I have written to a friend at the Royal Institution who deals with the science of combustion to ask if there is any way of recovering any information from the charred paper that we have. And let us keep watch on the vicarage. At the first sign of movement, we shall descend upon the Reverend Talfourd and I promise you that I will not let go until I have pressed every scrap of information out of him."

He went quiet.

She didn't say anything.

Eventually he said, "Aren't you going to caution me not to press him?"

"Absolutely not. We've been doing this long enough now, my dear. You press away."

⚜

TO MAKE THEIR OBSERVATION OF THE VICARAGE comfortable, they took a small private room upstairs on the first floor of the Mason's Arms that had a good view of the village green and the main roads in and out. It was approaching lunch time so they ordered some food and drink, and discussed Lord Morland.

There wasn't really much to say; both agreed that he was a sad case but a bounder nonetheless. As for a murderer, he certainly had an unshakeable belief in himself and his rights, and a very fixed idea of class. He came from the sort of line that did see the workers as an expendable resources, putting him quite at odds with Ramon and Margaret's more egalitarian leanings. But they understood why he liked to spend time with them. When he had spoken of his demons and of the comfort he found in

Ramon's company, he had spoken with a raw honesty they hadn't seen in him before.

But ultimately, he was a snobbish manipulator and Adelia wanted to wash her hands of him, and hoped that Margaret did too.

Because she was thinking about Lord Morland, at first, she mistook the male figure striding across the green towards the inn. But he was coming from the north, not from the direction of the manor, and he was burlier and bushier than the athletic figure of Lord Morland.

"Theodore, look, here comes Beaumont Sloane."

"He has a face like thunder."

"He always does. He doesn't look any angrier than usual but he's walking in a very determined way – oh, he's coming in. He doesn't have a shotgun with him, at least."

Theodore stood up. "I'm going to see what he wants."

"He won't want anything from us."

"I am only going to stand by the door as if I am contemplating going into the bar, and hopefully I can eavesdrop."

"If you are not going in, I can come too." She didn't let him object. Quickly they shot down the stairs and approached the open door of the public bar.

They could hear him ordering people about.

"You – you, I can't remember your name – but you have a cart, don't you? I need you and another to move some of the stalls out of my barn and start to set them up on the green. What? Yes, now. Well, that will have to wait. Hey, hey – where do you think you are going? I have jobs for everyone here. And I need everyone with a cart to come to my house as soon as the stalls are set up. I have more work for the lot of you. Personal work. None of your business! Yes, of course. What? No, of course I bloody won't pay you. It's your civic duty to get involved. Oi! Ho, there..."

There was general mutterings and she could hear objections and refusals, which seemed to astonish Sloane and make his manner even more rude and bullying. His voice was rising as he launched into a tirade about the laziness of the average worker in the village when a new and strange hush fell. Sloane himself stumbled to a halt. Adelia and Theodore could not help themselves. They inched to the door and peered through.

Mr Frederick Arbury had appeared.

He'd been distant with everyone at breakfast. Adelia had wondered what he was thinking. The proposal made by Ramon and Margaret was clearly bothering him but he wouldn't come out openly with his objections so they didn't really understand why he was reluctant to get involved. He had frowned a lot more than was usual, and disappeared from the table quickly. Margaret had said that she hoped he wasn't planning on doing a flit like Charlie Webb had, and Adelia had agreed. After all, she thought, he might actually be involved in her death. He had to stay.

But now here he was in the taproom and he was white-faced, brimming with suppressed emotion that made his cheeks tight. Whatever had been eating away at him was clearly coming to a head. He pointed a gloved finger at Beaumont Sloane.

"You owe me," he said.

Sloane laughed defiantly. "I don't owe you a second's thought."

"You still owe me."

"You've got it all back," he retorted. "Oh, the stuff that went in the pool, that was just a jape. And it doesn't matter because it's yours again now, so I can't see what you're complaining about."

But Adelia knew what Mr Arbury was talking about.

He said, "I have nothing of value returned to me. I mean

her. I mean my Jane. You stole her from me. You took my love."

To Adelia's astonishment, and indeed the whole gathering, Sloane said, "Oh, her? Well, you can have her. That is, if you can get her. We're leaving. I'm going to the continent and she's off to an asylum the minute that it can be arranged. That's why this ignorant lot need to sort out the stalls and then come to the house to help shift my stuff."

The men in the pub were already inclined to dislike the orders being handed out by Sloane. Being called ignorant and told they had to work for free was the last straw. Someone threw something and someone else laughed as a hard bread roll bounced off the side of Sloane's head.

Mr Arbury seized his chance. He said, far more sternly than he'd ever spoken before, "Look at this joke of a man! You all know what he did! You all know what deceit he is capable of, and what he did to me in the past. Is he not the murderer of Charlie Webb? Is he not the imprisoner of his innocent wife? How can you proud villagers even bear to have him in your inn?"

Someone else cheered and then a pint of ale was hurled over Sloane. He roared and made for the door, shoving Mr Arbury roughly into a table as he went, scattering tankards and plates and turning over chairs.

He stormed out as chaos raged behind him, shouting, "You yokels won't chase me out! You won't!"

"So is he leaving or not?" Adelia said to Theodore.

"And if he does go, does that not make him look more guilty?"

HARRIET AND MARGARET WERE IN THE MIDDLE OF consoling Gwen when Adelia and Theodore got back to the manor. She had left the state of copious weeping by now, and had moved into distraught fury, which was a healthy sign. Theodore retreated hastily at the sight of the women plotting violent revenges to be perpetrated upon Lord Morland, while Adelia stepped forward to take part with great glee.

It was good to see that Gwen was recovering. Margaret left with her a little while later, intending to walk her back to her house accompanied by a servant at a careful distance, but they had only been gone ten minutes when they all returned to the manor in a breathless rush.

"Mama, come and see what they've done!" Margaret said, laughing, and would not tell them anything else. "It is a surprise but oh, you will love it."

Adelia and Harriet went with them back to the village green. They had only got as far as the bridge when they could see that something was happening around the site of the old stocks. There was a crowd gathered around a figure that was sitting in the criminal's place, their wrists and neck trapped in the wooden frame while they knelt on the ground. Adelia's stomach lurched until she realised it wasn't a real person.

It was an effigy, made much in the manner of a scarecrow by clothes stuffed with straw, and a painted-on head. It was crude and indistinct but it was clearly based on a real person.

It was supposed to represent Beaumont Sloane, and he was being pelted with eggs and vegetable peelings.

"Oh my goodness," said Adelia. She was amused, but she was also horrified. There was a dangerous feeling of lawlessness to what was happening and it made her uneasy.

That feeling intensified when Beaumont Sloane turned up. Someone must have alerted him to some trouble on the green and he strode to the stocks, unable to see what was going on until he broke through the encircling crowd and finally laid eyes upon his homemade doppelganger.

"Who did this?" he roared as he went purple and then,

strangely, white in the face, as if all the blood was leaving his body. He lurched forward and grabbed the effigy, wrenching it backwards out of the stocks. Unfortunately the head popped off the body and he stumbled, half-falling with the body on top of him, spewing straw from its neck.

He jumped straight back to his feet, whirling the decapitated body around as he yelled, "Who did this? Which one of you ingrates did this? I'll have you arrested!"

Someone threw an egg and it burst on the side of his neck, the yolk oozing across his collar in a blooming stain of yellow.

"This is going to turn into a lynching," Adelia said in horror, starting forward in spite of her better instincts. She had no desire to protect the man, but she wanted to stop any rising feeling bubbling over; it would benefit no one if tempers snapped completely. There was no telling what the baying mob might do.

But as soon as he saw her, his own temper exploded. "You! Lady Calaway, you meddling witch!"

The crowd gasped in shock. Adelia was taken aback and could not think of a thing to say. She stopped. Had she really been about to step in and ask for mercy for this man?

He was furious. He yelled, "You started all of this! It was you! You brought him here, you and your idiot family. If you hadn't done *that,* none of this would have happened! It ought to be you in the stocks here. Someone grab her! Let's see justice done properly!"

But before he could take another step towards her, an absolute rain of eggs and stones was poured upon him from all angles. The villagers waded in, shouting and booing, hurling insults along with the projectiles, and chased him right off the village green and away.

Adelia watched them go.

Harriet said, "Well, they were certainly defending your honour."

"I rather feel it was a convenient excuse for them to finally unfurl their true feelings about the man."

"Even so, at least it was aimed at him and not us."

"Very true. You know, that was all a little too close for comfort. Come on, let's get back."

"Are you really shaken up?" Harriet asked with surprise. "You, who have weathered being kidnapped, and all manner of horrible threats?"

"I don't think one grows inured to such things. Yes, I am shaken. Perhaps it is because nothing did happen. When the worst happens, all one can do is deal with it. Imagining the worst happening is an ongoing process that nags at the mind ... when it does happen, it's always easier to cope with than you might have imagined it would be."

"Oh, you silly goose. Nothing happened and you mustn't waste a single more moment imagining anything that might have happened but did not."

"But can't you see the implications of what has happened?" Adelia insisted. "The feeling of the local people has always been against Sloane, and now they are finding that they can stand up to him. Until this point, they have been silently under his thumb. Now they are testing their boundaries and discovering the power that they hold. It started with the draining of the Holy Pool – he opposed it, but was defeated. And since then, defeat upon defeat has been piled upon him."

"But he deserves it. What are you upset about?"

"It starts with opposition to Sloane, yes. But where does it end?"

"Ah." Harriet linked her arm into Adelia's, and gave her hand a squeeze. They hurried back to the manor. It was a place of sanctuary – at least for now.

❧ 20 ❧

Theodore listened to Adelia's account of what had happened to Beaumont Sloane with a sinking feeling. He understood why she was concerned about the wider implications of the wild turn that the attitude of the village had taken. He had laughed about their ways, but now this was serious.

He, too, shared Adelia's misgivings. He was seeing a similar slide and decay in the social order all over the country. Had he not been treated with a worrying lack of respect the last time he had been in London? If he had been in his twenties, he might have welcomed such relaxing of the rules. Now he was older, and a grandfather, he could feel his own conservatism nudge him into a general unwillingness to accept any more change. He knew he was ridiculous – and that didn't stop him from being worried and not a little resentful.

He sat alone, later on, in the study, with his feet up on a leather stool, contemplating the person that was Beaumont Sloane. Specifically, he wanted to really consider if the man was a credible suspect.

Yes, he could be a murderer; Theodore could picture

many scenarios where the man's temper was so overwrought that he lost control of himself and struck out. But he could only imagine that happening to someone like Mr Arbury. Sloane had a long and historic problem with Mr Arbury, an established enmity, and if Mr Arbury turned up dead then Sloane would be the immediate suspect.

What Theodore could not unpick was a link between Sloane and Charlie Webb.

Except, of course, there had to be one, because Sloane had sought Webb out to threaten her in front of Adelia. And he had once again made the connection that very day, by accusing Adelia of meddling by bringing Mr Arbury to Greyhaven.

Once again, the lack of access to the parish records made everything more complicated.

Theodore began to imagine a new solution. This one chilled his bones for it would be far, far harder to unpick. What if there *was* a connection between the Talfourds with the parish records and Beaumont Sloane? What if they were all working together, in spite of the public spats? That could all be for show. If the three of them were complicit in some dreadful crime, that would account for all the misdirection. And hadn't Sloane proved himself capable of crime? And now he was openly planning to leave, abandon his wife, and start a new life abroad. Who would do such a thing but a profoundly guilty man?

He also wondered just how much Reverend Talfourd knew. Or did he merely suspect foul play and was content, as the dutiful son, to bury his head in the sand and let his mother direct matters?

Theodore reflected on the other controlling women he'd encountered in previous cases. There had been quite a few. And he cautioned himself not to assume that he was seeing the same thing here. It would be too easy to fall into that trap and spot patterns that did not actually exist.

He let his eyelids fall. Perhaps a short nap would help. He was sitting mostly upright so it didn't count as a proper sleep ... just a few winks ... he slid into a deep relaxation, only to be jerked awake almost instantly by shouting and running foot-steps. Someone knocked on the door and burst straight in without waiting to be summoned.

"What's happening?" Theodore stood up too quickly and had to grab the arm of the chair so he didn't fall back down at the feet of the breathless maid.

"Sir, begging pardon my lord but Mr Sloane is here and he's very angry. Mr Alfoxden is with him now but your pres-ence is expressly requested."

"Thank you," he blurted as he lurched past her. He didn't need to ask where they were. He could follow the shouting.

Mr Sloane was in the entrance hall, filling the space with his fury and cursing. Ramon was equally angry at the rude intrusion. Slow to anger he might be, quiet and mild in most ways, but this was his own house that was being violated. He was facing squarely up to Mr Sloane and demanding that he leave the place immediately. Already a butler was hovering in the corner, hefting a club with a certain confidence. Butlers with slightly dodgy pasts were the very best in such situations; every home should have one.

Theodore felt that he himself would be of less use in the current situation.

But Sloane was not here for Ramon. As soon as he spotted Theodore, he pointed and yelled, "You! Here you are, at last, you coward! Hiding behind the skirts of your wife!"

Theodore looked around with an exaggerated movement. "Where is she?"

"Get down here and explain yourself."

That made Theodore stop. He was halfway down the stairs but he would be ordered about by no man.

"No. I have nothing to explain. You, however, do."

"I do not! And yet I seem to be a suspect in your ill-judged investigation! Let it drop. No one is paying you to do this. The police are not interested. So give it up. It's clear you are only doing this to fuel your own swollen ego."

"I am doing this for justice."

Sloane swore. "What is that? If I am going to get scriptural on you, I'd remind you that God is the ultimate arbiter of justice. Leave it to Him, and leave me alone."

"I'll leave you alone when you tell me what linked you to Charlie Webb."

"Absolutely nothing."

"Yet you came here to threaten her, and you accused her of being the cause of the problems between you and Mr Arbury."

"The cause of *that* problem turned out to be your wife," Sloane spat out. "But Webb was still culpable. If she hadn't come here in the first place, she would not have asked any questions and she would not be dead. It's her own damn fault."

"Sir!" said Ramon in disgust, but Sloane was utterly unmoved. He sneered at Ramon and turned from him, instead approaching the foot of the stairs.

"Do you really think there is more to all this than what you already know?" Sloane said to Theodore.

"Yes, I do."

He could see that Sloane was vulnerable, somehow. And as he got closer, he could see the remains of egg staining his clothing, and his hair was matted and his general air was one of disarray. The villagers turning against him had unseated his deep-rooted confidence and shaken his notion of supremacy. He couldn't cope with feelings of anxiety and turned everything into anger. Theodore had seen that a hundred times in other men, and even found the tendency in himself; Adelia would not indulge such things and challenged him every time.

If, in his youth, he'd been as bad as Sloane was now, Adelia had been very brave to stand up to him, he thought.

Sloane was still standing there at the bottom of the stairs. Theodore walked the rest of the way down to him but stayed on one step above him, deliberately.

"Why don't you tell me everything," Theodore said. "Disregard what you think I already know. I'd like to hear the whole history of you and Mr Arbury from your own lips."

"Rather than the twisted lies he has spun you?"

"It would be interesting to compare the accounts and spot the lies," he said tactfully, wishing Adelia could hear how good he had become at being careful with his words.

Sloane was unimpressed. "Spoken like a true snake of a politician. Ha! Oh, you *lords*."

Theodore wondered, then, if the fact that Sloane had money, prestige, power but no title rankled him at all. Or perhaps it was good, old fashioned jealousy and no more.

He said, "Begin at the beginning. You are a little older than Mr Arbury so you must have known his family when it was one of the dominant ones in the area?"

"They were in decline when I was a youth. It was an open secret. They sent the boy away – he was a milksop, a drooping wet rag of a boy – and the house got shuttered up, bit by bit. I didn't care. I was here and there, travelling, spending time abroad; I became a man early and I took to my responsibilities quickly, unlike him. The Arbury family just faded away. No one cared. Oh, the Alfoxdens may lay claim to this area but I own half of it; their attention is elsewhere, their family too scattered, their interests too widely spread to take any notice of what one of their distant scions is up to."

He threw a scornful look at Ramon. Ramon did not rise to it and said nothing.

Sloane carried on. "This place, it's just a backwater for forgotten offshoots. And I came back here when my father died, and my mother was ailing, and took over. I wanted to marry before she passed away, to make her happy. Ah! That surprises you?"

"No," Theodore lied.

"I saw your face. Yes, I can be honourable. What man does not love his mother? I aimed high but luck was not on my side and time was pressing. Jane Walker-Andrews was a beauty, though I had disregarded her at first on account of her background."

"What background? She is a well-bred sort of lady, is she not?"

"It is true she had completed her education in Switzerland and she was a charming young lady, but a little parochial compared to the women I had known in London. And I'll make no secret of the fact that I hoped to marry a woman of more substantial ancestry. Not for myself, you understand, but to make my mother happy."

He was lying, but Theodore did not challenge it.

Sloane rested one foot on the lower step of the stairs and went on. "With time being limited, I broached the subject first with my mother, who adored Jane, and then with Jane's parents who were happy enough for me to pursue the match. Jane herself played the minx, I will confess, pretending to be innocent and unwilling to take part in the game of love."

Theodore frowned at him. He did not notice.

"All was going well until Arbury came back. I thought he was dead, if I thought of him at all. But he came back and I discovered that he and my love had been corresponding for years. I felt shocked and betrayed. What man would not?" Sloane said, challenging Theodore to agree with him.

"You just said she was unwilling to court with you. Why should she not set her sights upon another?"

"Why? Because my mother and her parents had agreed she was to be mine! How can a woman of that age and limited experience know her own mind? It was nonsense. And yet she had been indulging in a silly schoolgirl love affair with this penniless Arbury and I could not have it. She would make a laughing stock of me and worse, injure her own reputation. The whole business had to be stopped. So I did what I had to do."

Theodore waited.

"What, you want it spelling out to you? Very well, then! I let it be known that Arbury was utterly without money or prospect, and had not even completed his studies due to a lack of funds. When he came to me to ask for the best way to sell the things he had inherited, I gave him false information and waylaid him when he went as I had directed him to go. But as you know, I did not covet those items myself."

Sloane paused, looking around as if he expected praise.

No one moved or spoke.

Uncaring, he went on. "I like to think I acting with far greater integrity than any common thief. Why, if I had been like a run of the mill criminal, would I have not taken those things and sold them? No! I did the better thing; I cast them into the pool. And so I freed Jane from his clutches, and sent him away from here in shame, and was able finally to make my mother happy before she died. Every single thing that I have done, I have done from a position of good morals. It is impossible to see this in any other light."

Theodore felt slack-jawed in his admiration of the man's ability to twist his own actions in such a self-aggrandising way. It really was a feat of interpretation.

"And what of Charlie Webb?" he asked.

Sloane's face closed again. "What of her? I never knew

her. Why would I? I didn't know the family and I didn't know her. When she came back here in that stupid disguise, I didn't think twice about it until she started asking about Frederick damn Arbury. *That* was what alarmed me. That, and the draining of the pool. But you know why it alarmed me. There is nothing more to it than that."

Theodore began to think that if there had been more to it, Sloane would have told him – and told him in such a way to paint himself as the victor or hero in it all. Perhaps it really was as Sloane had just outlined.

But there was one more thing to put to the man. "What about the Talfourds?" he asked.

A flicker of genuine confusion passed over Sloane's face, turning again almost immediately to his default state of anger. "What?"

"What do you know about any connection between the Talfourds and Charlie Webb, or Mr Arbury or his family?"

"Nothing. Why should I? I don't care about either of them. I'm not hypocritical enough to go to church and pretend to listen to what he says. I have my own faith, of course, but it's a private matter: so it should be for any Englishman. Do you see me asking about your own faith?"

"No, and I wasn't really asking about yours."

"Good. Now I hope I've satisfied your idle curiosity and I won't hear another thing from you or your wife. You've stirred up enough trouble. The very least you can do is allow me and my own wife to leave this place in peace."

"When do you go?"

"None of your damn business," Sloane said, and he turned on his heel, and left.

That night at dinner, Margaret and Ramon were very excited to be able to discuss Beaumont Sloane's apparent fall from favour in the village. Adelia understood their glee, but found it a little inelegant.

Theodore remained sunk into a silence that a stranger might have considered sullen, but Adelia recognised as deep thought. They had discussed Sloane before dinner. Both agreed that he could be a murderer – but not of Charlie Webb. If he was going to kill anyone, it would be Frederick Arbury. And he hadn't, in spite of wanting to. He gained nothing, as far as they could tell, from Charlie Webb's death. He was still a suspect. He had to be. But he wasn't a convincing one.

Adelia was far more suspicious now of both Mr Arbury and Lord Morland. Again, Morland's apparent confession, if true, could explain his argument with Charlie Webb but it didn't remove his motive at all. He still came to dinner that night, but did not speak. Margaret and Ramon had chosen not to throw him out, and Adelia was grateful for that. It was hard for Margaret as she wanted to defend her friend and cast

Morland out for good. But Adelia and Theodore had begged her to keep her disregard for him under wraps while they investigated, and Margaret understood immediately.

"I hope he is the murderer, then he can be hanged," she said with a spiteful edge.

As for Mr Arbury, Adelia could not put her finger on why she still considered him to be a suspect, but he was. There were too many questions about the unsolved links between him and Charlie Webb; a secret past he claimed not to know about.

She was not sure that she believed him.

The talk that night, however, centred around the May Day fair. Margaret was pointedly ignoring Lord Morland, and instead talking eagerly about the fair and the future ramifications of it, including Mr Arbury in all her plans.

He was noticeably less enthusiastic. Adelia wanted to get a chance to talk to him about it. She wanted to know exactly why he didn't want to take up the offer to have his house and fortune restored. Granted, Greyhaven wasn't London, not by any means. The explanation could be that simple.

And of course, she realised, with a silent curse at her own blind idiocy – why would he want to stay in an area with so many bad memories as well as good ones? Even if Jane did leave along with Beaumont, this place was riddled with pain for the poor man. Adelia could hardly believe that she hadn't seen it before. She looked upon him with more sympathy, and resolved to speak privately with Margaret about it.

But no one could get a word in edgeways at the moment as Margaret talked at great length and great volume about how they could now "direct" the fair in the "most appropriate" manner, ensuring its "authenticity" and "honesty." Adelia tried to catch Theodore's eye from time to time, but he was lost in his own world. Ramon gazed at Margaret with nothing but love and support. But that love was blind love, and his unfailing support did not for one moment challenge her flights of fantasy.

"Now Sloane is no longer the respected and feared man he once was, we can ensure the maypole is erected just as it ought to be!" Margaret said for the third time.

"And what of Dorothy Talfourd?" Adelia was forced to say.

"Mama, I *told* you that the village has no real respect for her either. I *explained* all that."

Adelia bit her tongue and decided to concentrate on her food instead. She had to ponder whether the village respected Margaret and Ramon to quite the degree that they hoped.

ON SUNDAY, THE NEXT DAY, HARRIET DISAPPEARED OFF TO church. Adelia went with her for the first time since she'd been in the area. Harriet was surprised that Ramon and Margaret did not go, not even infrequently.

"I noticed that they don't even hold household prayers," she said. "As you know, I don't abide with the notion of the outward formality of meaningless rituals *but* ... well, it is a surprise. It's more about the example that they ought to be setting to people, you know?"

"I agree completely but she won't have it. She thinks that the example that they are setting to the village is one of industry and hard work."

Harriet laughed so much she had to stop walking and wipe her eyes. She pointed at the mill that was up ahead. "That factory there, that is industry and hard work!"

"I know, I know. But they have Camelot to build here, don't forget. Why do you think Mr Arbury isn't so enthusiastic about taking up their offer?"

"Ugh, why would he? He's a clever man and has his life in

London. I can't understand why he's here at all, or why he has stayed here."

"If he left straight after the murder, he'd look like a suspect."

"He is a suspect. Sloane's off, isn't he, somewhen?"

"He is. Lord Morland will slink away soon, I am sure, though I asked Margaret to try to get him to stay until this is solved."

"And what if it isn't?"

"We don't give up. We have tried to give cases up in the past and that never worked. So we will keep going until … well, until we can't, I suppose."

"If Sloane, Arbury and Morland all leave, you have to give it up. Or pin it on the Talfourds, like I've suggested before!"

"Harriet, I am shocked and appalled."

Harriet laughed and skipped ahead to the church. "Oh, you know I am joking."

"Do I?"

⚬⚬⚬

REVEREND TALFOURD DRONED ON AND ON, AND ADELIA sat in rigid horror in the very front pew. Alongside her to the left was Harriet. In the front pew on the other side of the aisle, to her right, was Dorothy Talfourd.

Behind them – no one.

No one at all.

There was not one single villager, not one visitor staying at the inn, not a traveller nor a soul from the cottages and outlying hamlets.

Just three worshippers sat in the chilly building as Reverend Talfourd's voice whined reedily upwards to be lost in the rafters amongst the birds' nests and cobwebs.

It was excruciating. Adelia went through the motions but

felt that his eyes were upon her far too much, and she could not bring herself to gaze up at him, which meant that it seemed as if she was ignoring the lesson. And she was ignoring it, because she couldn't follow his train of thought at all. Possibly it had involved owls and why they shouldn't be eaten, but she wasn't entirely sure.

And of course, at the end of the sermon, there was no escape. They all stood up as he walked down the aisle to the door. If there had been a large congregation now filing out to shake his hand and murmur their thanks, it was sometimes possible to slide out behind them all. But there was no way that Harriet and Adelia could hide behind Dorothy Talfourd.

She was staring at them with a silent hatred, anyway. Adelia didn't want to get close enough to be hit with her cane. She really hadn't been sure that Dorothy Talfourd was going to let her into the service at the beginning. But Mrs Talfourd had merely glared and said nothing.

No doubt she'd spent the whole service simmering with fury.

They stood back and waited, politely allowing Mrs Talfourd to lead the way out of the church. Harriet hissed in Adelia's ear. "Is it always like this?"

"I have no idea."

To Adelia's horror, then, Harriet asked the same question of Reverend Talfourd as they shook his hand. She started innocently enough, well, innocent for Harriet at any rate.

"Thank you for a lovely sermon, Reverend. I was particularly intrigued as to your reflections upon the accumulation of wealth. You were rather more accepting of it than many Christians tend to be. Almost ... approving."

Dorothy was in ear-shot, and she answered on behalf of her son. "We are simply keen to encourage people to be industrious in their lives so that they may reap the rewards of their labour and thus pay unto the church their tithe, as is right and proper. Without such funds, as you can see, we are in uncomfortable straits."

"The people?" Harriet said. "It is somewhat surprising to see such a lack of congregation today but I imagine it's to do with ... agricultural matters? Harvest?"

"In April?" snapped Mrs Talfourd. Her face was like a rusted trap, all closed in on itself, and her eyes were watering. She slammed her cane on the broken flagstones. "They mock us, more and more, with each passing week! Fewer attend. They don't contribute. They don't respect. They don't listen!" Her wheezing grew alarmingly hoarse. "And today – no one at all! No one!"

"*We* came..." Adelia said, concerned about the old lady's increasing agitation. She looked at Reverend Talfourd, nodding at him, trying to communicate that he needed to take his mother home.

"You?" Mrs Talfourd said. "What use are you? What use are any of you?"

She began to walk away. Reverend Talfourd finally moved himself, going to her side to reach out for her arm. She pushed him away, nearly falling over as she shoved him, and continued on her slow and painful progress. It was noticeable that, in spite of her infirmity, she did not need her son's assistance. He kept pace with her, at an arm's-length, twisting his hands around and around behind his back as if he were stopping them from reaching out.

What those hands would do if they did reach out was anyone's guess.

❦

HE CAME AFTER THEM ALMOST IMMEDIATELY. HARRIET AND Adelia had walked slowly over the village green, and then impulsively changed their minds and went together towards

Beaumont Sloane's house, intending to see if he really was leaving. So they were angling back at a diagonal to the church, and were intercepted by Reverend Talfourd who was in something of a state of distress.

"She won't come out!" he said, coming to a halt in front of them, his fingers still working and twisting together.

"Mrs Sloane?" Adelia said, thinking of Jane in her room, and the threat of being sent to an asylum. She should have tried to pay a call on her, she thought, feeling a pang of regret. Though Sloane himself would have no doubt waved a gun at her.

"No, my mother," the reverend replied, frowning and shaking his head. He gazed past them, not meeting their eyes at all. He looked so desperately sad. "She has locked herself in her room and she refuses to come out."

"I am so sorry," said Adelia.

"Shall we come and speak to her?" Harriet offered. "Or is there someone that she trusts, that we might fetch?"

He was still shaking his head. "No. Perhaps she is better locked in, if I am honest. She ... I am a sinner," he said, suddenly.

His sadness was changing. His face was hardening.

"Because you struggle to honour your mother, as we are instructed to?" Harriet said.

He could not speak. He clamped his mouth shut, his fingers still fretting over and over.

"You do as much as you are able to," Harriet said, and she spoke kindly. "God has given you the capacity to do what you are doing, and He expects no more than you are able to give."

"But I am so dreadfully afraid that..."

"What?"

"No," he said, his tone now as hard as his face. "No, I am not dreadfully *afraid*. I am angry. I am disappointed. I am let down and betrayed."

"By your feelings...?"

"By her," he said, in a snap.

Adelia said, cautiously, "Reverend Talfourd, might we beg you, might we beseech you, for access to the parish records? That poor soul, Charlie Webb, did not ever deserve what happened to her, and we must uncover what she was looking for. You do understand that, don't you?"

"I understand very well the firm hold that a past might have over someone in the present," he said bitterly. He turned around, his hands now balled into tight fists at his side. "Yes. Come with me."

They walked briskly alongside him as he headed back to the church. Adelia didn't want to mention what she and Theodore had seen in the grounds of Arbury House. She was keen, now, to pay close attention to his reactions as he showed them the parish records. Would they be complete, accurate and true? Or would there be a gap, and he would have an excuse already prepared?

They went back into the church and up to the end, where a small door led into an antechamber where the priests and choir could robe themselves in private before emerging into the view of the congregation. It was partly a storeroom, too, with heaps of books and bits of broken wood, scattered abandoned teacups and piles of folded, moth-eaten fabrics. Beyond that was another door, which was locked.

"Reverend," Adelia said as he hunted through a pile of keys. "Do you know anything about a tunnel that links the church to Arbury House?"

She expected a denial, she wasn't sure why. She was surprised when he said, "Oh, yes!" He smiled wistfully for a moment. "I used to hide in it as a child – when the others ... well, it was a cunning place to go, my secret. Just mine. The others used to think it was just a legend and no one else ever found it."

"No one knew about it? Are you sure?"

He shrugged. "I didn't think so, but this was many years ago. Maybe others have found it since, although I don't think anyone knows about it at the moment. I would be surprised if you could still get through. I wouldn't like to try it now. It's too risky. Who knows if the roof will stay up? But I don't see children playing around, and I would notice that, I think."

Harriet said, "Did your mother know where you were hiding?"

"Yes, I expect so," he said, turning away from them abruptly to fiddle with the lock. "She always knew everything. Ah, here we are. So we have records going back to 1598 although there is something of a gap in the 1640s, of course. But Charlie Webb was young, so we need to start with her birth, which will be in ... oh."

He had walked into the room, and Adelia and Harriet followed eagerly. It was a windowless place, with white-painted walls and a high ceiling. It was lit by a fogged skylight that was covered with leaves and dirt. In spite of the gloom, it was obvious that there was one huge gap in the ledgers that ranged along a sagging shelf.

"Someone's had this out already. It will be here, somewhere."

In confusion, he went to the table, even though it was clearly bare of anything. He looked underneath it. He circled the room twice, and then worked his way meticulously along the row of ledgers, examining each one, double-checking the dates on the spine and the dates written in the frontispiece.

Finally he stopped and faced them both. "It is gone. Do you think that she might have taken it?"

"Your mother?"

"No, I meant Charlie Webb!" he said in protest. "Why would my mother..." But he tailed off.

"Why, indeed," said Adelia. She was fairly convinced by

his utter confusion. "A few nights ago, we saw a figure burning books in the grounds of Arbury House. We approached, and they disappeared into thin air. The next day, we returned to investigate and we found the tunnel. It is still open and we walked the full length of it, coming up here by the church. And the things that had been burned were thoroughly destroyed, though a few scraps remained."

"Burned?" he said in a low tone. "Destroyed?"

"Indeed so. My husband is trying to discover how they might be analysed." She waved at the leather-bound tomes around them. "But enough of the spine remained to convince me that it matched these here exactly. Someone burned that particular ledger, Reverend Talfourd, and we think that it was the work of your mother."

He paled. Adelia expected him to protest, quite naturally so. He'd say she could not walk so far. That she could not have carried a heavy book. That she was incapable of such an act of deceit.

But instead he said, "Was the figure that you saw wearing a long cloak?"

"Yes."

"And it would have been damp at the bottom when they returned, I imagine," he said, now musing to himself. "And hung up in the hallway, smelling of the undergrowth and dark tunnels, with weeds caught in it, and smoke in the fibres. And the owner of that cloak would cough late into the night and demand brandy for her lungs, and grow angry when asked if she had been out."

Adelia had never seen the man look so furious. She simply nodded in sympathy and encouragement. Harriet, too, managed to remain silent.

He raised his head. He grew three inches in stature and confidence, buoyed on by righteous anger. He spoke now in a voice that would have commanded a village to its knees had he thundered from the pulpit in the same vein.

"I vow to you now, before my God, that I will get to the bottom of this wicked, wicked business."

"How? You must stay safe. And what do you plan to do? You cannot act alone," Adelia said. "Come to the manor and speak first to Theodore."

He looked at her with a flat, blank stare. He didn't really see her. He was looking right through her as if his whole life was unravelling. A thread had been tugged and now it was all disintegrating around him.

He said, "No."

And he strode past them and down the aisle of the church, his black robes flapping like a raven descending, leaving every door unlocked and paying no heed at all.

"Oh, goodness me," said Harriet in a small voice.

"An avenging angel?"

"Have you read Revelations? The angels are not really the pretty slim youths in pink and blue that we like to see in paintings. Oh dear."

❧ 22 ❧

Harriet and Adelia needed to hurry back to the manor. Sunday lunch was always rather late, traditionally so to give the servants time to return from church – if they went, which they clearly did not – before the servants got back to work preparing the food, mostly cold meats and so on.

But as they were walking over the bridge, they were waylaid by Nanna Black who was sitting on the sunny side of the bank with two small children at her knee, and a third one wading in the muddy dregs of what was left of the river. He was smeared with black mess up to his thighs, yet still dipped his net into the foetid swampy pools with glee and unconcern.

Nanna Black waved and wished them a good day. Her hands, like the hands of all good women, were perpetually busy. Unlike most good women, however, she seemed to be making a kind of poppet out of dry, twisted strands of long grass. Adelia was fascinated and repelled, and hoped that Harriet had noticed. She didn't want to ask what it actually was, as she didn't trust Nanna Black to give her a true answer.

Nanna Black asked if they were intending on staying for the May Day fair in a few days' time.

"Certainly we shall," said Harriet. "I cannot wait to take part in a simple, pure pastoral celebration. It will be soul-affirming, I am sure."

"What?" said Nanna Black, laughing. "I'm not sure if I understand all that perhaps. I'm an innocent country woman and everything." She fashioned two long arms on the poppet, holding it up as if now challenging them to query what she was doing.

No, thought Adelia, *you understood perfectly but you know the part you like to play. And that poppet is part of the game.* She said, "And what of the maypole that the Alfoxdens have had carved?"

"What of it?"

"Well, it seems that Mr Sloane is not as involved in the running of things as he had once been. The power is returning to the people, you might say. So there is no reason why the maypole can't be erected in pride of place, right in the centre, as it ought to be."

Nanna Black laughed loudly, and the children laughed too, out of duty.

She said, shaking her head kindly, "Oh, no, pet. We shan't be having that thing at all."

"The maypole? But it's been made for the fair. It's a tradition. And you seem to be inclined towards traditions. Don't worry about what the Talfourds will say."

"No one has ever really worried about what the Talfourds would say. I hear, anyway, that old Dorothy is having a right fit about what her son is up to. Says he is 'in league' with us, with the village. I don't know what's happening there. Maybe he's discovered a backbone! And she's not happy at all."

"Very well, but still – what does the village think about the maypole?" Adelia said in growing alarm.

"What about it? It isn't our tradition, hen; it's nothing to do with us. It might be all right for pretty maids down south where the sun shines all the time and flowers grow in your hair, but that's not how we do things up here. Spend a winter on this hill and then you'd see. *Then* you'd see."

She shook the poppet at them. It was made in the rough shape of a man, complete with his *parts*, and Adelia wanted to snatch it out of Nanna Black's hands and hurl it into the water before the children saw it.

But they wouldn't understand what they were looking at. And Nanna Black was trying to shock Adelia and Harriet. When one of the children came up to Nanna Black, she tucked the poppet into her hand, hiding it from innocent eyes.

The child was holding out a small daisy to Nanna Black, saying, "Flower! Flower!" Nanna Black turned her attention very deliberately to the child, and Adelia did not know what to say. They hurried off.

As they got nearer to the manor, Adelia said, "I am not sure that we ought to say anything to Margaret. What do you think? Was Nanna Black telling the truth?"

"I think she was jesting with us," Harriet said. "I don't know the woman but she seemed to be one of those yokels who like to take any opportunity to get one over on other people. They see us as the enemy. As for that *thing* she was making, that was no pagan artefact, created in league with the Devil. It was a silly notion and nothing more. I would wager that the village cannot wait to have the maypole erected. Think of the fun that the children will have! And she clearly does love the children – that is to her credit."

"True. But what about the things she said about it not being their tradition? She has a point about that." In spite of Harriet's calming words, Adelia still remembered the rags in the hawthorns. The hints that the village had their own way of keeping children safe. Safe from what? Suddenly the bright day seemed darker.

"She's trying to scare you," Harriet told her. She ascended the steps and the door was swung open for her. "Ignore her country nonsense."

Adelia followed, but she was slower. She was worried, and she had to speak to Theodore as soon as possible.

❧❧

THEODORE COULD NOT CONTAIN HIMSELF. AS SOON AS HE saw Adelia coming into the room, before she even had a chance to divest herself of her hat and gloves, he dismissed Smith and said, "He's gone!"

"Who has gone? Sloane?"

"Lord Morland."

"Oh! Where? And how? What happened? Did those dreadful men catch up with him again?"

"No. I gather that Ramon had words with him, strong words, and Morland stormed out. Margaret tried to keep the peace, but I don't think that's her strongest skill to be honest. Anyway, so that's that. The man's off."

"Where?"

"I am not sure. I did have a horrible feeling he was going to ride directly over to Miss Fitzroy-Harris's house and throw himself at her feet, crying for forgiveness."

"No, that's not his style. A knight would not do such a thing," Adelia said. "Those men were all so assured of their rightness, just as he is so assured that whatever he does is somehow right, no matter what. He would not ask for forgiveness. He still believes in unrealistic love. He would be far more likely to kidnap her and throw her over his horse and ride away, all the while telling himself he was acting honourably."

Theodore grimaced. "Do you think she is in danger?"

"No. She lives with her parents and they must have servants. And he will quickly regret his actions. He is no Lancelot, not really. Thank goodness."

"Your interpretation of the Knights of the Round Table are markedly different to mine," Theodore said.

"That is because you are a man. Try reading those stories as a woman," she replied.

"Margaret enjoys them."

"Our dear daughter is quite a force," Adelia said with a laugh which soon died. "Although I suspect her stubborn pig-headedness and lack of real empathy is going to bring her some pain soon. Listen to what has happened today. Mrs Talfourd, Reverend Talfourd, Nanna Black ... oh Theodore, I am not at all happy about this May Day fair."

ADELIA SPENT THE AFTERNOON TRYING TO FIND MR Arbury. She wanted to understand his misgivings about the proposal for Arbury House. She eventually tracked him down in the rather bare-looking rose garden at the back of the manor.

"Lord Morland has left," he told her as he sat morosely on a stone bench.

His clothing was not quite as impeccable as usual. There was dust on his trouser hems, and a wrinkle in his shirt front that ought not to have been there. His gloves were crooked.

"I have heard. Do you know where he went?"

"He claimed that he intended to see Gwen but I think that was bluster. I imagine he will continue to run from his creditors. At least he had the decency to leave. He won't bring any more trouble to this house."

"And yourself?"

"Do I have the decency to leave, do you mean?"

"No, not at all. Indeed, what do you think about my daughter's suggestion that Arbury House be returned to its former glory? Is it not an appealing proposition? Or do you think you will miss London too much?"

"I miss London already but when I am there, I miss Greyhaven. But perhaps it is the people that I miss; and those people are not real. They are just memories."

"Jane."

"Yes, Jane." He laughed drily. "Tell me, Lady Calaway, what are the chances of me being able to break her free of whatever asylum that pig puts her in?"

"Fairly slim."

"I thought so. But consider this: what were the chances of me making a success of my life, when I was young and penniless? Yet I did! Life is a vale of tears and sorrow, and it is brief and meaningless. I might as well try to do something, might I not, however insane it all sounds? However doomed to failure it might be?"

"Oh, Mr Arbury, you are so full of sadness."

"I am sorry. I ought to not burden you with my darkness. It is not right, and ought to remain hidden. It is undignified of me."

"Not at all. You must talk to someone and why not me?" She was surprised at the depth of his sorrow and his bleak outlook, but tried not to show it.

He shook his head. "Thank you. No, indulging such feelings must be a sin, I am sure, and I will not do it."

"Speaking is not indulging."

But he would not be drawn. He closed up like a clam, and sighed.

He said, in a brighter tone, "Anyway, as for dear Mrs Alfoxden's plans for the house, they were kindly meant but I cannot accept. I shall, instead, gift her the place."

"She will not take that gift!"

"Well, then, she can offer me some money – a token amount – and that way she can do whatever she likes with the house, and I am free of it at last. The place is surely worthless and I cannot in all conscience sell it for a large sum."

"Mr Arbury, did you ever find out what linked your family to Charlie Webb?"

He snorted. "I found out nothing. I can only imagine that her family was in service to mine, perhaps over the generations, and that some legend was passed down and grew in the retelling into myth and lies. But I have no evidence for that, and no real way of knowing."

"Did she not speak to you?"

"She did but it made no sense."

"What exactly did she say?" Adelia pressed on, though she knew from his expression that she was on dangerous ground.

She had pressed too far.

He shuffled his feet, readying himself to stand up. "I am sorry, Lady Calaway. She was disturbed, quite disturbed in the mind – the evidence was plain for all to see. I took care to avoid being alone with her because I was unsettled by her, though I did not know why at the time. My instincts have been proved correct. I do not think it does us any good, now, to think upon her troubled life and rake over the past. You will excuse me."

He bowed, and walked away. He went briskly, too briskly.

He was *desperate* to get away.

He knew something, Adelia thought. She had a favourable impression of him, still, but there was something he was not yet telling her.

THE EVENING MEAL WAS MUCH SMALLER THAN IT HAD BEEN of late. No Gwen, of course, and now no Lord Morland. Mr Arbury likewise made an excuse to be absent. Adelia suspected that he was packing to leave, and wondered if he had told Margaret yet.

She thought that he had not, because in spite of it all, Margaret was in an enthusiastic and ebullient mood. She even mentioned something that Iseult had done and spoke with pride in her voice.

Adelia asked something that had been bothering her for a while. "Margaret, are there plans for brothers and sisters for little Iseult? She's all alone here."

"Alone?" Margaret looked blank. "She is not. We are all here and she is constantly with her nurse."

"She needs playmates of her own age."

"Oh, mama. You know I am a modern and practical woman. Give me the credit, if you will, of having thought about it."

"I am sure you have. I was wondering what your thoughts were," Adelia said, as snippily as Margaret.

"Well, is it not obvious that everything about our way of life here is concerned with honest toil and a return to the idylls of the past? I shall be positively encouraging Iseult to join in with the play of the village children – yes! I know that it shocks you and all of society, too. But this way she will learn to deal with everyone in a warm and natural manner, like I do."

Theodore began to cough as some food went down the wrong way. It had nothing to do with Margaret's words, of course. Adelia had to bend her head to hide her expression for a few seconds.

Eventually she mastered herself and was able to say, "Margaret, dear, the past was even more hierarchical than the present day."

"This is why I speak of idylls," Margaret said crossly. "I am under no illusions that the past was better in all ways. We simply seek to recreate the best bits, but under a more egalitarian rule."

"Those two words don't go together," Theodore pointed out.

The opposition to her ideas was riling her and Margaret appealed to Ramon for help. "Iseult does not strike you as lonely, does she?"

"Not at all. Why, I saw her yesterday and she was happily babbling to herself while she sat on the lawn with her dolls, the perfect picture of childhood contentment."

"You had many sisters, Margaret, and Edith will be here tomorrow or the next day. Don't you wish for the same for Iseult?"

Margaret gave but the briefest shake of her head. "Perhaps," was all she said, and Adelia had to reflect that Margaret's relationship with her sisters wasn't exactly "the perfect picture of childhood contentment."

Ramon said, "Anyway, this will be the first May Day fair that she is old enough to really enjoy and remember. Perhaps she'll dance with the others around the maypole!"

Adelia did try not to let anything show on her face but she could not help but catch Theodore's eye. And Margaret noticed.

"What?" she demanded, still spiky and argumentative.

"Nothing, dear."

"Nothing," echoed Theodore, but he was a poor liar and the doubt in his voice was obvious.

"Papa," said Margaret. "What are you not telling me?"

He looked rather pleadingly at Adelia, and said, "Nothing, dear one. Only that you must not try to take over quite so much."

"Take over? Beaumont Sloane has dropped all involvement, which means that the whole thing will fall apart unless we step up to direct things."

"Do you not think the villagers themselves will run it the way they want it to be run?"

Margaret frowned with utter incomprehension on her face. "The villagers?"

"Yes," said Adelia firmly, her patience unravelling at last. "You know, these honest labourers, these sons of toil that you idealise so much. Surely their *natural* connection with the land and the soil will somehow just *spring* out of them and they will celebrate May Day in the most *pure* form without outside interference."

Margaret's face was absolute thunder. Her hand trembled where she was gripping her knife so hard. She let the cutlery drop with a clang.

"You are mocking me. I thought you were able to treat me as an adult at last, but I see that I was wrong."

"I will treat you as an adult when you behave like one."

Theodore stepped in, ever the peace-maker, albeit a blundering one. "Please, Adelia, Margaret, this is a simply misunderstanding. Margaret, we only wish to protect you from disappointment and heartache."

"What disappointment?" she screeched.

"The fair might not turn out as you hoped."

"Why wouldn't it?"

"The villagers..."

"The villagers work hard but they have not had a chance to allow their finer feelings to develop yet. We will show them how. Can't you see that? We are not telling anyone what to do. We are not taking over. We are simply acting as benevolent parents." She jumped to her feet. "But perhaps you do not recognise that sort of act."

She flung down her napkin and stormed out of the room.

Ramon coughed awkwardly and reached for his wine glass. He did not speak.

Adelia stared at Theodore. He simply raised his eyebrows and shrugged.

It wasn't the first time that Margaret had dramatically left a meal, after all. Adelia remembered the incident when the Duchess of Cornwall had been present, and shuddered. At least this time her daughter's idiotic arrogance was only shown to family.

And then they heard the scream.

Now they were all on their feet, and rushing to the door. They were only halfway across the hall, with concerned servants streaming in from all sides, when Margaret burst back into the manor, yelling and screaming at the top of her voice. She must have gone outside, albeit briefly. She ran straight for Ramon who grabbed her and held her tight.

"It is gone!" she bawled. Then she broke one arm free and pointed it at Adelia. "It is gone – the maypole is gone – and you *must have known*."

❧ 23 ❧

Nothing could calm Margaret. She insisted that they follow her outside.

They all rushed out to the workshop and found that the door had been levered open, leaving rough splinters around the lock. Inside there was no disturbance. Everything was laid out just as it had been left – except for the long trestles laid out in a row which were now empty, supporting nothing at all.

Ramon was wide-eyed and furious, too, but his anger was tempered by his concern for his wife. He took a calm control of the situation. He quietly requested that Theodore and Adelia go back inside, and finish their meal. He allowed no opposition and they had to acquiesce.

Whatever he said in private to Margaret was their business, but it must have worked. She did not reappear again that evening, but Ramon came down to the drawing room later on, when Adelia was growing bored of waiting for news and Theodore was staring glumly at the fire, lost in thought and unwilling to talk.

Ramon stalked over to the brandy decanter and poured himself a large glass before turning to speak.

"She is better now," he said. Adelia could see the suppressed anger still bubbling in him. His knuckles were pale, and the skin around his eyes was tight. He moved like a wild cat. "With all due respect to our bonds of blood and your status, Lady Calaway, but my primary loyalty is to my wife and so I must ask you, on her behalf, did you know anything about this?"

She sat up straight, and fought her inclination to be offended. She knew why he was asking it, even if she thought it was utter nonsense.

"I knew nothing. I am as shocked and confused as you all."

"Yet you clearly warned her, and indeed both of us, that things might not go to plan. Why?"

"I have been talking with and listening to the villagers. They said to me, quite plainly, that they had what they called 'their own traditions' and implied that they thought the maypole was something more in keeping with the rituals of southern England, inappropriate to the north country."

He frowned. Then he sighed and took a seat, heavily thumping down into it, and swigged back the drink in one movement.

He waited a moment then said, "I warned her, too, you know."

"I thought you were both as keen as mustard on this whole thing?"

"Oh, we are. But you know what she's like. When I am with her, I am consumed by her brilliance. Her fire. Her passion."

Adelia had to lower her eyes. Was he really describing Margaret? Her daughter was brilliant in many ways, yes, but she had never shown a great deal of fire and passion. Rather, to Adelia, she was cold and logical and brittle and easily offended. Adelia did not recognise the woman that Ramon saw.

She wondered if the fault was in herself.

Ramon went on. "When she talks, everyone listens, because she speaks from a place of knowledge. I have seen a room full of men hang upon her every word. At the anti-quarian society of which I am a member, she is actually welcomed; and that cannot be said of many women. She speaks, and they listen, and I cannot tell you how proud I am of her. She has such a depth of passion for the old ways and expresses the things that I have no words for."

Adelia was astonished. She had not heard Ramon speak at such length before. And she began to understand that Margaret had seen past his silences to the man's heart within, and given voice to it, and made him feel understood. No wonder he had such devotion to her. No wonder he thought that she completed him. She did.

But she also overshadowed him, eclipsed him, a fact that he was perfectly happy to accept. They had their roles and were content.

Except, of course, in this matter, when he had tried to warn her that the village might not accept the maypole. He was explaining this now.

"I, too, had heard in the village and the inn that the local people were not as keen on the maypole as we were. But I thought that the bulk of their antipathy was to Sloane's involvement, and I do believe that now he has gone, or as good as gone, there is a gap to be filled. Without the direc-tion of someone, without some leadership, the fair will be nothing but a group of people wandering around on the green. There is an emergency meeting tomorrow to discuss this," he added.

"That will be the day before the fair itself," Adelia said. "And Edith should be here by tomorrow too."

"It will be a busy day," Ramon said. "Hopefully Margaret will be feeling better. I am sure that this is a jape by the villagers and we can sort it all out tomorrow. I told her to take heart and see it as a good sign. One only plays jokes on those one likes, isn't that true?"

Adelia could not bring herself to make a comforting reply.

❧

EDITH ARRIVED, TO EVERYONE'S GREAT DELIGHT, THE NEXT morning. Adelia had not seen Margaret at breakfast. Mr Arbury had made a brief appearance and then disappeared when the post arrived. Adelia knew for certain, then, that he was making arrangements to leave.

She wondered about Gwen, and thought perhaps that Margaret had gone to see her, but a servant told her that Mrs Alfoxden was in the rose garden with her daughter.

Edith stayed in the manor, chatting to Theodore and Ramon about the journey, while Adelia headed out to find Margaret, dismissing the maid who was with her. She wandered out across the lawns which were springing up with the year's new growth, making it a soft and delightful surface to walk upon. She could hear Margaret's voice as she got closer to the trellises and brick walls that screened the more delicate flowers.

"Small roses!" said Iseult, laughing.

No roses were yet in flower. Adelia could not see them and she slowed her pace, listening.

Margaret replied very precisely. "No, Iseult, it is not the season for the roses yet. Indeed, it is very early for the rosemary to be blooming. It is only because it's in such a sheltered part of this garden. Do you see the wall? It protects the plants here from frost and there has been a lot of sun on that patch. Look over there. That is also rosemary but there are no flowers at all. That is more normal for this time of year."

"Rosemary," said Iseult. "It's a name, isn't it, mama?"

Adelia rolled her eyes and braced herself for more tedious lecturing from Margaret. But she was surprised.

Margaret said, with a more lyrical tone to her voice, like a storyteller not a schoolmistress, "Rosemary – *ros marinus*, the dew of the sea. Do you see how blue the flowers here are? They used to be white until when the Virgin Mary herself was fleeing to Egypt and she hid by the bush, and where her cloak touched the flowers, they were blessed and turned blue. Blue is her colour, you see, a sacred colour. And it's a flower of remembrance."

"What's *membrace?*"

"Remembrance. Memory. So this flower is said to stop you forgetting things. You will be able to recognise it now in the paintings I show you in London."

"I will need this."

"What are you doing? Oh – take just one or two sprigs, then. Cook will be annoyed if you strip the plant bare."

"I need them all, mama, so you won't be so angry with me for forgetting."

"Iseult! I am never *truly* angry with you, my darling, sweet girl. And ... I am sorry if I sometimes seem to be so. Come here. I am sometimes impatient, I know, but that is not with you. It's with the world."

Adelia held her breath. This was not the right time to interrupt.

Whatever else was said, it was low and muffled. Adelia withdrew as silently as she could, counted to sixty twice, and then approached the rose garden from the gravel path, noisily calling as she went.

Iseult came running towards her with armfuls of rosemary

and Margaret followed on behind. She wasn't exactly smiling, but she wasn't angry either.

ADELIA WAS HUGELY GRATEFUL FOR THE ARRIVAL OF EDITH. She was the perfect intermediary between Margaret and the rest of them. She was younger than Margaret but as ferociously clever as her sister but in a different way; she had a mind that made connections. She saw patterns in things and was able to step away and see the way things all fitted together. It was logic of a very particular sort. She had had an idea for a very special sort of travel business, and was keen to talk to Margaret all about her latest plans.

Iseult was handed back to the nurse and whisked off to the nursery out of sight and earshot, and they all spent a happy luncheon catching up.

The murder of Charlie Webb, however, was only briefly mentioned. Theodore morosely glossed over it, and even Adelia was half-convinced that he was no longer interested in it. She watched him carefully. It would not be like him to admit defeat, although the fact that more than half of their principle suspects were leaving or had already left was something of a problem.

The problem, such as it was, then shifted rather strangely at the impromptu meeting about the May Day fair that afternoon.

Everyone went to the inn, even Edith. Mr Arbury was asked if he would join them, and he prevaricated, saying he would catch them up in a moment if they went on ahead. Adelia looked back as they left, and there was no sign of him at all.

The inn was crowded and no one gave them a second glance as they pushed into the large lounge on the ground floor. Any nervousness that Adelia still felt about being a woman in a male space was utterly unfounded. Edith and Margaret had all the confidence of youth, being the new sort of woman, and Harriet of course felt her status as the bishop's wife gave her free access to anywhere.

But as the meeting got underway, Adelia realised something else was afoot. No one looked their way because they were all totally irrelevant.

A tall man stood up on a chair and everyone cheered. He was clearly well-known and well-liked. Adelia whispered to Margaret, asking who he was, but Margaret just shook her head. That might have meant she didn't know, or she didn't want to reply. He began to explain that now they were free of Sloane and his "ideas", they were going to have the fair the way they had always had it in the past.

"Turn up early and set up your stall. Mick'll be doing the drinks, will ye not, Mick?"

The landlord roared a yes from behind the bar.

"Aye, so play fair and support the inn. They'll be a hog roast right enough, and big thanks to Archie the Knife for that." Another cheer went up. "Again, do right by him and fetch him a few coins. We've the music all sorted – are ye ready, lads?"

A rag-tag of young men hollered from the back of the room and someone whistled a few bars. "And let's not any of us worry about a thing. For one day, we'll dance up the sun and drink it back down again. Hooray!"

The room erupted into cheering and clapping and the stamping of feet.

Ramon looked unhappily at Margaret. She was white in the face, and she elbowed her way past everyone, right up to the man on the chair. He looked down at her and he laughed.

"Where's my may pole?" she demanded.

Someone shouted something very crude in reply. They were hushed but the laughter continued.

"It is theft!" she said. "I shall involve the police, you know."

"How do you know we didn't take it so we could put it up on the green?" he asked.

"Oh. Did you?"

He sniggered. "No, of course not. I don't know what you're talking about. Call the police if you like, but it's obvious you all stick together."

"What do you mean?"

The man laughed again and looked around the room. When his eyes alighted on Theodore, he pointed.

"See you, there! Lord what's-yer-face. Found the murderer of that wee lassie yet?"

"Perhaps."

The man grinned and shook his head. "Now, here's what I want to know. You're all looking at this person and that person but you've not investigated yourselves, have you? I mean the Alfoxdens and whoever the hell you lot are. What about her?" he said, pointing now at Margaret. "Or him? He's far too quiet. Has some claim to these lands, does he?"

He jabbed a finger towards Ramon before turning back to Theodore. "We all know you've been running around asking questions, a bit of a game I suppose for the likes of you, but you don't take it seriously enough to really look for the real culprit. It must be one of you four and it's all part of your little game. I am surprised you haven't pinned it on one of us for a joke."

"And who do you say that culprit is?" Theodore demanded. "Which one of us?"

The man on the chair was enjoying his time in the lime-light. He put one hand on his hip and said, "Well, let's look at who you've been investigating, first of all."

He looked around and the crowd clapped and laughed.

Adelia wondered if the man on the chair really believed the murderer was Ramon or Margaret, herself or Theodore. He seemed to be making it up as he went along.

He cried, "Beaumont Sloane, that oaf, he was one you was looking at. He thinks he's one of you lot but he's not really a toff, is he? He's not one of you and I am sure you don't like him. Who does? And he was just scared of everyone finding out that he was a bully, when really we all already knew. Didn't we? You could have made him out to be the murderer. But he ain't, I don't think."

The crowd agreed.

"Next, there was that proper toff, Lord Morland. Fancy horse, fancy ways. But his debts caught up with him and have run him out of town – good riddance! Maybe he did it? Maybe?"

"Hooray!" shouted the drinkers. Some people called that he was guilty, and others that he was not.

"You were asking about Dorothy and Thomas Talfourd, too. We've seen you talking to them, and sneaking about, and thinking you were so clever to find that tunnel. *Everyone* knows about that tunnel. But old Dorothy is as mad as a hatter inhaling mercury, and our Reverend can't have done anything bad. He's good, because he's too stupid to be bad. Am I right?"

"Yes!" The villagers were loving every minute of it all.

"Finally there's that shiny young man from London, the one who thinks that because he was born in Arbury House before it fell down around the old man's ears that he has some kind of link to this place. That family never were a part of things and never will be again, as far as we can see. So he didn't do anything because he would not have risked staining his satin slippers. We've seen him struggle to open a door. He could not kill someone."

There were cries of "fop!" and "dandy!"

Someone shouted, "Go home to London!" and someone else began banging a tankard in a rhythm on a table.

Others joined in. The mood was turning, just as it had done when the villagers had made the effigy of Sloane and put him in the stocks.

"So it's one of you!" he finished, pointing at them.

The crowd turned to stare at them. The shouting continued.

Adelia put a hand on Theodore's arm. He understood. She moved backwards to the door with Edith and Harriet, while Ramon and Theodore went forward to persuade Margaret to withdraw. Adelia held her breath, praying her wayward daughter would not indulge her stubborn tendencies.

She did not.

They all tumbled out into the late afternoon, followed by nothing worse that shouted curses and mocking laughter.

From the look on Margaret's face, though, those things hurt as much as any blows.

❧ 24 ❧

Adelia hung back with Theodore, Harriet and Ramon. Edith walked alongside Margaret, and Adelia could hear snatches of the sisters' conversation.

"...how can you live here with people like that?" Edith was saying, aghast.

Adelia didn't catch Margaret's reply. Edith shook her head in despair.

"...my business but..."

"...search for the maypole? It can't be..."

"...hang it all, Margaret, and let them rot," was Edith's final and loudly stated opinion.

She stopped speaking as they approached the manor, because waiting outside, looking nervously about him, was Reverend Talfourd. He was clutching a book to his chest, and hurried forward to meet them on the gravel drive.

"I fear that I have found something," he said in a wavering voice. He looked distinctly unhappy.

"Right. Let's get inside." Ramon said.

He quietly and calmly led the way into the house, ordering servants around with a cool manner. He hustled everyone into the dining room where the reverend could lay the large leather-bound book down on the table.

"So it wasn't destroyed," said Adelia, in confusion. "Theodore, have you heard back from your correspondent in London regarding the burned papers?"

"Yes, and there was nothing to report," he said. He, too, was transfixed by the book in front of them all. "I wonder what we saw burned that night? Might it not have been linked at all?"

"Oh, it was linked," Reverend Talfourd said. He twitched and chewed his lip. "The whole ledger for the decade in which Frederick Arbury was born was destroyed. And I have reason to believe that other things were also set alight that night."

"Evidence?"

"Potentially."

"What is this, then?"

"The copy of the original ledger at least. They are regularly copied at the end of certain cycles of years, depending on how busy the parish is, and kept in safe places away from the church. Not everyone keeps up with it. Many of us grow lax. My mother does not know all the day to day workings of my life, believe it or not. She chooses not to bother with the tedious business matters. Such as this." He waved his hand at the ledger, but kept his distance, as if he was afraid now to touch it.

"May I?" said Theodore.

Reverend Talfourd nodded.

Theodore opened the book with a certain amount of exaggerated respect and care, but that soon faded as his eagerness to find the right entries overtook him. He flicked quickly through while they all watched.

"1867. Do we know the month? Oh, there are not so many children born in a year here ... here we are. Frederick St John

Hammerton Arbury, a son, born to Hammerton Julian Angelus Arbury – goodness, there's a name to conjure with – and Mary Grace Arbury, of Arbury House, blah blah blah. Um, the twelfth of October." He looked up. "There is nothing here of any note," he said. "What am I missing?"

"Look at the deaths."

Theodore sighed. "Ah, I see. The mother died in childbirth. Did Hammerton marry again?"

"No. And so Frederick was the only son and heir," Reverend Talfourd said. He pointed towards the bottom of the ledger. "Now, look at who made the official declaration."

"Was it not the father? Oh, no, I see – I suppose he was sunk into grief. Yes, the nurse came to inform the parish of the birth. Nurse Williams."

Everyone looked curiously at Reverend Talfourd. He wetted his lips. "Nurse Claire Williams," he said. "My aunt. My mother's younger sister."

"Oh yes," said Adelia, looking at Ramon who nodded. "The midwife."

"She was, indeed. And a few months after that birth, the sister of that midwife, Dorothy Williams, was married and I was born, and I was raised in a far more wealthy household than the Williams family could have ever expected, and far beyond the means of my father, too."

"What did your father do?"

"He was a weaver, nothing more and nothing less."

"Yet you went to study theology?"

"I did. And even then, though I was raised in a strict and narrow way, I could see that the food on the table that my mother enjoyed was of the best quality. My education likewise was of the highest. My father, a good man and industrious, passed away and yet we continued to live like nothing was of any problem to us at all. Consider – a widow, who had been a bitter spinster until she was thirty, now living in comfort and ease! From where did this money come? For it was not from the fruits of *his* labour."

Adelia thought of a dozen ways that a woman might make money, but when she lined them up in consideration against Dorothy Talfourd, she could not countenance any of them.

Except, perhaps, blackmail.

They had long been suspicious of the Talfourd's background and wealth, had they not?

Theodore was examining the ledger again. "Charles Webb is recorded here too, being born in the same week."

"Charles?" cried Margaret. "A boy? How is that possible?"

"I do not know. I will swear on my very life that the Charlie Webb that we knew was a woman. Yet here the birth is, and he is a boy."

"I had been beginning to think this was a case of switched at birth," Adelia said.

Theodore nodded. "Me too."

Her head was spinning and she stood up to walk to the window. She hardly knew what to think, now.

"If you had told me that Charlie Webb was recorded as a girl," she said, "I would have assumed that the Arburys had had a girl that night, and in desperation at the death of Mrs Arbury, the girl had been swapped with a boy from the village, so that the Arburys had an heir. That would mean Frederick was originally from the poor Webb family, and that Charlie Webb was the Arbury child, raised in poverty. But that does not follow if both are boys. Oh, this is all nonsense. What else in that ledger could possibly be hiding something so desperate that a person is killed, and the records destroyed?"

"Is blackmail not enough?" said Margaret.

Edith said, logically, "What is there to be blackmailed about?"

"Oh."

"I have it," said Theodore suddenly. "Did I not attend enough births as a doctor? Admittedly I was rarely called to the bedside of a poor villager. Which makes me now ask you all – in those cases, who *does* attend the lying-in of a commoner?"

"Oh," said Adelia. "Her family and her neighbours. Usually there will be a local woman of particular skill and knowledge who can assist if things go wrong."

"Indeed. So there were plenty of people, I would argue, at the birth of Frederick when he was born to the Webb family in some dingy cottage. They all knew that Mrs Webb had been brought to bed of a boy. Now, if Goodwife Williams, Mrs Talfourd's sister, was then tasked with finding a suitable boy to swap, that's all very well – no doubt the Webbs were paid handsomely to hand Frederick over, and take the girl in substitute – but how do they then account for the change in gender?"

"They don't," said Adelia. "Oh my goodness. That poor mite was told she was a boy all her life. If that is how she was raised, how could she then stop? She would not have known anything was amiss at first."

"And they moved away when she was five years old," Reverend Talfourd said. "As far as I can tell, from talking with my fellow vicars, and listening to unhealthy village gossip, the Webb family frittered away whatever money they had, and continued to live a low, mean life."

"I wonder what they told Charlie?" Margaret said. "How on earth could they account for her living as she did? As she grew older ... she would have known, surely?"

"It is impossible to say. I can find no record of them currently living. Nor did the police."

"They didn't look very hard," said Theodore. "But I, too, have had no luck. We can imagine, then, that they are dead, and Charlie was quite alone, with nothing but vague memories, rumours, half-truths, and the knowledge that her whole life was built on a lie – and she didn't know why."

"How awful!" Margaret said.

They were all moved to some extent. Harriet looked furious.

"And meanwhile," said Reverend Talfourd in bitter unhappiness, "My own mother was blackmailing the Arbury family with the knowledge of their deception that she had gained from my aunt. Blackmailing, bleeding them dry, and using that money ... for me. I feel soaked in guilt."

He paused. No one jumped in to assuage his feelings. It was all too complicated, too new, and too raw.

"Does your aunt still live?" Adelia asked.

"To be brought up as a witness, you mean? I don't know. Our family cut off all contact with her and I have never known her. I was told it was because she had done something unspeakable. Now I wonder. I suspect my mother simply didn't want anything to do with her because she knew too much."

"Is it possible that your mother's greed was the ultimate cause of the fall of the Arbury family?" Adelia said. "Do you really believe that she bled them dry, as you say?"

"She must have been one large part of it. All my studies were paid for. How could someone from my background get the education and career that I did?" he said. "I was always told that I owed everything to her, to my mother, and I grew up under a huge obligation to obey her in all things."

"And that is why you took up the living here," Adelia said. "You didn't want to return to Greyhaven at all, did you?"

"I've never felt particularly at home here, no. I was happy in Doncaster – Doncaster of all places! But then this position arose and mother commanded me to return. She was ill, she reminded me. Frail. I had a duty to her and to God. So of course I came back." He looked sick at the thought of it. "Here I am. Honouring my mother," he added bitterly.

"Does she know that you have this copy of the ledger now? Does she know that you know what has been going on?" Theodore asked.

"I don't know, and I am not sure if I care any longer. What will she do?"

Adelia said, gently, "More to the point, what will you do now?"

"I will move on to pastures new. I'll say this: whoever Mr Arbury is, and whether he knows the truth of his background or not, he has been something of an inspiration to me. He has been brought low, defeated by life, and yet he brushes himself off and starts again. That is both amazing and humbling. I can do it too, don't you think?"

He was looking past them as he spoke, his eyes fixed on the view through the window. He exhaled as if he were letting all his past drift out of him, and then he left abruptly, with the barest of farewells. He merely nodded at the book on the table.

"Keep it, do what you will with it. As for my mother – well, she is still locked in her room, sulking that the village seems to have turned against her."

"There is more to that," Adelia said. "She is scared of what is being discovered."

"Quite possibly. I do not care." Reverend Talfourd left.

They all looked at the open ledger.

Then Edith said, "So, does Mr Frederick Arbury know about his past – or not?"

❧ 25 ❧

Theodore wanted nothing more than utter solitude, total peace, a private room of calm, and possibly a small tot of whisky and a pork pie. Maybe some chutney, too. Instead he was forced to spend the rest of the evening amongst the clamour and endless chatter of his dearly beloved family who, he had to admit, were driving him to complete distraction. Even Ramon was shaking off his usual reticence to look up from his book and contribute the occasional sentence or two.

Talk mercifully paused at dinner that night, however, because Mr Frederick Arbury was there.

Theodore braced himself for supreme awkwardness but he was impressed, as usual, by the deftness with which Adelia handled the situation. Margaret, too, was a capable hostess. Edith and Harriet took up the slack and the conversation remained light and fizzing and totally innocent throughout the meal. If Theodore and Ramon were unable to contribute, it was unlikely to have been noticed. Anyway, Mr Arbury was himself somewhat subdued and quiet.

At the end, he made his announcement.

He tapped a cake fork on his glass and coughed. Everyone felt silent. Theodore knew what he was about to say.

"I would like, first of all, to thank Mr and Mrs Alfoxden for their generous hospitality over the past two weeks. They have shown kindness beyond all measure to an utter stranger who wandered into their midst. I came here with nothing but my name and my background to recommend me, and they could have easily left me lodging at the inn, but instead they opened their arms, their hearts and their house to me, and I will forever be grateful to them. Such openness has moved me beyond words."

They all nodded and smiled. But Theodore could not help but search his words for hidden meanings. When Mr Arbury spoke of his "name" and his "background", what did he mean? What did he know? He looked so open and innocent. Yet did he conceal the serpent within his breast?

"But the Chinese have a famous proverb, I believe. Houseguests are like fish. After three days, they begin to stink. I cannot outstay my welcome – indeed, I fear that I ought to have left many days ago. I came here on a quest, a fool's errand if we are honest, and I must leave none the wiser. I wanted to know about my family and its decline, and when I heard that someone was asking about the very same things, of course I took the chance to visit."

He nodded at Adelia, who looked a little strained. Theodore knew she still blamed herself for the events that unfolded. He was infuriated and frustrated that he couldn't make her see that she was being irrational.

"You have been a wonderful guest and our house is always open to you," Margaret said.

"Thank you. And I must extend the same courtesy to you all, though my situation in London is rather modest."

It was merely social convention speaking. Theodore didn't

expect that Margaret and Ramon would be rushing to the capital to spend time with Mr Arbury.

"When do you leave?" Harriet asked, a little bluntly.

"Tomorrow. I have stayed, I confess, out of curiosity for the fair. But by the mid-afternoon, I shall be gone."

"Ugh, the fair," said Margaret. "I am not even sure if I want to go any more." She was clearly upset about the loss of Mr Arbury and the dashing of her dream to renovate Arbury House but she would not say so in front of everyone.

"After all this?" cried Edith. "What about Iseult? She was babbling to me earlier about all the things she was going to see."

"You can take her."

"I shall. But Margaret, you must come."

Margaret huffed. "As I said, I am *not sure*. I will decide tomorrow." Then she pasted on a polite smile, and changed the subject, and the ladies withdrew.

Theodore, Ramon and Mr Arbury did not linger with their cigars. Mr Arbury went up to his room – final packing arrangements, he said – and Ramon insisted that Theodore come to the drawing room.

He did so reluctantly. He had a lot of thinking he wanted to do. And he had to do it before Mr Arbury left.

❧

THEODORE WOKE WHILE IT WAS STILL DARK. HE LAY IN THE bed, staring up at the ceiling. He was in that cosy state where everything was exactly the right temperature for comfort. He didn't want to move. Adelia snored very lightly, a fact that he loved. He loved, too, that she didn't know that she snored. He would never, ever tell her. She would be mortified and he hugged the secret to his heart instead.

But gradually he became aware of his pressing bladder.

His shoulder ached. He was finding, lately, that lying in one position for too long made his whole arm go numb. He had self-diagnosed an issue with a nerve. It was likely that his joints were growing arthritic and the wearing-away of the bone was causing issues. There was nothing he could do about it. He wriggled his toes. Were they more tingly than usual? Perhaps his bed-socks were too tight. Tight bed-socks were one of those things that he had always been warned about, along with going out with wet hair, and eating raw fruit. No good could ever come of such actions.

He smiled into the darkness. The only thing wrong with him, really, was age. But as the body inched its way along its inevitable downward path, at least he could hopefully ascend in experience if not wisdom.

And that brought his musing back to the death of Charlie Webb.

A kind of calm excitement settled on him. He knew, now, who the killer was and he knew why they had done it.

Everyone would be at the village green that day. He was sure, knowing Beaumont Sloane, that he would not be able to resist making a last visit. Lord Morland had gone, they said, but Margaret was not so sure; Gwen, she said, "was foolishly entertaining notions of a reconciliation." Mr Arbury had said he would certainly be at the fair. And as for the Talfourds, he knew that the reverend would be present. If the son went, then surely the mother would not be able to miss out.

Things had caught her up in such a whirl, lately, that she could not risk being absent.

Slowly, Theodore sat up. Adelia rolled over and whispered, "What's wrong?"

"I'm getting up."

"Is it time?"

"Soon."

"Have you made your plans?"

"I think so. I don't think we'll ever see official police justice served unless the community is convinced there is a case to answer, and *they* insist upon it. It's different up here, isn't it?"

"It is. I wish Margaret could see it. We didn't raise her well enough to cope with how it is here."

"She's an adult, now. She made her own choices. You must forgive yourself."

"I am a mother. I will dwell on my mistakes until the day that I die. And then, from beyond the grave, I shall haunt my daughters endlessly."

"You already do. Margaret speaks to Iseult how you used to speak to Margaret."

He felt the bed shift, and a looming dark shadow appeared next to him as Adelia sat up.

"I do *not*," she hissed in horror.

He grinned at her, though she could not see it. "Don't worry. It's not too bad."

"I worry about how she is raising that child."

"Don't. This afternoon she'll be dancing with the others at the May Day fair, maypole or not. She's a bright, lively child. She'll start to make friends, I am sure. Remember that she has not been brought up with airs and graces; she is not going to go down into the village with a prim attitude and a high-minded manner. She'll go with her tales of dragons and knights, and who can't fail to love that?"

"I hope you are right," said Adelia. "And I hope Margaret does decide to come with us."

"She will. She's already decided to, but she can't possibly admit it yet, that's all."

"I AM *DEFINITELY* COMING WITH YOU," SAID MARGARET, her face red with fury that morning. She was already dressed for the day, and she held a hand-delivered note. "Gwen says that she will be there."

"Oh, how lovely," said Adelia.

"No, mama!"

"Ah." Adelia's heart sank in sympathy with Margaret's plight. She guessed immediately what the matter was. "She's taken up with Lord Morland again, hasn't she? They said that he was intending on winning her back."

"I cannot believe how silly she is being. I must persuade her to throw him over for good. But then part of me cannot be bothered. If this is her choice, her true choice, then she has made her bed and I will let her lie in it. But mama, what on earth is she thinking?"

Adelia sighed. "She is thinking of old tales and stories, where people are redeemed and knights ride out of the mist to sweep ladies off their feet, and if she cannot forgive his mistakes and his past then what hope has she?"

"But she hasn't made any mistakes in her own past."

"We all think that we have, no matter the view from the outside."

Margaret stilled. She closed her mouth, stopping whatever was about to tumble from her lips, and she looked at Adelia with a sudden intensity. Adelia felt a jolt as she recognised her own eyes looking back at her.

Nothing needed to be said.

They were interrupted by Harriet bursting into the room, closely followed by Edith who walked with far more decorum as if she were the older, more mature one of the pair. Ramon appeared, looking tight-lipped, glancing around.

"Where's Calaway?"

"He's on his way."

"I've been trying to catch him all morning. I feel sure he's planning something. Has he decided if the murderer is still here? Is he going to do something dramatic?"

"I doubt it," said Adelia. "Here he is now."

"Calaway! Might I have a word?"

"Of course," said Theodore, taking great pains not to be drawn off to one side. "Let's talk as we walk, shall we?"

It wasn't at all what Ramon wanted. But he had to put up with it as Theodore would not be hustled off to be spoken to in private.

Mr Arbury appeared at last, dressed in his very finest clothes; he'd have to change before setting off again when he left for good that afternoon, but for now, he was the very glory of the village. Adelia thought he was going to look like a peacock that had been dropped into a hen coop.

The nurse came down with Iseult dressed in her prettiest dress, and Margaret reached out for her daughter's hand. She told the nurse she could have the day at the fair herself, if she wanted, and to pass that on to the rest of the servants. The nurse bobbed a curtsey. Adelia smiled to herself. She had a feeling that half the household had already decided they were going to the fair anyway.

And off they went.

❧ 26 ❧

They spotted Gwen and Lord Morland first, because they were standing on the bridge to the south of the green, evidently waiting for everyone from the manor to pass by.

Theodore felt Adelia stiffen and he understood the distaste that she felt for the duplicitous man. Harriet tutted and Margaret hissed something to Ramon, who murmured a placatory response.

Lord Morland winced a little as they approached but his natural self-confidence, which was definitely very close indeed to sheer aristocratic arrogance, soon asserted itself. He bowed low with his hat in his hands, and then straightened up to resume his tight hold of Gwen.

There were some muttered pleasantries and they turned to approach the green. Morland and Gwen went first, followed by Ramon and Margaret with Iseult currently in Ramon's arms. Harriet was like a child, keen to explore the fair, so she surged on ahead.

Theodore said to Adelia, "You know, I think Morland really does love Gwen."

"Pah. She deserves better and he is a mere cad and a user of women."

"No, really. He sees something pure and good and wonderful in her. She might save him, you know, like you did me. He has a title even if he is penniless so he could have his pick of women."

"He could not," Adelia said. "Any decent woman would turn him down flat."

"Well, maybe so. But consider, also, all the rich widows who would accept him. If he were interested in wealth, he would drop Gwen and find one of those vultures."

"Oh, Theodore. Anyway, I did not save you. You had to want to be saved. And I certainly didn't accept you because I thought I could *be* any kind of saviour."

"Yet you did." He reached out and caressed her hand swiftly and secretly.

She smiled but returned to the topic. "If Gwen is under that illusion, then I pity her, for it will surely fail. And as for Morland returning to her, if I am honest, I think it was done out of his need to be proven right. He hated being rejected. He could not bear it. Men like him don't get rejected, in his world. So he had to persuade her to take him up again, that's all. It's pride, nothing more."

"I am sure he is in love with her," Theodore said stubbornly.

"Maybe he is."

"Then why are you arguing with me?"

"Because love is not all there is in a marriage," she said, sliding a sideways glance at him. He thought she was teasing him but wasn't entirely sure.

"Is it not enough?"

She rolled her eyes with a snort. "I doubt we would have got this far on love alone. Now look – oh, goodness me. This fair. It looks nothing more than any common street market."

"And still no maypole," said Theodore as he scanned the tawdry display on the village green.

He had half-hoped that the village might have erected it anyway, as some kind of surprise for Margaret and Ramon. But even as he looked for it – as if it could be hidden! – he knew he was doomed to failure. It was gone. There was, however, a merrily burning bonfire that had been lit rather too early in the day, with a great pile of logs heaped ready next to it, and his suspicions flared.

Well, he thought. *This is the villagers' day, not ours.*

All around the green, people had spread their wares out to be sold. They had flooded in from miles around, and there was a good amount of travelling tinkers and the like, too. Some had tables or at least wooden boards propped up on trestles, but many had simply spread a blanket or cloth on the ground, and tipped their knick-knacks out in a jumble.

There were some professional and semi-professional showmen of a very low sort, unattached to any carney, running their non-stop patter at the passers-by, challenging people to ha-penny card tricks and memory games, sleight of hand moves and tests of skill that were so obviously rigged.

There were plenty of food sellers and a few lowly sorts defying the request to leave the alcohol business to the Mason's Arms. They sidled up to people and offering tots of home-brewed liquor from brown jars and stained bottles. The musicians had not turned up yet, and the hog roast was only just getting going; it would not be ready until much later that night. Theodore shuddered to think about how the fair would progress once darkness fell.

Margaret and Ramon had drawn off to one side and were having an intense, private conversation. Iseult was standing close by, holding on to Margaret's skirt, but she was staring around in wonder. None of this was at all how Margaret had imagined it would be, or should be, but the little girl was in a new paradise.

Lord Morland was as appalled as the other adults at the shabbiness and ordinariness of the fair. He kept Gwen's arm tucked into his own. Theodore tried to see it as an act of love, but now that Adelia had sown doubt into his mind, he could only see possessiveness. Morland's eyes flicked constantly around.

Theodore could not help himself. He said, "You seem nervous, Lord Morland."

"Oh – it is only that I fear that those crude men, those so-called bailiffs, might not give up the chase yet. I have sent money, more money," he added, a little wildly. "It is not that I think I owe them anything more, but it was a token to get them off my back. I would consider anything further to be blackmail."

"Blackmail?" Theodore said. "Is that something you know about?"

"I? No! Of course not!"

"You know, I have plans to expose the murderer today," Theodore said as casually as he could, just to provoke a reaction.

He got one. Lord Morland started and said, "Here? He is here?"

"Oh yes, they are very much here."

"They?"

"Yes." Theodore smiled.

Morland looked both confused and panicked. "Good," he said with a squeak that he turned into a manly cough. "Gwendolen, my dear, shall I buy you some pretty ribbon for your hair?"

He led her away.

Adelia had been close enough to listen to it all. She raised one eyebrow at him, but all she said was, "Ribbons for the hair. Honestly, what is it with men thinking that it's the most longed-for gift you can give a woman?"

"I bought you ribbons."

"You did."

"What did you really want?"

She laughed. "A pair of greyhounds."

They were interrupted, to his relief, by the arrival of Reverend Talfourd. He had spotted them from some distance away and made a very determined beeline right through the crowds to get to them. People parted to let him pass, and a few touched the brims of their caps, but there was no fawning or real respect shown.

"Lady Calaway. Lord Calaway," he said.

"Good morning, Reverend. How is your mother?" Adelia asked politely. Anyone listening would have thought nothing of it.

He twitched, the skin around his eyes tightening. "She remains in her room, confined to her bed."

"She might wish to be present here," said Theodore. "I had thought she might attend. I plan on revealing the murderer in our midst very soon." He spoke loudly and deliberately so.

Heads began to turn. People nudged one another.

"That is entirely up to her. She can come or go as she pleases."

"Is that so?"

"Yes," said Reverend Talfourd. His words were now attracting even more attention. The villagers goggled to see their meek, mild churchman suddenly declare himself with such finality. "I have made some new plans for my future and they do not include *her* at all."

"Ooh!" said a young woman standing nearby with her friends. They clustered together and whispered, giggling.

"You are becoming brave and bold," said Adelia warmly.

"I am becoming my own man, at last," he said. "And she can deal with the consequences of her own choices. You know that she was far more involved in all of this than she would ever admit to."

"Oh yes, we know," said Adelia.

A ripple of excitement went through the crowd. People didn't pretend to be occupied with other things. They were openly listening as they made a little circle around the group, and as was always the way of things, the fact that some people were looking made others come and look, too.

The Reverend nodded gravely at them all, and then held his head high and walked away, stiff-backed, his robes fluttering with far more gravitas than they had done before. Perhaps it was all in the way he kicked his legs. He was no longer scuttling, with his surplices jittering in agitation. Now, he sailed away upon waves of dignity.

Mr Arbury was watching as keenly as everyone else.

He sidled up to Theodore and said, "Is the murderer really here?"

"Indeed they are."

"Ought we not send for the police?"

"They have proved useless so far."

"True, true. Oh, this is all so strange!" he burst out.

"The fair?"

"Yes. And ... well, none of this is what I expected to happen when I first came back." He snorted with a self-deprecating laugh. "I suppose I ought to be grateful. I have a few items of my inheritance back in my possession."

Margaret came over. "And the possibility of a new life and future. Our offer still stands, you know. Let us manage the redevelopment of Arbury House and build a centre for craft and artisanship here. It will give you direction and purpose, too."

Mr Arbury just shook his head sadly.

To fill the awkward silence, Theodore said, "Do you really think the villagers will welcome such a venture? You know, after all this business with the maypole?" He regretted his words instantly. He had tried to make things better but it simply angered his daughter.

She frowned, glowering, making her face quite ferocious. She folded her arms and glared around at the shabby fair on the green. A worker from the mill was already being sick in a bush, while a stout woman stood by with a stick in her hands as if she were going to beat him the minute he felt better.

Theodore wondered if the Knights of the Round Table ever got so drunk that they threw up in public in the middle of the day.

Margaret said, snappily, "I don't know any more. I don't know what the villagers want or would welcome. It's just..."

"What?"

Margaret blinked rapidly and stopped talking for a few seconds. She looked again at the scene around her. People laughing, shouting, sometimes arguing. Many people simply standing silently and watching them. Watching *her*.

Theodore said, "If you don't know what the villagers want..."

He didn't need to finish the sentence. He saw something suddenly make sense to her. She pursed her lips and prised Iseult's hand from her skirt, handing her over to Ramon.

It looked as if she were about to try and solve things immediately. He tried to stop her. He said, going after her, "Wait, Margaret, think about it first..."

But she paid him no heed. She reached Nanna Black.

"Nanna Black," said Margaret.

The old woman was surrounded by a collection of people with faint family resemblances but she stepped forward. "Mrs Alfoxden."

"We must take tea together soon."

"Where will we take it? Where does tea want to go?" Nanna Black said, and the villagers laughed.

It was mostly in good humour. *Mostly*.

"Perhaps it will go wherever it wants to go. And likewise, the village."

"Eh?"

Theodore thought that Nanna Black looked genuinely confused now, and was not merely playing the part of slack-jawed yokel.

"What does the village want from us? If anything at all? How can we be of service to you all?" Margaret said with honesty and forthrightness. Theodore was proud of her, and cringed all the same.

Nanna Black grinned, frowned, shook her head, and laughed, all at the same time. "I don't know," she said. "We want beer and soft beds."

Someone cheered.

"I appreciate I have sprung an unexpected question on you," Margaret said. She spoke awkwardly and formally. She lacked the common touch that Adelia had, Theodore realised with regret. But Nanna Black inclined her head and listened anyway. "Please do think about it and in a week or so, we'll talk. Or you'll talk. And I will listen. I really do want to ... be a part of this village. Properly, I mean."

Oh, stop now, Theodore thought. *You mean well, I know...*

Someone shouted something derogatory in disbelief. If Margaret had expected the village to raise her aloft with rousing cheers of gratitude, she was going to be disappointed.

But maybe, Theodore then thought, *he was doing his daughter a disservice*. She didn't look surprised by the reaction and she didn't press the matter home either. She left it at that for the moment, which was very wise. She didn't press Nanna Black for any kind of affirmation – she knew she'd never get one.

Would things work out? Would they ever take tea together? Theodore doubted it.

Mr Arbury seemed to breathe out in relief. While everyone's eyes remained on Margaret, Theodore turned his attention to Mr Arbury. He fiddled with his hat, and glanced around. He began to slip away. He had attended, he had shown his face to the world, and now he could disappear without a shred of criticism attaching to him.

Theodore let him get to the stocks at the edge of the green. Before Mr Arbury stepped off the grass onto the track that led to the bridge, Theodore said in his loudest, and most compelling voice: "Stop."

Mr Arbury did.

"Mr Frederick Arbury," Theodore said, attracting everyone's attention. "You will stop right there."

Mr Arbury tensed, as if he could run. Jack Fletcher and some other men materialised around him.

He was going nowhere.

✥ 27 ✥

He tried to bluster, of course.

He stammered out, "I say, I don't know what you mean by this, but you know that I am leaving today and I've arranged with the coachman to take me to the station so if you'll excuse me ... time and tide wait for no man, as they say, ha ha!"

The nervous desperation in his voice alerted everyone to the unfolding drama.

Theodore had rehearsed this whole thing in his head many times over the past twenty-four hours. He knew he was acting the showman, but he allowed himself the indulgence. His previous cases had rarely allowed him to have his moment in the limelight quite so neatly.

"The only place you will be going is the courtroom," Theodore said.

The crowd erupted with cries of "What's he done?" and "Did he do it?" and "What's happened?" and the occasional "I knew it all along, didn't I say? Didn't I?"

"I am innocent," Mr Arbury said, and there was none of

Lord Morland's arrogance in his unhappy face. His eyes were shining with tears though he did not let them fall.

"You were innocent of the initial wrong that was done to you, yes," Theodore said. "It was not your fault that you were taken from your birth family and given to another to be raised in what ought to have been luxury and ease."

Everyone gasped.

Theodore went on. "When did you discover this terrible truth about your background?"

"What? What truth? I don't know what you are talking about. I still do not believe it. It is terrible but it is not a truth."

"Mr Arbury, it is true." Theodore looked at the confusion on the man's face and made a guess. "You have only recently found out, haven't you? Charlie told you everything."

"He – she spun her lies to me, yes. But you can all remembered how I avoided her. I had nothing to do with her. Ever."

"You avoided speaking to her because you could not face the facts. It fitted together. She had proof, didn't she? She said she had seen the records. I am not sure if they were the original parish records or some other proof from her family."

"I tried to see those records myself but I was not allowed. Then I heard they had been destroyed. Maybe she saw them before that. Maybe *she* destroyed them because there *was* no evidence."

"There was a copy. There is *always* a copy. And it confirmed that what she said was, indeed, the truth."

"Oh." Mr Arbury let his shoulders rise and fall. In a smaller voice, he said, "Please, Lord Calaway, I beg of you now: tell me the truth. Who am I?"

It was the most plaintive of questions.

"You were born to the Webb family in poverty and squalor. You were taken by Nurse Williams, the younger sister of Mrs Talfourd, and swapped with the rightful child of the

Arbury family. That child was Charlie, who was raised in the house that you should have occupied. But as all the neighbours knew that Mrs Webb had given birth to a boy, Charlie was raised as if she had been a boy."

"And she was the true Arbury, and I am nothing?"

"You are not nothing," Harriet said suddenly. Theodore cursed inside. He really didn't want the bishop's irritating wife spoiling his flow. "You are a child of God."

"I think I have forsaken my place at His knee," Mr Arbury said.

Before Harriet could launch into a lecture about redemption and forgiveness, Theodore said, "Charlie kept coming after you, wanting to know the truth, didn't she?"

"But I didn't know the truth. She thought that I had known all my life, and I swear that I had not. You must believe me. I thought that I was ... I was me. Frederick Arbury. Son of my father."

"Are you claiming that you are the victim here?" Margaret said harshly.

He went red and hung his head, shaking it mutely.

Theodore had not accounted for the contributions of other people when he'd rehearsed all this in his head. He ignored Margaret and said, "So she came after you again and again, asking for something you could not give her: an explanation."

"Yes. And I was scared, because although I have nothing to my name, and there is nothing that she could have claimed as her own – except perhaps Arbury House itself, and who would want that? – I was still scared. I think I was afraid that she would take the last thing I really had, which is my name itself. I didn't know what would happen."

"So you killed her."

"No! I couldn't understand any of this, and I didn't know that she was a woman, so it made no sense why we had been swapped at birth. I thought she was a madman, if anything, and dangerous. Whether it was true or not was almost irrelevant, perhaps. She kept on finding me and I wanted to leave, but Mr and Mrs Alfoxden were so kind and ... and ... and there was Jane."

"Ah. Jane Sloane."

"Sloane? Don't sully her by attaching that brute's name to hers! She ought to have been mine and when I saw how desperately unhappy she was here, I thought I ought to do something about it. Steal her away, if I could. So I stayed, in spite of everything, trying to find a way to bring some good into her life at least. But Charlie Webb found me early one morning, walking. I saw her from a distance, on the bridge, and I changed direction. I ended up by the Holy Pool."

"And she followed you."

"She did. He did. I swear, I did not know she was a woman! I saw only a man, a crazy man, with lies and half-truths, ruining everything. I just wanted him to go away. Her to go away. I just wanted things to be as they were. But he came at me and I hit him."

"You hit *her*."

"I didn't know!" Mr Arbury looked at his own hands in horror. "I swear I would never strike a woman. But she wasn't a woman, not then. And when he – she – turned, I struck ... *her* ... again, on the back of her head, and she fell, and she was dead. Instantly dead. I was sick, so sick to my stomach. I never ever meant to kill anyone. But I had. I rolled the body into the pool and realised that I could not now leave. I had to stay for Jane, and I had to stay for if suspicions were raised, I would look guilty if I fled straight away."

"What about Sloane?" someone cried.

Mr Arbury shook his head. "I didn't know that the pool would be drained. And I didn't know that it was Sloane, all those years ago, who had stolen my things and thrown them in there, just so that he could steal my love from me. Everything unravelled. I should have left straight away. But Jane, oh my Jane!"

There was such a plaintive note in his voice that Theodore was struck with the sorrow that Mr Arbury must have carried with him for years. He did not speak.

"I went there late last night, you know," Mr Arbury said. "I went there, but she was locked in her room and the servants loosed their dogs and I ran like the coward that I am. I must go back! I *must* release her."

"You are going nowhere," said Jack.

"Has someone sent for the police yet? Now we have a public confession, they must act at last," Theodore said.

But his command was pointless. Someone had already gone for the police, and another man went to help Jack take Mr Arbury to the stables behind the Mason's Arms where one particularly secure tack room could be used to contain him.

Looking at the pathetic, dejected figure, Theodore thought that Iseult herself had the strength to hold him. All the fight had gone out of him, and he walked with a docile, broken air, needing no chains or irons but instead trapped firmly by the guilt he had brought upon himself by his actions.

❦

ADELIA RESTRAINED HERSELF BUT SHE WANTED TO CHEER. She looked around for Harriet, surprised that she wasn't applauding Theodore's show, but her friend was in deep conversation with Reverend Talfourd now. They appeared to be having an animated discussion but both were happy to be having it. That was something, at least. Adelia was worried about her friend and her reactions lately, and she still had to get to the bottom of this business with her mother.

Then her musings were interrupted by Edith appearing at her elbow.

"Mama, well done, the pair of you."

"I don't think I did anything this time," she said and felt a little dejected. "Except perhaps start it all off. If I hadn't written to my friends in London and called Mr Arbury here, Charlie would still be alive."

"Don't be ridiculous. I rather fear that all this would have happened somehow."

"You are good to say so. I'll never quite shake the feeling that I did something wrong, however."

"Let us do something right, then."

"What?"

Edith smiled wickedly. "Poor Jane Sloane is locked up in her house, is she not? I have just heard someone say that a carriage is coming for her from the asylum. Is it right that she is committed?"

"I am not a medical expert so..."

"Mama, is it *right*?"

"No."

"Then it would be right of us to prevent the dreadful injustice of having an innocent woman taken to an asylum. Come on!" Edith took her mother's hand and pulled her before stopping. "Which way to their house?"

"Edith, we cannot."

"Of course we can. And as you say, you have not contributed much this time. So, here is your chance to do one good thing."

Adelia threw caution to the winds. She gathered herself and off they went.

THE OVERHEARD CONVERSATION ABOUT THE CARRIAGE WAS correct. There was a sombre-looking vehicle standing outside Beaumont Sloane's house and a number of grey-suited men were in a little cluster, discussing something. Adelia glanced behind. Quite a few of the villagers had followed them from the green, keen to witness the next exciting event. Now that Mr Arbury had gone to his temporary lock-up, there was nothing else to see there.

"This was your idea," Adelia said, her steps slowing as the men in grey all looked up at her. They immediately looked away, dismissing her as someone of no importance in the current matter. "Now what do you propose that we do?"

"We will simply walk in and bring Mrs Sloane out with us. From everything I have heard about her from you and papa and Margaret, she will not resist. She will be glad to come."

"And her husband?"

"Surely won't dare to raise his hand to two ladies."

"Oh, Edith, this man is a beast."

"All beasts can be tamed."

Edith strode up to the door. The men were conversing amongst themselves. A servant came to the door and opened it politely, inviting Edith to step into the hall and explain her business. Adelia caught up with her and the manservant did not even blink in recognition. He had not had time to speak when Beaumont Sloane came running down the stairs.

He was shouting in a wile manner. "Gentleman, she refuses to take the medicine but I am sure that with a few more hands to assist me, she can be persuaded – you!" He stopped as he saw them. "And you, whoever the devil you are. What do you want? Can't you see we are in the middle of things? Just get gone, and leave me alone. This is my last day here anyway." He waved his hands at them, as if he were using a broom to brush them out of the hallway.

Adelia looked at Edith with her eyebrows raised but they

were interrupted by two of the grey-suited men appearing in the doorway, dark against the bright May Day sunlight behind them.

"Mr Sloane, if we might have a word about the paperwork?"

"Paperwork be damned! I've signed what I need to sign."

"You have signed, yes, but we have a query about the doctor's signature. Mr Chappell has the documents outside. If you would just step this way to clarify the last few points? Thank you."

The men withdrew.

Sloane growled and stamped outside.

Edith looked squarely at the manservant. "How loyal are you?"

"My lady..." he said, uncertainly.

"Excellent. A loyal idiot would have had no hesitation in their reply. You, however, are a clever man with morals, I would wager. Let us spring Mrs Sloane from her prison without delay."

Adelia was impressed and for a moment considered if their investigative agency might be enlarged. She had no more time to ponder as the manservant was leaping up the stairs with Edith hard at his heels.

He led them along a corridor that was lavishly furnished in a rather ostentatious way. Their feet sank into the deep Turkey-red carpet, and every inch of the walls was crammed with dark paintings showing square-bodied cattle and pigs of unfeasible bulk. The horses were all bays with spindly legs and a rather uncoordinated approach to jumping over hedges. They came to a stop outside a wide door that had a lock, but no key.

The manservant turned to them, shrugged briefly, and then without any further warning, spun around and slammed his heeled boot directly into the wood below the lock.

It splintered. Inside, a woman screamed.

The man cried out, perhaps a little late, "Mrs Sloane, stand away at the window!"

He kicked again and this time the door panel burst open around the lock, which remained for a moment in the frame before it tumbled to the carpet with a thud.

The manservant grinned. Then he bowed, and retreated, his pace picking up as he got further away, until he was running out of sight.

And that, thought Adelia, *was the last that anyone would see of that particular hero in Greyhaven.*

Jane Sloane was standing with her back to the window, clutching a hairbrush as if she might hurl it at them. When she saw who was standing there, she burst out laughing almost hysterically. Adelia remembered how reliant she had become on laudanum and alcohol in general, and quickly went over to her so that she might calm the woman down.

But as she got closer, she could see that Jane's eyes were bright and clear, and she soon quelled her laughter.

"Lady Calaway! What brings you here? And this must be your daughter – I can see the same determined chin."

"Edith Ivery, Baroness Ivery, of Ivery Manor."

"Pleased to meet you, Mrs Sloane," said Edith, with a formal shake of the hand.

"Pleased to meet you, Lady Ivery."

Adelia clapped her hands. "We are not at a garden party! We must go. If you want to take this chance, of course?"

Jane Sloane was already grabbing a few things from her dressing table, noticeably ignoring the vials of laudanum and bottles of pills.

"I will seize it immediately, without question. No; I have many questions. But they will wait."

The three of them trooped down the stairs.

"There will be a back way out of here," Adelia said as they

reached the ground floor. "It would be stupid to risk the front door."

"I don't know about that," said Edith, skipping ahead to peer out.

The double doors were open and there were dozens of people outside now. Beaumont Sloane was ranting and raving, and the three men were huddled by the carriage clutching their paperwork. And all around them like the audience at an open-air prize-fight, was half the village.

In spite of themselves, Adelia and Mrs Sloane crept forward warily. Someone outside spotted them, and pointed. Beaumont Sloane whirled around and began to scream at them, but before he could approach, he had been grabbed by two of the villagers. He flailed his arms, yelling incoherent insults as he tried to shake them off.

Jane Sloane shrank against Adelia, who put her arm around her waist and told her not to worry. Meanwhile, Edith strode out onto the top step of the porch and pointed dramatically at Beaumont.

"You ought to be ashamed of yourself! Your wife is as sane and calm as a nun. You're a weak-willed spineless coward and no one wants you here! You said you were leaving? Then go!"

He wrestled himself free of the grasp of the villagers. He paused and stared at the three grey-suited men. One of them held the papers aloft, and all of them shook their heads.

With a strangled curse, Beaumont Sloane stalked past them all and headed out along the road north. He had nothing in his hands, and no horse to ride.

He would have to return to collect a few things.

But for now, pride and fear kept him going, and the chorus of cheers and mockery from behind preventing him from turning around again.

❦ 28 ❧

The men from the asylum didn't leave empty-handed after all.

They were just climbing into the carriage when Reverend Talfourd came up to them and engaged in an urgent conversation.

Edith leaned closer to Adelia. "Is he doing what I suspect he is doing?"

"It wouldn't surprise me if he tried," Adelia said, feeling somewhat sceptical that he would succeed. "I think we ought to leave that sad business alone. It does not concern us. Mrs Sloane, have you friends or family you might stay with now?"

"I..." The excitement of having broken free of her husband now faded and she looked down at the bag in her hands. "I should go back," she whispered.

"You could, because he is not there," Edith said happily.

"He might come back at any moment," said Adelia. "And no, you should not go back. Life is going to be harder for you now, of course, and you will need support. Come back to the manor first."

"What will Mrs Alfoxden say?"

Edith laughed. "She can say what she pleases but she is my sister and I will bring her round."

Mrs Sloane was reluctant but she saw that she had no choice. They set off along the track and the crowd of villagers parted to let them pass. Some of them called words of support and praise. Gradually, Mrs Sloane's head lifted and her step grew more confident.

The village was happy to have her back.

❧

THERE WAS NO SIGN OF THEODORE. THE MAY DAY FAIR was in full swing, however. That meant people were sitting around, eating, drinking, laughing and talking. Children played, hustlers swaggered around, girls flirted and boys watched them with uncertain eyes. There were a few coaches from the police station by the inn, and Adelia had to persuade Edith that it was not their place to go and intrude.

Instead they headed back to the manor, where they found Margaret, Ramon and Harriet lounging around in the second-best sitting room. Iseult had been taken up for an afternoon nap, replete with all the sweet foods she had eaten.

Margaret looked tired. She listlessly rang a bell when they entered, and eventually the sole remaining maid came in with a tea tray and some refreshments.

Adelia explained what had happened, and Margaret accepted Jane Sloane's presence without a protest. "I do believe we are becoming quite the little sanctuary," she said.

Adelia winced. Lord Morland had been running from his debts and Mr Arbury from his crimes; but Jane Sloane, as far as she could see, was perfectly innocent.

"I will not intrude for long," she replied. "Though I am aware that you may have certain trepidations about my stay. I have not behaved well on previous occasions. I offer no excuses. Only a promise that such ... *absurdities* ... will not happen again."

"My dear, we are more than open to absurdities in this house," Margaret said. "What we don't want are travesties, and the only true travesty was your husband."

Adelia felt a bloom of pride in her daughter.

"Thank you," said Mrs Sloane, with a wry smile.

Theodore burst in then, and Adelia could not help but gasp in horror. He was about to tell everyone what had happened – and no one had yet informed Jane Sloane that her first love, her dear Frederick Arbury, had finally confessed to murder.

❧

THEODORE SAW A LOOK ON ADELIA'S FACE THAT MADE HIM stop before he had even started. She got to her feet and put a hand to Mrs Sloane's shoulder.

What on earth was she doing here? Theodore then realised that his news would have to wait.

Gradually everyone else began to understand that something wasn't being said.

And unfortunately all eyes turned to Mrs Sloane, and she frowned. "What is happening? Has he returned?"

"Ah, Mr Sloane?" said Adelia. "No, I doubt it. You are quite safe."

"She is going to have to know sooner or later," said Edith pragmatically.

"Edith," said Margaret warningly but as Edith looked at her, she fell into silence. She didn't know what to say, either.

In the end it was Harriet who took up the charge. She asked Mrs Sloane to walk with her in the rose garden, and led her out, leaving the rest of the room sitting in an excruciating stillness that was broken, at last, by Edith slapping her thigh and declaring, "Well, papa, is it all over?"

"Not by a long way. But if you mean *has he been arrested* then yes, the police came and he confessed to them instantly, crying as he did so. He will go up before the judge, and he will hang for it."

"But he was a nice man," Margaret said glumly. "Why must it happen like this?"

"Nice?" Theodore shook his head. "He had admirable qualities, I do not doubt that. But he was scared, and weak, and foolish too. He killed in a panic and then he hid that fact. No, he was not a nice man, not once you scratched the surface."

"They are all turning out to be brutes," she said. "Lord Morland has disappointed me hugely, and Gwen alongside. How can we rescue her from his clutches?"

Adelia said, "Just urge her to make the engagement a very long one. I have little doubt in my mind that something else will happen to that unfortunate man rather soon. It's in his nature. She will be crushed, all over again, but hopefully emerge a little wiser."

"Are there no good men in this village?" Margaret said in frustration.

"I like to consider that I might be one," Ramon said mildly.

"Oh, you don't count."

"How charming."

"I didn't mean that."

Theodore found himself smiling at their bickering. They were secure enough in one another's love to tease one another, and it was reassuring to see.

He said, "You know, I am going to suggest that Reverend Talfourd is one of those good men too."

"The reverend? Papa, you are surely joking."

"Not at all. He has struggled with his past and he was brought up to be deferent in all ways to his controlling mother, but he has broken free at last, and I think that he will be a better man for it. And as for her, well, those gentlemen from the asylum were very interested to meet her. I don't think her reaction did her any favours at all."

"Have they really taken her away?"

"Temporarily, I believe, to make an assessment. But I don't think we will be seeing her again."

"Goodness me," they all muttered in various ways.

With poor Jane Sloane out of the room, they then pressed Theodore to talk again about what had happened. How had he known? What had Mr Arbury said? What did the police think? He pulled up a chair and happily went over it all again, and again.

❧ 29 ❧

The rain came streaming down and hammered on the roof of the garden room. Adelia was trimming some of the indoor plants that Margaret had sadly neglected. She didn't call it "neglect." She preferred to see it as "the art of nature making its own beauty." Adelia could not stop herself from taking up some shears and pruning, just a little. Margaret lounged back in a wide wicker chair and criticised from a distance.

Edith sat alongside, reading a terribly dull pamphlet about labour-saving devices for clerks. She had arranged to stay with Margaret for a week or so. Otherwise it would not have been worth the effort of the long journey. And they argued, but in a comfortable sort of way.

"We did not see Iseult last night," Adelia said. "Is she well?"

"She was exhausted, according to nurse. She had spent the day playing with Nanna Black's ... grandchildren? Nephews and nieces? It is impossible to work out. The mothers were a little worried at first, apparently, in case she tore her dress or got dirty. But they all soon relaxed."

"That is wonderful to hear. And I am glad that you aren't treating her like a precious ornament. It's good for her to run and play with the other children."

"Yes," said Margaret in an off-hand manner. "I always knew that it would be. I don't know why you are talking to me as if I had any other plans at all."

Adelia bit her tongue. The result was a good one, regardless of how they had come to it.

Harriet popped her head into the room. It was time for her to leave. "Reverend Talfourd is waiting for me," she explained.

Margaret sprang to her feet and they embraced with genuine warmth, spilling out "thank you" and "do come again" and "any time at all" in a rush.

"Are you both going all the way to York together?"

"Yes. The Bishop is keen to meet him. We might have somewhere more suitable for him. Did you meet the new incumbent?"

"I have not," Adelia said, but she nodded at Margaret. "Didn't you go over this morning?"

"I could not wait. The house was full of people! Reverend Talfourd looked very happy about his replacement. The new vicar has a wife, and simply dozens of children, half of them almost grown up. Some of the sons were particularly tall and handsome. Courteous, decent, honourable..."

"They sound just like knights," said Adelia. "Which reminds me. Have you heard from Gwen?"

"She is at home waiting for letters from her swain. I have told her not to waste time waiting too long. He claims to have popped to Dublin."

"No one merely *pops* to Dublin."

"Indeed."

Harriet kissed them all again. As she got to the door, it

opened before she reached out for the handle. Reverend Talfourd apologised for the intrusion, but they called him in.

"We cannot tarry," he said.

"Then go, go; but before you do, how was ... he?" Margaret said.

"Mr Arbury?"

"Yes. They say you went to visit him yesterday."

"He was a sad and broken man. He knows what awaits him now. He is bleak and defeated and accepting of his fate."

Harriet could not let herself leave under such a gloomy cloud. She went around the room and embraced each one again. When she got to Adelia, she held her particularly close.

"Adelia, you and I, we ought to meet soon – when there are no murders or anything like that – and we must talk. There I things that I should unburden myself of. To you."

"Please, I would like that very much. Do look after yourself."

Harriet pulled away, laughing. "Goodness, no, I have no intention of doing *that*. I have a husband whose job *that* is."

She finally allowed the reverend to tow her out through the rain to the waiting carriage.

⚜

THE MAYPOLE NEVER DID TURN UP. IT DID NOT GET mentioned again. Nor did Margaret talk about her plan to bring craftsmen to the area and set up her idealistic commune. Adelia pondered those things as she settled back into the comfort of a first-class coach. Theodore sat opposite her and carefully placed the bag of provisions on the seat next to him. She could tell, from his face, that he was already itching to begin on the cold meat pies. The train had barely left.

"What did Nanna Black say to you in the village?"

Theodore asked. He had been buying a few last-minute articles in the grocer's, while Adelia had been waylaid by the ancient matriarch.

"She was telling me that Beaumont Sloane had come back in the night with hired men and carts, and stripped the manor bare. She expects it to be put up for sale."

"It is," he said. "The man in the shop told me so. He wanted to know where Mrs Sloane had gone, so I told him she was off to be a companion to some distant family member."

"A maiden aunt. There are worse things to be. I hope she finds herself in the right household. Margaret tried to persuade her to stay, but how could Jane accept that offer? There are far too many bad memories for her here."

Theodore nodded.

"Oh, I did ask Nanna Black if she has taken tea with Margaret yet. I didn't dare ask Margaret in case she took umbrage. Anyway, she said no, not yet, but maybe. Or maybe not. She then asked why the village couldn't just roll along as it always has? So I said to her, in that case, you would have no new steam engine."

"How did she take that?"

Adelia laughed. "Oh, she said that I had scored a point, and she didn't seem to have any malice in her when she said it. And she was happy that Iseult was playing with the village children, too. I was going to ask her about Iseult but..."

"What? You look downcast."

"No, I am unsettled." Adelia dug into her bag and pulled out a piece of plaited string. Dangling from the end of it was a small, round stone. The string passed through a hole in the middle of the stone. "Before I could ask her anything else, she gave me this. She folded it into my hand and told me that it was for my protection. I was so alarmed I could not speak."

"I would wager that she danced away, cackling at how she has managed to spark a reaction in you."

"Perhaps. Or perhaps she really believes it."

"That is not the point. Do *you*? That is where the power lies, you know. In your own belief, not anyone else's."

Adelia held the string high in the air. The stone turned lazily. She peered through it at the passing countryside.

"I believe in the power of change," she said at last.

There was one other thing that she had been given before she had left. It was not from Nanna Black. It was from Margaret.

Theodore took the stone and examined it. In his hands, it became nothing more than geology. He put it on the seat and it lay there, inert and dead now.

"Anyway, don't you think that we got a marvellous result in the end?"

Adelia said, "It was a good result in the end, I suppose, all round. Justice has been done, at least."

"You still look sad, dear heart. What is it? Is it because I can claim all the credit?"

"Ha! I am only sad because with each success rests on an initial act of terrible brutality. Without that, we would not now celebrate. Isn't that awful?"

"I don't see it that way. I would go mad if I did. Anyway, I suppose I cannot claim very much credit. I did very little real detection. I didn't get to use any tricks or knowledge. It was just dogged policework, eliminating suspects and working out motives."

"No," Adelia said. "Don't play it down. After all, you spotted that a crime had been committed in the first place. And you did not let go, even when it seemed hopeless."

"You taught me that," he said. He could not stop himself. Almost without being consciously aware of his movement, he reached out into the bag for a small pie.

"Now, I hope you are able to stop dwelling on your part in all of this?"

She shook her head. "I had until you just brought it up again."

They laughed.

She said, "Well, in honesty, I think I will always remain a little sad about it. But I won't let it gnaw away at me."

"Good."

"And we did well building bridges with our daughters, too," she went on, thinking again of the other thing in her bag. Margaret had pressed a letter into her hands as Adelia had boarded the train. *Read it,* she had said, *when you are home. It says the things I cannot say. I love you, mama, and I will do better.*

"I had not been aware that bridges needed to be built. What had Margaret done?"

"Oh, she was just being so very Margaret. But Edith is good for her. They can talk to one another in a way that I cannot."

"Well," said Theodore. "That is good, isn't it? And Iseult is a little darling."

"She is. I am hopeful she'll have a happy childhood if Margaret can relax her expectations just a little."

"If you hadn't had high expectations, you would have been a poorer mother and our daughters would have suffered," Theodore said.

Adelia had not thought about that. She remained silent for a moment before saying, slowly, "Perhaps. But let us talk a little more about building bridges," she went on, more brightly. "And with sons, not just daughters."

He ate a pie with studied attention. But she knew that he was listening and considering her words.

"Yes," she pressed, feeling that the time was right, not least because he was happily enjoying a meat pie and was therefore more inclined to be charitable. "Now that we have begun to bring Bamfylde back into the fold and he has revealed himself to be rather more than either of us imagined, or dared to hope, then let us continue with the reconciliation. Have you not thought this yourself?"

"I have," he admitted at last, brushing crumbs from his lap. "But so much is at risk."

"What?" she scoffed.

He would not answer.

"You have to risk it," she urged gently. "You have to risk getting hurt. You have to take the chance that you might get it wrong. I know that not acting seems like the safest option, but that's ..." She trailed off.

"Cowardice," he finished for her.

"I didn't say that. I mean, I didn't mean it."

"But you would be right." He reached out to take her hand. "And I cannot bear to be a coward in your eyes. I will write to him tomorrow."

She considered that a victory and did not insist on anything more.

END OF BOOK SIX

Thank you for reading *The Countess's Deadly Discovery*! I hope that you enjoyed it and are able to leave a review which will help other readers decide if this book is for them.

The next book in the series is *The Lady's Scandalous Secret*. It's released on 26 March 2021 and you can buy it here:

The Lady's Scandalous Secret

ABOUT THE AUTHOR

Issy Brooke writes light, refreshing Victorian mysteries set in her native Britain. She has a master's degree in Nineteenth Century Literature and a passion for historical authenticity.

Her current series is *The Discreet Investigations of Lord and Lady Calaway*, which follow the exploits of an older married couple. They are detectives to the upper classes and their adventures take them the length and breadth of the UK. The series begins with *Murder at Mondial Castle* and continues through six more books (and ongoing). There is also a novella, *The Killer on the Belltower*, which can be read at any point in the series.

Her first series was *Lady C Investigates*, which is complete at five books beginning with *An Unmourned Man*. All five books are also available as a box set.

Fans of the wonderful scientific discoveries of the Victorian age will also enjoy the trilogy *The Investigations of Marianne Starr*.

When not reading about the Victorians, thinking about them, writing about them and watching films about them, Issy enjoys travelling and walking, eating cakes and drinking tea.

You can sign up to her mailing list here for notifications of new releases. http://issybrooke.com/newsletter

THE END

Made in the USA
Las Vegas, NV
15 October 2021

32392900R00173